THE MYSTERY OMNIBUS

Ruskin Bond is known for his signature simplistic and witty writing style. He is the author of several bestselling short stories, novellas, collections, essays and children's books; and has contributed a number of poems and articles to various magazines and anthologies. At the age of twenty-three, he won the prestigious John Llewellyn Rhys Prize for his first novel, *The Room on the Roof*. He was also the recipient of the Padma Shri in 1999, Lifetime Achievement Award by the Delhi Government in 2012 and the Padma Bhushan in 2014.

Born in 1934, Ruskin Bond grew up in Jamnagar, Shimla, New Delhi and Dehradun. Apart from three years in the UK, he has spent all his life in India, and now lives in Landour, Mussoorie, with his adopted family.

RUSKIN BOND
THE MYSTERY OMNIBUS

Published by
Rupa Publications India Pvt. Ltd 2023
161-B/4, Gulmohar House,
Yusuf Sarai Community Centre,
New Delhi 110049

Sales centres:
Bengaluru Chennai
Hyderabad Kolkata Mumbai

Copyright © Ruskin Bond 2023

This is a work of fiction. Names, characters, places and incidents are either the product of the author's imagination or are used fictitiously and any resemblance to any actual person, living or dead, events or locales is entirely coincidental.

All rights reserved.
No part of this publication may be reproduced, transmitted, or stored in a retrieval system, in any form or by any means, electronic, mechanical, photocopying, recording or otherwise, without the prior permission of the publisher.

P-ISBN: 978-93-5702-590-4
E-ISBN: 978-93-5702-591-1

Fourth impression 2025

10 9 8 7 6 5 4

The moral right of the author has been asserted.

This book is sold subject to the condition that it shall not, by way of trade or otherwise, be lent, resold, hired out, or otherwise circulated, without the publisher's prior consent, in any form of binding or cover other than that in which it is published.

Contents

Introduction   *vii*

TALES OF HORROR

The Shadow on the Wall	3
The Doppelgänger	10
Haunted Places	15
Eyes of the Cat	23
A Face in the Dark	26
Ghost Trouble	29
Susanna's Seven Husbands	41
The Man Who Was Kipling	47
Wilson's Bridge	51
A Face Under the Pillow	57
Some Hill Station Ghosts	60
Fairy Glen Palace	67
The Haunted Bicycle	73
Whispering in the Dark	76
The Skull	82
The Ghost and the Idiot	88
The Overcoat	92
Bhoot Aunty	96
From the Primaeval Past	99
A Traveller's Tale	103

The Chakrata Cat	109
A Dreadful Gurgle	113
The White Pigeon	116
The Trouble with Djinns	118
Pistols at Twenty Paces: A Duel at Poona	123
Phantom Lover	126
Do You Believe in Ghosts?	127
Whistling in the Dark	128
The Skeleton in the Cupboard	134
Hill of the Fairies	146
Reunion at the Regal	150
The Monkeys	155

TALES OF MYSTERY

He Who Rides a Tiger	163
He Said It with Arsenic	166
A Job Well Done	175
The Wicked Guru	181
A Hill Station's Vintage Murders	184
Strychnine in the Cognac	188
A Case for Inspector Lal	198
In a Crystal Ball: A Mussoorie Mystery	206
Death of a Familiar	212
Panther's Moon	229
The Night Train at Deoli	260
Killer with a Knife	266
Born Evil	277
The Late Night Show	287
The Last Truck Ride	297

Introduction

The dark has never really bothered me. I have always imagined it to be home to friendly, mischievous or peculiar creatures and enjoyed the solitude that comes with it. And yet, living in the mountains for long, I have heard stories and experienced things that still make a chill run down my spine. Over the years, I have realized that darkness may lurk in the hearts of the most idyllic places and the most cheerful people, cropping up when and where you least expect it.

In *The Mystery Omnibus*, I bring you a collection of stories and essays exploring two enigmas of existence: horror and mystery. The first section includes tales of horror—like 'A Face in the Dark' and 'The Haunted Bicycle'—full of spectral beings and supernatural incidents. I hope they make you question your understanding of the limits of the world we inhabit.

My writing has often drawn upon the endearing qualities of the people I have encountered. Occasionally, though, I have met or heard of people who cast darker shadows than the rest of us. Their actions are crueller than most, terrifying yet fascinating in their uniqueness. The stories in the second section of this collection—like 'Strychnine in the Cognac' and 'He Said It with Arsenic'—include tales about such mysterious people.

While most of these stories aim to elicit a sense of fear or unease, I also hope that some of them—like 'The Skull' and 'The Overcoat'—show you that you need not always be afraid of what lurks in the dark. There is so much mystery, intrigue and perhaps even humanity and kindness to be found in the shadows. So, go ahead, take the plunge, step into the darkness. Who knows? You might just meet a friendly ghost or a perfectly charming murderer!

TALES OF HORROR

The Shadow on the Wall

When I was in my early twenties, a struggling freelance writer, I rented two small rooms above a shop in Dehradun, and settled down to make my fortune as an author. Or so I hoped.

The rooms were without electricity, the landlord (the shop owner) having failed to pay the electricity bills for several years; but this did not bother me. Dehra wasn't too hot in those days, and I had no need of a ceiling fan. And I thought an oil lamp would be sufficient and even quite romantic. Hadn't the great authors of the past penned their masterpieces by the light of a solitary lamp? I could picture Goethe labouring over his *Faust*, Shakespeare over his *Sonnets*, Dostoyevsky over his *Crime and Punishment* (probably in a prison cell) and Emily Brontë composing *Wuthering Heights* by the light of a flickering lamp while a snowstorm raged across the moors that surrounded her father's lonely parsonage.

Many geniuses would have written by lamplight— Premchand in his village, Keats in his attic, poor John Clare in a madhouse... Well, I was no genius and I had no wish to enter a madhouse, but I liked the idea of writing by lamplight, so I invested in a lamp and a bottle of kerosene, set up the lamp on an old dining table (I took my meals at a dhaba down the road), brought it to a fine glow, and wrote a new story under its benediction.

I don't remember what the story was about, but it wasn't a bad effort, and I sold it to a Sunday magazine.

Every evening, after taking my meal in the dhaba, I would light the lamp, settle down at the table, and toss off a story or an article. I enjoyed the lamplight, even when I wasn't writing. There was something soothing about its soft glow. It threw my shadow on the wall on the other side of the desk; and whenever I got up and paced about the room (as I often do when writing) my shadow would follow, prowling about on the walls of the room, almost as though it were taking on a life of its own.

The shadow was always a little larger than life. The lamp seemed to magnify my image. Probably this had something to do with the glass or the position of the lamp. And late one evening, while I was in the middle of a story, I chanced to look up—and there, beside my shadow on the wall, was another shadow. It was the shadow of someone who was standing behind me.

Someone was in the room, looking over my shoulder, reading what I was writing.

It is always irritating to have someone watching you while you work. Even in an exam hall I could never proceed with my essay or answers if the supervisor was standing over me; I would wait for him to move on, so that I could concentrate properly.

So now, disturbed, I turned around to see who was looking over my shoulder.

There was no one behind me, no one was in the room.

I can't say I was frightened. But I felt extremely uneasy. Had I imagined the shadow on the wall—the shadow of the watcher? I looked again. It was no longer there.

I returned to my writing. But I was uneasy. I couldn't help feeling that I was not alone, that someone was reading my manuscript even as it was being written.

Well, doesn't every writer cherish a reader? Why complain?

If there can be ghostwriters there can be ghost readers.

And when I looked up again the shadow was there, standing beside my own seated shadow, very still, studying the page, my words, my stream of consciousness.

It was the shadow of a woman, of that I was certain. Her hair fell to her shoulders, the outline of her figure was feminine, and she was wearing a gown that trailed behind her. All this the shadow told me; but no more.

I put down my pen, covered my manuscript with a paperweight, put out the lamp, and went to bed. In the dark there are no shadows.

◆

The dark has never really bothered me. With my poor sight I am just as home in the dark as I am in a well-lit room. That's why I like the lamplight. It is not too harsh, too intrusive; and beyond its circle of light, there is darkness, the friendly dark that is home to little bats, timid mice, and shy humans.

But lamps throw shadows. And when I sat down at my desk the following evening, I was expecting the shadow of my solitary reader.

I had written a page or two before I became aware of her presence. I knew she was there without looking up to see if her shadow was there on the wall. The room had become suffused with an unmistakable fragrance—attar of roses! She was speaking to me through the perfumes of her favourite flower.

But I was not to be seduced!

I carried on with my story—'Time Stops at Shamli'—completed a few pages, covered them up, put out the lamp, and went to bed.

My visitor must have been annoyed, because the scent of roses vanished, to be replaced by the strong odour of crushed marigolds. I covered my head with a blanket and shut out all scents and shadows.

Next morning I found the pages of my manuscript scattered about the floor of my room. Perhaps the dawn wind had disturbed them. The window was half open. Could my visitor have disturbed them? She was doing her best to make her presence known.

I started working in the mornings instead of at night. The lamp would be given a rest except when really needed. Let the shadows rest. Let the phantom lady rest....

She did not like being ignored.

Late one night—it must have been about two in the morning, the witches' hour—I was awakened by the most terrible shrieks. The room vibrated with the sounds of a shrieking woman.

Scared out of my wits, I leapt out of bed and lit the lamp, which now stood on the dressing table. The shrieking stopped. And shadows scurried about on the walls.

This happened night after night, for almost a week. Shrieks would wake me in the middle of the night, and would stop only when the lamp was lit. No longer did fragrance fill the air; just the smell of oil and something burning.

I confided in Melaram, the owner of the dhaba where I took my meals. He twirled his luxurious moustache, nodded sagely, and said: 'It seems your landlord kept something from you—the tragedy of the woman who perished in your flat some five or six years ago. They were a childless couple, she and her doctor husband. They quarrelled a lot. One day, when she was in the kitchen preparing their dinner, the petromax stove burst, burning oil fell on her clothes and soon she was covered in flames. She ran on to the balcony, screaming for help, but by the time we could get to her she was in a terrible state.'

'And where was her husband?'

'Out, visiting a patient. He followed us to the hospital, but by then she had gone. In fact, there wasn't much left of her.'

'So it was an accident?'

'The police called it an accident. But there were rumours—there are always rumours in such cases, and when the doctor left town and set up his practice in Delhi, there were more rumours. And then of course he married again...'

'All speculation,' I said, 'But I've had enough of the lady's presence. Her shadow seems real enough—and now those shrieks! I'm moving into the station hotel, and then perhaps you can help me find another flat.'

But I could not move immediately. Two suitcases held all my clothes and personal effects, but I had accumulated a cupboard full of books, and these, along with my notebooks and manuscripts, had to be carefully packed. It meant another night in my haunted rooms.

I went to bed as late as possible. I went to bed in the dark. Well, it wasn't too dark, because a full moon threw its beams across the balcony. But I did not light the lamp; I'd had enough of shadows.

I had asked Melaram's young assistant to bring me a glass of hot tea at daybreak. I slept soundly. There was no shrieking that night. But I was awakened by a push on my left shoulder. And I started up and called out 'What's up? Why so early?' thinking it was the boy with my tea. The moonlight had gone and it was dark everywhere.

I got no answer. Instead I received another push.

This annoyed me and I said, 'Why don't you speak, boy? Is something wrong?'

Still no answer, and as I began to sit up I felt a human hand, warm, plump and soft, slip into mine.

Still thinking it was the boy, I held the hand; but my free

hand encountered a wrist and arm, a long sleeveless arm. I felt along the arm, but when I reached the elbow all trace of the arm ceased. I was left holding a disembodied arm!

You can imagine my fright. I dropped the arm, tumbled out of bed, and rushed to the balcony calling for help. Melaram was up by then, and he and his boy came rushing to my aid with torches and an old firearm. But there was no one in the room, no remnants of a burnt or dismembered body. And soon it was daylight.

◆

After a few nights in the station hotel, I found a bright, cheerful flat just behind the Odeon cinema. It had electricity too. Although we were subject to long power cuts, I was no longer dependent on the oil lamp, which I still possessed—just in case I couldn't pay the light bills!

But somehow I missed the gentle glow of my oil lamp. I had a feeling that I wrote better by lamplight than by daylight or the harsh light of electricity. The lamp provided the right kind of atmosphere for my writing; it created the mood I wanted, a touch of mystery, a touch of melancholy, of emotions undefined...

And so one evening I lit the lamp, sat back on an easy chair, and watched the shadows on the wall.

But there were no shadows apart from mine, no one looking over my shoulder. In the words of the old song, it was just 'my echo, my shadow and me....' And we weren't really company.

I decided to visit a friend at the other end of town. I returned home late. I was too tired to do any work, so I left the lamp burning and went to bed. Outside, on the street, a clock struck twelve.

I was slipping into a dream when I felt that soft hand on my shoulder. Then the other hand touched me. I shivered with fright and apprehension. The hands moved across my chest and arms, there was nothing disembodied about them. I lay perfectly still.

A soft, warm, plump arm brushed against my cheek. I put out my hand to discover, to touch her face. But there was nothing to touch. She was headless!

As I tried to get up, her free arm stretched out, stretched right across the room, and switched off the lamp. I was in bed with a headless woman!

And that's when I woke up. That's when I always wake up. For it's a dream, a nightmare that has pursued me over the years, slowly driving me out of my mind as I try to imagine what the missing head looks like.

The Doppelgänger

It was in 1960, or thereabouts, that I first met a doppelgänger. There, I have at least spelt it right. It's a German word but you can find it in the *Oxford Dictionary of English*, where so many exotic words turn up.

I was twenty-six at the time. I'd had a novel published in London, but very few people bought it, and my freelancing efforts in New Delhi were appreciated but seldom rewarded. I had taken a job with CARE, an American relief agency, and they sent me to Darjeeling (among other places) to see what help could be given to the Tibetan refugees who had arrived there.

So I was a nobody, trying to be a somebody.

When I entered the portals of the old Everest Hotel, I found it full of somebodys. There was Shammi Kapoor and his Bollywood crew, engaged in making a romantic film called *Professor*. And there was Satyajit Ray and his crew from Kolkata, engaged in making an artistic film called *Kanchenjunga*.

Kanchenjunga was the name of the majestic peak visible from Darjeeling, and while I was there I had a glimpse of it as well as a few glimpses of the shooting of these two contrasting films. But this is not the story of those films, or of my work with the Tibetans, but of an encounter that took place because of them.

Free one afternoon, I was strolling along the Darjeeling Mall when I heard a stentorious voice call out, 'Mr Bond! Have you got my Henry Green?'

It was Marie Seton.

I had met Marie Seton a few times in New Delhi, having been introduced to her by the chief of CARE, who had written a book about Laos. Marie was much older than me, but she was good company, and we would often meet at the India Coffee House and have long, gossipy chats over a pot of strong coffee. She was a film enthusiast, had edited Eisenstein's unfinished *Que Viva Mexico*, which I had seen in London, and was now engaged in writing the filmography of Satyajit Ray's films. That accounted for her presence in Darjeeling.

'Your Henry Green?' I countered, as we came face to face, 'I have never read Henry Green.' He was an author who was currently in fashion, but I had yet to meet someone who had read his works.

'I am sure I lent it to you,' she said vaguely. 'Or maybe it was to Khushwant. Anyway what are you doing up here? You're not with that lot from Bombay, are you—singing and dancing on the railway tracks?'

'No, of course not.' But I felt a little guilty, because only that morning I had exchanged a few words with the charming Geeta Bali, Mr Kapoor's wife. She was not in the film—had retired from filming because of poor health—but was still very attractive in her own unique way.

'I can't sing and I can't dance,' I said. 'But come and have a coffee, and I'll tell you why I am here.'

So we sat at the wayside café and chatted about books and films and the British royal family (she was an expert on the royal family and knew all of them, apparently), and even promised to introduce me to the great Satyajit Ray later that evening.

And so we parted, and I went about my work, returning to the hotel at about six in the evening. The lobby was full of all the film people, but there was no sign of Marie Seton, and when I enquired at the reception I was told that no one by that name was staying there.

Never mind. She must've been staying somewhere else, in a more modest hotel, and presumably at her own expense. I went for a long walk in Darjeeling's December mist, and forgot all about our encounter.

A few weeks later I was back in New Delhi, strolling around Connaught Place in search of a bookshop, when I heard that familiar voice. 'What have you done with my Henry Green?'

It was Marie Seton again.

'You know I don't have it,' I protested. 'I haven't read Henry Green and have no desire to read his damn book. So come and have a coffee and bring me up to date on all the royal gossip.'

We went into Nirula's and caught up with each other's news.

'So tell me,' I asked, 'how did the shooting go in Darjeeling? We were supposed to meet, but I couldn't find you at the hotel—'

'What hotel? What are you talking about?'

'Last month in Darjeeling. Don't you remember? We met on the Mall, while Ray was filming *Kanchenjunga*.'

'My dear boy, I've never been to Darjeeling. You've been imagining things—reading too much Anaïs Nin! I wish I'd been there, though. Watching Ray at work—just what I need for my book. But it was not to be. I was down with flu at the time.'

'But you were there—we met on the Mall—you asked me for your wretched Henry Green!'

'Nonsense! I couldn't have been in two places at once.'

And then it occurred to me—perhaps she was a doppelgänger, capable of being in two places at once! I gave a little shudder. Somehow a doppelgänger was scarier than a ghost; a living person with supernatural qualities. Was she, even now, real? Or was she just an apparition sipping coffee with me? Of course she had been in Darjeeling that day. And perhaps she was somewhere else, even now. She could be having tea at Buckingham Palace! No wonder she was so well-informed on royalty...

I got up to leave; made some lame excuse about a prior appointment; promised to meet her again.

'Farewell, dear boy,' she said with a sinister smile. 'And don't forget my Henry Green.'

◆

Well, I had yet to come across a copy of a Henry Green novel, although I know that such a writer did exist; forgotten, if he was ever remembered. And I did not see Marie Seton again for a couple of years, although I felt sure she was doppelgänging all over the place.

And then one day I was at the New Delhi railway station, accompanied by a young writer called Sasthi Brata, who was to make a name for himself with a confessional novel called *My God Died Young*. We were seeing off Professor P. Lal, an academic whose Writers Workshop in Kolkata was the last resort for many an aspiring writer.

We had paid our respects to the great man, and the train was beginning to move, when I caught sight of Marie Seton in the next compartment. She was reading a book. I called out to her, and she looked up, but I don't think she saw me, as just then the train picked up speed, and her compartment swept past me.

'Who did you call out to?' asked my companion.

'Marie Seton,' I said. 'She's always turning up in unexpected places.'

'It couldn't have been her,' said Sasthi B. 'She died on a film set in Bhutan about two months ago.'

'It was Marie Seton in that carriage,' I insisted.

'Then you saw her ghost,' he said. 'Or someone who looked just like her.'

So now even her ghost was a doppelgänger!

I gave up. And when I got home to my room in East Patel Nagar I wasn't a bit surprised to find a Henry Green novel on my desk.

While rounding of this little tale it has occurred to me that everyone mentioned in it—writers, actors, directors, singers, academics—have all made their exits from life on this particular planet and have, hopefully, moved on to a better place—or to complete nothingness—leaving behind some memorials to their artistry: books, films, songs, poems, creative contributions big or small to the passing show.

There is a Latin proverb—

Ars longa, vita brevis...

Art is long life is short.

Or, to turn it around: life is short, but art is long.

Haunted Places

The Rocking Chair

Yes, sometimes old houses do give you a feeling of still being occupied by the ghosts or spirits of long-dead occupants—people who once lived and loved beneath that weathered roof and between those listening walls.

The walls listen to us by day; and when, late at night, the residents are asleep, they and the rest of the house come to life, gossip among themselves, and discuss the strengths and weaknesses of the human guests. Those walls, those pictures, those old tables and armchairs have seen triumph and tragedy, and sometimes they resonate with these things and release some of what they have absorbed.

Like that old rocking chair I picked up in the antique shop near Landour's clock tower. I had no desire to purchase or own a rocking chair, but when I spotted it in a corner of the shop I couldn't resist sitting down in it; and finding that it suited my ample proportions I remained seated for some time, becoming increasingly aware that I belonged to it in some way and that I ought to possess it.

We haggled over the price, and I ended up paying more than it seemed to be worth, although the shop owner maintained that it had once belonged to a royal family. A Nepali labourer carried it on his back and delivered it to my rooms higher up the hillside, and I found a place for it in a corner of my sunny bedroom.

Every afternoon I would settle into that rocking chair, read a little, and then rock myself to sleep until Beena woke me up with a cup of tea. I had the rocking chair all to myself—by day, that is…

It was only at night, late at night, that someone else seemed to occupy it.

The chair had been in my room for a few days, getting used to its new surroundings I suppose. Then, one night, I was woken by a rhythmical creaking sound, and switching on the bed light I saw that the rocking chair was in motion, oscillating back and forth as though it had an occupant.

Well, there was no one in it, and I came to the conclusion that it had been set in motion by the light breeze from my open window, kept open on summer nights.

This happened on several occasions and I was getting quite used to it when, late one night, the rocking was more rapid and vigorous than usual, and I turned on the light to see a tiny old woman sitting in the chair, rocking to and fro, and grinning at me in a rather childish manner. There were rings on her fingers and she appeared to be dressed in an expensive gown. But she had no teeth, and this gave a sort of malevolent leer to her grin.

I shot out of bed, and as I did so the figure of the old woman vanished. The empty chair kept rocking.

Next day I removed it to the attic. If the ghost of old ladies wanted to use it, they were welcome to do so, but not in my bedroom. And when I spoke to the antique shop owner about this vision of mine, he confessed that the rocking chair had once belonged to the Rani of —, and that she had died in it, at an advanced age.

The rocking chair is still in my attic. I don't go up there at night. But the other day, while reading in my little sunroom, I heard the creaking of the chair and felt bold enough to climb the stairs to see if it had a visitor.

It was only the neighbourhood cat, a large tabby, curled up in the middle of the chair, enjoying its motion.

Perhaps the old rani likes having a little company, because the cat is there quite often, purring contentedly, while an unseen hand strokes it behind the ears. I don't disturb them. Cats see more than we do. And if the rocking chair can give pleasure to the ghost of an old rani, she's more than welcome to it.

But I don't go up to the attic at night. I might just see her again.

♦

A Haunted House

Back in the 1950s, when I was still in my teens, I would often wander up the Rajpur Road, a quiet tree-lined highway with a few old bungalows scattered here and there. One of them, a two-storeyed building, had lain empty and abandoned for several years. It was reputed to be haunted, and no one was interested in buying or renting it. Even passers-by gave it a wide berth.

I had seen the house from outside, but I had never ventured into its grounds. The story of the haunting, if indeed it was a haunting, went like this: An elderly English couple, childless, had owned the house and lived in it for many years. But when they grew old their income from investments dwindled, and at the time of Independence they were really hard up. Being old and reclusive, they had been forgotten by the rest of the community, most of whom were busy making arrangements to leave the country. By the end of 1948 most of the Anglo-Indians and Europeans in Dehra had left for 'home' (the UK) but the old couple had stayed on, more from compulsion than desire. They had, indeed, been quite forgotten—until, one day, a bill collector (for light or water or some unpaid services) entered the house and found the old couple dead in their large four-poster bed. They had died of starvation, probably within a few hours of each other. The post-mortem revealed that their stomachs were empty.

It was a sad story and a depressing one, and people did not want to talk about it. It was nobody's fault, but we all feel a little guilty when a fellow human dies of neglect.

I was curious about the deserted house but I was afraid to enter it on my own. Instead I wandered about the grounds, a wilderness of overgrown shrubs and dying rose bushes. Here and there a flowering plant had struggled to survive but tall grasses and weeds were taking over.

As I was about to leave from the broken gate, I was hailed by my cousin Ronald, who was passing by on his bicycle.

'Hey, Ruskin, what are you doing there? Have you become a ghost-hunter now?'

'Just looking around,' I said, feeling a bit foolish. Did I really expect to see a couple of ghosts?

'I'll come and join you,' said Ronald. 'But first let me fetch some grub. You can't look for ghosts on an empty stomach.' And off he rode, in the direction of the Ellora Bakery.

He was an impulsive fellow, and I wasn't sure if he'd come back; but twenty minutes later he came cycling through the open gate, his shopping basket topped up with pastries, buns, cheese rolls, chicken patties, sandwiches…. Ronald's pocket money far exceeded mine. His father owned a cinema; my stepfather owed money all over the town.

'Let's go inside,' said Ronald. 'It's hot out here. And ghosts don't sunbathe.'

So far I'd remained in the garden, reluctant to venture into the house on my own. But Ronald showed no compunction about going in; I simply followed.

Most of the furniture had gone from the rooms. In the hall was a sofa with the stuffing exposed; in the dining room a table and a couple of broken chairs; in the bedroom a large double-bed without any mattress or coverings. Anything that could be sold had been taken away, probably by vandals.

We weren't vandals, but we were a couple of ghouls, picnicking in the ruined home of people who had died in tragic circumstances. But Ronald was very blasé about the whole thing. For him it was enormous fun.

'Tuck in, Ruskin,' he said, spreading out all the delicacies on a dressing table, its mirror broken. 'They must have looked in it every day, except towards the end.'

I was beginning to lose my appetite. Those old people had starved to death, and here we were, glutting ourselves on cakes and savouries. When I commented on this fact, Ronald said, 'Pooh! It wasn't our fault, what happened. They're welcome to join us, if they are still around.'

But no one was around. A haunted house? The rooms were entirely without any atmosphere. Just dust everywhere, and cobwebs.

A large spider ran across the bed.

'We'll leave a pastry for the spider,' said Ronald. And since you're not eating anything, we'll leave the rest for the old folk,'

'Don't leave any food here,' I said. 'It seems rather—'

'What?'

'Well, disrespectful.'

'You are an old-fashioned fellow, Ruskin. Come on, let's go. I want to catch the matinee at three. They're showing *Ben-Hur* at the Odeon.'

I walked with him to the gate. No, I had no premonition of disaster, but I declined his invitation to take a ride on his pillion, and as for *Ben-Hur*, those quasi-Biblical spectacles, with their 'casts of millions', failed to excite me.

Ronald hopped on to his bicycle and, as was his habit, rode off at speed as though he were in a cycle race. Always up to new tricks, he grabbed the fender of a small truck and allowed it to carry him some distance. As it picked up speed, he let go and swerved into the centre of the road. At the same time an army truck, coming from the opposite direction, slammed straight into the cyclist, sending him sprawling and then running over the helpless boy.

It all happened very suddenly. I stood there, petrified. People ran to Ronald's aid, and within minutes the truck driver and his mates had taken the badly injured boy to the army hospital in the nearby cantonment. But Ronald did not survive the impact of the collision. It was no one's fault, just the logical outcome of his reckless nature.

And we hadn't seen any ghosts. But had they seen us? Do we see the stars at noon? They are there all the same, looking down at us, and it is we who cannot see them.

Ronald's parents were devastated by the tragedy, for he had been their only son. I had never been very close to him, but I had seen the accident and it scarred my memories for many years. It helped to convince me that life is not about rewards and punishments, but about consequences.

◆

A Haunted Planet

There is no ghost more dangerous or intractable than the Covid virus that has infiltrated the human race in the course of the last two years. Invisible! Unstoppable! Everywhere at once. Baffling and teasing scientists, rendering the gurus and godmen bereft of platitudes, bringing out the best in some of us, the worst in others.

A true ghost, travelling the globe without passport, without hindrance. Happiest in a crowd, moving unseen among the revellers or protestors or worshippers, regardless of what brings people together. A lover of crowds, this ghost, but it will follow you to a distant village or lonely hilltop if it so wishes.

Is it nature in revolt, now telling us that we are not the masters after all, and that there is a limit to how much we can destroy and poison and desiccate this unique planet...who knows?

Perhaps the haunting will subside and we will know then. Or is it too late to learn from our follies?

◆

2 a.m.

Two o'clock in the morning—the darkest hour, when our energy, mental and physical, is at its lowest. For those who are critically ill, the tide is running out. For those who cannot sleep it is a dead, depressing hour.

Because of a prostate problem I have to get up at least three times in the night to ease the pressure on my bladder. Twelve o'clock or thereabouts; at about 2 a.m.; and then at about four in the morning. At twelve o'clock there are some who are still awake. At four in the morning there are some who are getting up because they have a busy day ahead—a plane to catch or a long road journey. But at two or three in the morning nobody's about. The silence is deafening. Even the dogs have stopped barking; the neighbourhood dogs who bark simply because other dogs are barking.

And then, the other night, something unusual happened.

I had just returned from the bathroom and was about to hop into bed when I heard a loud knocking on the front door.

A visitor at 2 a.m.? I couldn't think of anyone who would want to drop in for a chat in the dead of night. It had to be an emergency. I put on my dressing-gown, went to the front door and opened it without hesitation.

Standing there, about nine or ten feet tall, was a woman in black, towering over me. It could have been a man, but I had the impression it was a woman, possibly a nun, because she was dressed in black from head to foot. I couldn't see her face, but I saw her hands—large hands with long scabrous fingers.

I had the fright of my life. This was Death's Dark Angel, if ever there was one. I tried to close the door, but she had slipped that questing hand between the doors and was pushing against them. In desperation I caught one of her fingers and bent it backwards, and finally she drew her hand away and I was able to shut and bolt the door.

I returned to my bedroom, unsure if I was enacting a dream or experiencing something very tangible and real. I sat on the edge of my bed, knowing I wouldn't be able to sleep. I turned off the light. And then, just as I did so, the knocking started again. But this time it was at the window. Someone was standing on the window-ledge, two storeys above the road, tapping on the windowpanes.

The curtains were drawn. I made a dash for them, pulled them aside, and opened the window. Opened it wide. This was an impulsive act, not a brave one. But I felt I had to confront this awful visitor.

There was no one there. She had made her presence felt, and then she had gone.

2 a.m.

The dead of night. When the dead still roam.

Eyes of the Cat

I wrote this little story for the schoolgirl who said my stories weren't scary enough. Her comment was 'Not bad', and she gave me seven out of ten.

Her eyes seemed flecked with gold when the sun was on them. And as the sun set over the mountains, drawing a deep red wound across the sky, there was more than gold in Kiran's eyes. There was anger; for she had been cut to the quick by some remarks her teacher had made—the culmination of weeks of insults and taunts.

Kiran was poorer than most of the girls in her class and could not afford the tuitions that had become almost obligatory if one was to pass and be promoted. 'You'll have to spend another year in the ninth,' said Madam. 'And if you don't like that, you can find another school—a school where it won't matter if your blouse is torn and your tunic is old and your shoes are falling apart.' Madam had shown her large teeth in what was supposed to be a good-natured smile, and all the girls had tittered dutifully. Sycophancy had become part of the curriculum in Madam's private academy for girls.

On the way home in the gathering gloom, Kiran's two companions commiserated with her.

'She's a mean old thing,' said Aarti. 'She doesn't care for anyone but herself.'

'Her laugh reminds me of a donkey braying,' said Sunita, who was more forthright.

But Kiran wasn't really listening. Her eyes were fixed on some point in the far distance, where the pines stood in silhouette against a night sky that was growing brighter every moment. The moon was rising, a full moon, a moon that meant something very special to Kiran, that made her blood tingle and her skin prickle and her hair glow and send out sparks. Her steps seemed to grow lighter, her limbs more sinewy as she moved gracefully, softly over the mountain path.

Abruptly she left her companions at a fork in the road.

'I'm taking the short cut through the forest,' she said.

Her friends were used to her sudden whims. They knew she was not afraid of being alone in the dark. But Kiran's moods made them feel a little nervous, and now, holding hands, they hurried home along the open road.

The short cut took Kiran through the dark oak forest. The crooked, tormented branches of the oaks threw twisted shadows across the path. A jackal howled at the moon; a nightjar called from urgency, and her breath came in short, sharp gasps. Bright moonlight bathed the hillside when she reached her home on the outskirts of the village.

Refusing her dinner, she went straight to her small room and flung the window open. Moonbeams crept over the window-sill and over her arms which were already covered with golden hair. Her strong nails had shredded the rotten wood of the window-sill.

Tail swishing and ears pricked, the tawny leopard came swiftly out of the window, crossed the open field behind the house, and melted into the shadows.

A little later it padded silently through the forest.

Although the moon shone brightly on the tin-roofed town,

the leopard knew where the shadows were deepest and merged beautifully with them. An occasional intake of breath, which resulted in a short rasping cough, was the only sound it made.

Madam was returning from dinner at a ladies' club, called the Kitten Club as a sort of foil to the husbands' club affiliations. There were still a few people in the street, and while no one could help noticing Madam, who had the contours of a steam-roller, none saw or heard the predator who had slipped down a side alley and reached the steps of the teacher's house. It sat there silently, waiting with all the patience of an obedient schoolgirl.

When Madam saw the leopard on her steps, she dropped her handbag and opened her mouth to scream; but her voice would not materialize. Nor would her tongue ever be used again, either to savour chicken biryani or to pour scorn upon her pupils, for the leopard had sprung at her throat, broken her neck, and dragged her into the bushes.

In the morning, when Aarti and Sunita set out for school, they stopped as usual at Kiran's cottage and called out to her.

Kiran was sitting in the sun, combing her long black hair.

'Aren't you coming to school today, Kiran?' asked the girls.

'No, I won't bother to go today,' said Kiran. She felt lazy, but pleased with herself, like a contented cat.

'Madam won't be pleased,' said Aarti. 'Shall we tell her you're sick?'

'It won't be necessary,' said Kiran, and gave them one of her mysterious smiles. 'I'm sure it's going to be a holiday.'

A Face in the Dark

It may give you some idea of rural humour if I begin this tale with an anecdote that concerns me. I was walking alone through a village at night when I met an old man carrying a lantern. I found, to my surprise, that the man was blind. 'Old man,' I asked, 'if you cannot see, why do you carry a lamp?'

'I carry this,' he replied, 'so that fools do not stumble against me in the dark.'

This incident has only a slight connection with the story that follows, but I think it provides the right sort of tone and setting. Mr Oliver, an Anglo-Indian teacher, was returning to his school late one night, on the outskirts of the hill station of Shimla. The school was conducted on English public school lines and the boys, most of them from well-to-do Indian families, wore blazers, caps, and ties. *Life* magazine, in a feature on India had once called this school the 'Eton of the East'.

Individuality was not encouraged; they were all destined to become 'leaders of men'.

Mr Oliver had been teaching in the school for several years. Sometimes it seemed like an eternity; for one day followed another with the same monotonous routine. The Shimla bazaar, with its cinemas and restaurants, was about two miles from the school; and Mr Oliver, a bachelor, usually strolled into the town in the evening, returning after dark, when he would take a short cut through a pine forest.

When there was a strong wind, the pine trees made sad, eerie sounds that kept most people to the main road. But Mr Oliver was not a nervous or imaginative man. He carried a torch and, on the night I write of, its pale gleam—the batteries were running down—moved fitfully over the narrow forest path. When its flickering light fell on the figure of a boy, who was sitting alone on a rock, Mr Oliver stopped. Boys were not supposed to be out of school after 7 p.m., and it was now well past nine.

'What are you doing out here, boy?' asked Mr Oliver sharply, moving closer so that he could recognize the miscreant. But even as he approached the boy, Mr Oliver sensed that something was wrong. The boy appeared to be crying. His head hung down, he held his face in his hands, and his body shook convulsively. It was a strange, soundless weeping, and Mr Oliver felt distinctly uneasy

'Well—what's the matter?' he asked, his anger giving way to concern. 'What are you crying for?' The boy would not answer or look up. His body continued to be racked with silent sobbing.

'Come on, boy, you shouldn't be out here at this hour. Tell me the trouble. Look up!'

The boy looked up. He took his hands from his face and looked up at his teacher. The light from Mr Oliver's torch fell on the boy's face—if you could call it a face.

He had no eyes, ears, nose, or mouth. It was just a round smooth head—with a school cap on top of it. And that's where the story should end—as indeed it has for several people who have had similar experiences and dropped dead of inexplicable heart attacks. But for Mr Oliver it did not end there.

The torch fell from his trembling hand. He turned and scrambled down the path, running blindly through the trees and calling for help. He was still running towards the school buildings when he saw a lantern swinging in the middle of the path. Mr Oliver had never before been so pleased to see the night watchman. He stumbled up to the watchman, gasping for breath and speaking incoherently.

'What is it, Sir?' asked the watchman. 'Has there been an accident? Why are you running?'

'I saw something—something horrible—a boy weeping in the forest—and he had no face!'

'No face, Sir?'

'No eyes, nose, mouth—nothing.'

'Do you mean it was like this, Sir?' asked the watchman, and raised the lamp to his own face. The watchman had no eyes, no ears, no features at all—not even an eyebrow!

The wind blew the lamp out, and Mr Oliver had his heart attack.

Ghost Trouble

I

It was Grandfather who finally decided that we would have to move to another house.

And it was all because of a *pret*, a mischievous North Indian ghost, who had been making life difficult for everyone.

Prets usually live in peepul trees, and that's where our little ghost first had his home—in the branches of a massive old peepul tree which had grown through the compound wall and spread into our garden. Part of the tree was on our side of the wall, part on the other side, shading the main road. It gave the ghost a good view of the whole area.

For many years the pret had lived there quite happily, without bothering anyone in our house. It did not bother me, either, and I spent a lot of time in the peepul tree. Sometimes I went there to escape the adults at home, sometimes to watch the road and the people who passed by. The peepul tree was cool on a hot day, and the heart-shaped leaves were always waving in the breeze. This constant movement of the leaves also helped to disguise the movements of the pret, so that I never really knew exactly where he was sitting. But he paid no attention to me. The traffic on the road kept him fully occupied.

Sometimes, when a tonga was passing, he would jump down

and frighten the pony, and as a result the little pony cart would go rushing off in the wrong direction.

Sometimes, he would get into the engine of a car or a bus, which would have a breakdown soon afterwards.

And he liked to knock the sun helmets off the heads of sahibs or officials, who would wonder how a strong breeze had sprung up so suddenly, only to die down just as quickly. Although this special kind of ghost could make himself felt, and sometimes heard, he was invisible to the human eye.

I was not invisible to the human eye, and often got the blame for some of the pret's pranks. If bicycle-riders were struck by mango seeds or apricot stones, they would look up, see a small boy in the branches of the tree, and threaten me with terrible consequences. Drivers who went off after parking their cars in the shade would sometimes come back to find their tyres flat. My protests of innocence did not carry much weight. But when I mentioned the pret in the tree, they would look uneasy, either because they thought I must be mad, or because they were afraid of ghosts, especially prets. They would find other things to do and hurry away.

At night no one walked beneath the peepul tree.

It was said that if you yawned beneath the tree, the pret would jump down your throat and give you a pain. Our gardener, Chandu, who was always taking sick leaves, blamed the pret for his tummy troubles. Once, when yawning, Chandu had forgotten to put his hand in front of his mouth, and the ghost had got in without any trouble.

Now Chandu spent most of his time lying on a string-bed in the courtyard of his small house. When Grandmother went to visit him, he would start groaning and holding his sides, the pain was so bad; but when she went away, he did not fuss so much. He claimed that the pain did not affect his appetite, and he ate a normal diet, in fact a little more than normal—the extra amount was meant to keep the ghost happy!

II

'Well, it isn't our fault,' said Grandfather, who had given permission to the Public Works Department to cut the tree, which had been on our land. They wanted to widen the road, and the tree and a bit of our wall were in the way. So both had to go.

Several people protested, including the Raja of Jinn, who lived across the road and who sometimes asked Grandfather over for a game of tennis.

'That peepul tree has been there for hundreds of years,' he said. 'Who are we to cut it down?'

'*We*,' said the chief engineer, 'are the PWD.'

And not even a ghost can prevail against the wishes of the Public Works Department.

They brought men with saws and axes, and first they lopped all the branches until the poor tree was quite naked. It must have been at this moment that the pret moved out. Then they sawed away at the trunk until, finally, the great old peepul came crashing down on the road, bringing down the telephone wires and an electric pole in the process, and knocking a large gap in the raja's garden wall.

It took them three days to clear the road, and during that time the chief engineer swallowed a lot of dust and tree pollen. For months afterwards he complained of a choking feeling, although no doctor could ever find anything in his throat.

'It's the pret's doing,' said the raja knowingly. 'They should never have cut that tree.'

◆

Deprived of his tree, the pret decided that he would live in our house.

I first became aware of his presence when I was sitting on the verandah steps reading a book. A tiny chuckling sound came from behind me. I looked around, but no one was to be seen. When I returned to my book, the chuckling started again. I paid no attention. Then a shower of rose petals fell softly on to the pages of my open book. The pret wanted me to know he was there!

'All right,' I said. 'So you've come to stay with us. Now let me read.'

He went away then; but as a good pret has to be bad in order to justify his existence, it was not long before he was up to all sorts of mischief.

He began by hiding Grandmother's spectacles.

'I'm sure I put them down on the dining table,' she grumbled.

A little later they were found balanced on the snout of a wild boar, whose stuffed and mounted head adorned the verandah wall, a memento of Grandfather's hunting trips when he was young.

Naturally, I was at first blamed for this prank. But a day or two later, when the spectacles disappeared again, only to be found dangling from the bars of the parrot's cage, it was agreed that I was not to blame; for the parrot had once bitten off a piece of my finger, and I did not go near him any more.

The parrot was hanging upside down, trying to peer through one of the lenses. I don't know if they improved his vision, but what he saw certainly made him angry, because the pupils of his eyes went very small and he dug his beak into the spectacle frames, leaving them with a permanent dent. I caught them just before they fell to the floor.

But even without the help of the spectacles, it seemed that

our parrot could see the pret. He would keep turning this way and that, lunging out at unseen fingers, and protecting his tail from the tweaks of invisible hands. He had always refused to learn to talk, but now he became quite voluble and began to chatter in some unknown tongue, often screaming with rage and rolling his eyes in a frenzy.

'We'll have to give that parrot away,' said Grandmother. 'He gets more bad-tempered by the day.'

Grandfather was the next to be troubled. He went into the garden one morning to find all his prize sweet peas broken off and lying on the grass. Chandu thought the sparrows had destroyed the flowers, but we didn't think the birds could have finished off every single bloom just before sunrise.

'It must be the pret,' said Grandfather, and I agreed.

The pret did not trouble me much, because he remembered me from his peepul tree days and knew I resented the tree being cut as much as he did. But he liked to catch my attention, and he did this by chuckling and squeaking near me when I was alone, or whispering in my ear when I was with someone else. Gradually I began to make out the occasional word. He had started learning English!

III

Uncle Benji, who came to stay with us for long periods when he had little else to do (which was most of the time), was soon to suffer.

He was a heavy sleeper, and once he'd gone to bed he hated being woken up. So when he came to breakfast looking bleary-eyed and miserable, we asked him if he was feeling all right.

'I couldn't sleep a wink last night,' he complained. 'Whenever I was about to fall asleep, the bedclothes would be pulled off the bed. I had to get up at least a dozen times to pick them off the floor.' He stared suspiciously at me. 'Where were *you* sleeping last night, young man?'

'In Grandfather's room,' I said. 'I've lent you *my* room.'

'It's that ghost from the peepul tree,' said Grandmother with a sigh.

'Ghost!' exclaimed Uncle Benji. 'I didn't know the house was haunted.'

'It is now,' said Grandmother. 'First, my spectacles, then the sweet peas, and now Benji's bedclothes! What will it be up to next, I wonder?'

We did not have to wonder for long.

There followed a series of minor disasters. Vases fell off tables, pictures fell from walls. Parrot feathers turned up in the teapot, while the parrot himself let out indignant squawks and swear words in the middle of the night. Windows which had been closed would be found open, and open windows closed.

Finally, Uncle Benji found a crow's nest in his bed, and on tossing it out of the window was attacked by two crows.

Then Aunt Ruby came to stay, and things quietened down for a time.

Did Aunt Ruby's powerful personality have an effect on the pret, or was he just sizing her up?

'I think the pret has taken a fancy to your aunt,' said Grandfather mischievously. 'He's behaving himself for a change.'

This may have been true, because the parrot, who had picked up some of the English words being tried out by the pret, now called out, '*kiss*,' whenever Aunt Ruby was in the room.

'What a charming bird,' said Aunt Ruby.

'You can keep him if you like,' said Grandmother.

One day Aunt Ruby came into the house covered in rose petals.

'I don't know where they came from,' she exclaimed. 'I was sitting in the garden, drying my hair, when handfuls of petals came showering down on me!'

'It likes you,' said Grandfather.

'What likes me?'

'The ghost.'

'What ghost?'

'The pret. It came to live in the house when the peepul tree was cut down.'

'What nonsense!' said Aunt Ruby.

'*Kiss, kiss!*' screamed the parrot.

'There aren't any ghosts, prets or other kinds,' said Aunt Ruby firmly.

'*Kiss, kiss!*' screeched the parrot again. Or was it the parrot? The sound seemed to be coming from the ceiling.

'I wish that parrot would shut up.'

'It isn't the parrot,' I said. 'It's the pret.'

Aunt Ruby gave me a cuff over the ear and stormed out of the room.

But she had offended the pret. From being her admirer, he turned into her enemy. Somehow her toothpaste got switched with a tube of Grandfather's shaving cream. When she appeared in the dining room, foaming at the mouth, we ran for our lives, Uncle Benji shouting that she'd got rabies.

IV

Two days later Aunt Ruby complained that she had been struck on the nose by a grapefruit, which had leapt mysteriously from the pantry shelf and hurled itself at her.

'If Ruby and Benji stay here much longer, they'll both have nervous breakdowns,' said Grandfather thoughtfully.

'I thought they broke down long ago,' I said.

'None of your cheek,' snapped Aunt Ruby.

'He's in league with that pret to try and get us out of here,' said Uncle Benji.

'Don't listen to him—you can stay as long as you like,' said Grandmother, who never turned away any of her numerous nephews, nieces, cousins or distant relatives.

The pret, however, did not feel so hospitable, and the persecution of Aunt Ruby continued.

'When I looked in the mirror this morning,' she complained bitterly, 'I saw a little monster, with huge ears, bulging eyes, flaring nostrils, and a toothless grin!'

'You don't look *that* bad, Aunt Ruby,' I said, trying to be nice.

'It was either you or that imp you call a pret,' said Aunt Ruby. 'And if it's a ghost, then it's time we all moved to another house.'

Uncle Benji had another idea.

'Let's drive the ghost out,' he said. 'I know a sadhu who rids houses of evil spirits.'

'But the pret's not evil,' I said. 'Just mischievous.'

Uncle Benji went off to the bazaar and came back a few hours later with a mysterious, long-haired man who claimed to be a sadhu—one who has given up all worldly goods, including most of his clothes.

He prowled about the house, and lighted incense in all the rooms, despite squawks of protest from the parrot. All the time he chanted various magic spells. He then collected a fee of thirty rupees, and promised that we would not be bothered again by the pret.

As he was leaving, he was suddenly blessed with a shower—no, it was really a downpour—of dead flowers, decaying leaves, orange peel, and banana skins. All spells forgotten, he ran to the gate and made for the safety of the bazaar.

♦

Aunt Ruby declared that it had become impossible to sleep at night because of the devilish chuckling that came from beneath her pillow. She packed her bags and left.

Uncle Benji stayed on. He was still having trouble with his bedclothes, and he was beginning to talk to himself, which was a bad sign.

'Talking to the pret, Uncle?' I asked innocently, when I caught him at it one day.

He gave me a threatening look. 'What did you say?' he demanded. 'Would you mind repeating that?'

I thought it safer to please him. 'Oh, didn't you hear me? I said, "*Teaching the parrot, Uncle?*"'

He glared at me, then walked off in a huff. If he did not leave it was because he was hoping Grandmother would lend him enough money to buy a motorcycle; but Grandmother said he ought to try earning a living first.

One day I found him on the drawing room sofa, laughing like a madman. Even the parrot was so alarmed that he was silent, head lowered and curious. Uncle Benji was red in the face—literally red all over!

'What happened to your face, Uncle?' I asked. He stopped laughing and gave me a long, hard look. I realized that there had been no joy in his laughter.

'Who painted the washbasin red without telling me?' he asked in a quavering voice.

As Uncle Benji looked really dangerous, I ran from the room.

'We'll have to move, I suppose,' said Grandfather later.

'Even if it's only for a couple of months, I'm worried about Benji. I've told him that I painted the washbasin myself but forgot to tell him. He doesn't believe me. He thinks it's the pret or the boy, or both of them! Benji needs a change. So do we. There's my brother's house at the other end of the town. He won't be using it for a few months. We'll move in next week.'

And so, a few days and several disasters later, we began moving house.

V

Two bullock carts laden with furniture and heavy luggage were sent ahead. Uncle Benji went with them. The roof of our old car was piled high with bags and kitchen utensils. Grandfather took the wheel, I sat beside him, and Granny sat in state at the back.

We set off and had gone some way down the main road when Grandfather started having trouble with the steering wheel. It appeared to have got loose, and the car began veering about on the road, scattering cyclists, pedestrians, and stray dogs, pigs, and hens. A cow refused to move, but we missed it somehow, and then suddenly we were off the road and making for a low wall. Grandfather pressed his foot down on the brake, but we only went faster. 'Watch out!' he shouted.

It was the Raja of Jinn's garden wall, made of single bricks, and the car knocked it down quite easily and went on through it, coming to a stop on the raja's lawn.

'Now look what you've done,' said Grandmother.

'Well, we missed the flower beds,' said Grandfather.

'Someone's been tinkering with the car. Our pret, no doubt.'

The raja and two attendants came running towards us.

The raja was a perfect gentleman, and when he saw that the driver was Grandfather, he beamed with pleasure.

'Delighted to see you, old chap!' he exclaimed. 'Jolly decent of you to drop in. How about a game of tennis?'

'Sorry to have come in through the wall,' apologized Grandfather.

'Don't mention it, old chap. The gate was closed, so what else could you do?'

Grandfather was as much of a gentleman as the raja, so he thought it only fair to join him in a game of tennis. Grandmother and I watched and drank lemonade. After the game, the raja waved us goodbye and we drove back through the hole in the wall and out on to the road. There was nothing much wrong with the car.

We hadn't gone far when we heard a peculiar sound, as of someone chuckling and talking to himself. It came from the roof of the car.

'Is the parrot out there on the luggage rack?' asked Grandfather.

'No,' said Grandmother. 'He went ahead with Uncle Benji.'

Grandfather stopped the car, got out, and examined the roof. 'Nothing up there,' he said, getting in again and starting the engine. 'I thought I heard the parrot.'

When we had gone a little further, the chuckling started again. A squeaky little voice began talking in English in the tones of the parrot.

'It's the pret,' whispered Grandmother. 'What is he saying?'

The pret's squeak grew louder. 'Come on, come on!' he cried gleefully. 'A new house! The same old friends! What fun we're going to have!'

Grandfather stopped the car. He backed into a driveway, turned around, and began driving back to our old house.

'What are you doing?' asked Grandmother.

'Going home,' said Grandfather.

'And what about the pret?'

'What about him? He's decided to live with us, so we'll have to make the best of it. You can't solve a problem by running away from it.'

'All right,' said Grandmother. 'But what will we do about Benji?'

'It's up to him, isn't it? He'll be all right if he finds something to do.'

Grandfather stopped the car in front of the verandah steps.

'I'm hungry,' I said.

'It will have to be a picnic lunch,' said Grandmother. 'Almost everything was sent off on the bullock carts.'

As we got out of the car and climbed the verandah steps, we were greeted by showers of rose petals and sweet-scented jasmine.

'How lovely!' exclaimed Grandmother, smiling. 'I think he likes us, after all.'

Susanna's Seven Husbands

Locally, the tomb was known as 'the grave of the seven-times married one'.

You'd be forgiven for thinking it was Bluebeard's grave; he was reputed to have killed several wives in turn because they showed undue curiosity about a locked room. But this was the tomb of Susanna Anna-Maria Yeates, and the inscription (most of it in Latin) stated that she was mourned by all who had benefitted from her generosity, her beneficiaries having included various schools, orphanages, and the church across the road. There was no sign of any other graves in the vicinity, and presumably her husbands had been interred in the old Rajpur graveyard, below the Delhi Ridge.

I was still in my teens when I first saw the ruins of what had once been a spacious and handsome mansion. Desolate and silent, its well-laid paths were overgrown with weeds, its flower-beds had disappeared under a growth of thorny jungle. The two-storeyed house had looked across the Grand Trunk Road. Now abandoned, feared and shunned, it stood encircled in mystery, reputedly the home of evil spirits.

Outside the gate, along the Grand Trunk Road, thousands of vehicles sped by—cars, trucks, buses, tractors, bullock-carts—but few noticed the old mansion or its mausoleum, set back as they were from the main road, hidden by mango, neem and peepul trees. One old and massive peepul tree grew out of the ruins of the house, strangling it much as its owner was said to have strangled one of her dispensable paramours.

As a much-married person with a quaint habit of disposing of her husbands, whenever she tired of them, Susanna's malignant spirit was said to haunt the deserted garden. I had examined the tomb, I had gazed upon the ruins, I had scrambled through shrubbery and overgrown rose-bushes, but I had not encountered the spirit of this mysterious woman. Perhaps, at the time, I was too pure and innocent to be targeted by malignant spirits. For, malignant she must have been, if the stories about her were true.

No one had been down into the vaults of the ruined mansion. They were said to be occupied by a family of cobras, traditional guardians of buried treasure. Had she really been a woman of great wealth, and could treasure still be buried there? I put these questions to Naushad, the furniture-maker, who had lived in the vicinity all his life, and whose father had made the furniture and fittings for this and other great houses in Old Delhi.

'Lady Susanna, as she was known, was much sought after for her wealth,' recalled Naushad. She was no miser, either. She spent freely, reigning in state in her palatial home, with many horses and carriages at her disposal. You see the stables there, behind the ruins? Now, they are occupied by bats and jackals. Every evening she rode through the Roshanara Gardens, the cynosure of all eyes, for she was beautiful as well as wealthy. Yes, all men sought her favours, and she could choose from the best of them. Many were fortune-hunters. She did not discourage them. Some found favour for a time, but she soon tired of them. None of her husbands enjoyed her wealth for very long!

'Today, no one enters those ruins, where once there was mirth and laughter. She was the zamindari lady, the owner of much land, and she administered her estate with a strong hand.

She was kind if rents were paid when they fell due, but terrible if someone failed to pay.'

'Well, over fifty years have gone by since she was laid to rest, but still men speak of her with awe. Her spirit is restless, and it is said that she often visits the scenes of her former splendour. She has been seen walking through this gate, or riding in the gardens, or driving in her phaeton down the Rajpur road.'

'And, what happened to all those husbands?' I asked.

'Most of them died mysterious deaths. Even the doctors were baffled. Tomkins Sahib drank too much. The lady soon tired of him. A drunken husband is a burdensome creature, she was heard to say. He would have drunk himself to death, but she was an impatient woman and was anxious to replace him. You see those datura bushes growing wild in the grounds? They have always done well here.'

'Belladonna?' I suggested.

'That's right, huzoor. Introduced in the whisky-soda, they put him to sleep for ever.'

'She was quite humane in her way.'

'Oh, very humane, sir. She hated to see anyone suffer. One sahib, I don't know his name, drowned in the tank behind the house, where the water-lilies grew. But she made sure he was half-dead before he fell in. She had large, powerful hands, they said.'

'Why did she bother to marry them? Couldn't she just have had men friends?'

'Not in those days, dear sir. Respectable society would not have tolerated it. Neither in India nor in the West would it have been permitted.'

'She was born out of her time,' I remarked.

'True, sir. And remember, most of them were fortune-hunters. So, we need not waste too much pity on them.'

'*She* did not waste any.'

'She was without pity. Especially when she found out what they were really after. The snakes had a better chance of survival.'

'How did the other husbands take their leave of this world?'

'Well, the Colonel-sahib shot himself while cleaning his rifle. Purely an accident, huzoor. Although some say she had loaded his gun without his knowledge. Such was her reputation by now that she was suspected even when innocent. But she bought her way out of trouble. It was easy enough, if you were wealthy.'

'And, the fourth husband?'

'Oh, he died a natural death. There was a cholera epidemic that year, and he was carried off by the haija. Although, again, there were some who said that a good dose of arsenic produced the same symptoms! Anyway, it was cholera on the death certificate. And, the doctor who signed it was the next to marry her.'

'Being a doctor, he was probably quite careful about what he ate and drank.

'He lasted about a year.'

'What happened?'

'He was bitten by a cobra.'

'Well, that was just bad luck, wasn't it? You could hardly blame it on Susanna.'

'No, huzoor, but the cobra was in his bedroom. It was coiled around the bed-post. And, when he undressed for the night, it struck! He was dead when Susanna came into the room an hour later. She had a way with snakes. She did not harm them and they never attacked her.'

'And, there were no antidotes in those days. Exit the doctor. Who was the sixth husband?'

'A handsome man. An indigo planter. He had gone bankrupt when the indigo trade came to an end. He was hoping to recover his fortune with the good lady's help. But our Susanna-mem, she did not believe in sharing her fortune with anyone.'

'How did she remove the indigo planter?'

'It was said that she lavished strong drink upon him, and when he lay helpless, she assisted him on the road we all have to take by pouring molten lead in his ears.'

'A painless death, I'm told.'

'But a terrible price to pay huzoor, simply because one is no longer needed…'

We walked along the dusty highway, enjoying the evening breeze, and some time later we entered the Roshanara Gardens, in those days Delhi's most popular and fashionable meeting place.

'You have told me how six of her husbands died, Naushad. I thought there were seven?'

'Ah, a gallant young magistrate, who perished right here, huzoor. They were driving through the park after dark when the lady's carriage was attacked by brigands. In defending her, the gallant young man received a fatal sword wound.'

'Not the lady's fault, Naushad.'

'No, my friend. But he was a magistrate, remember, and the assailants, one of whose relatives had been convicted by him, were out for revenge. Oddly enough, though, two of the men were given employment by the Lady Susanna at a later date. You may draw your own conclusions.'

'And, were there others?'

'Not husbands. But an adventurer, a soldier of fortune came along. He found her treasure, they say. He lies buried with it, in the cellars of the ruined house. His bones lie scattered there, among gold and silver and precious jewels. The cobras guard them still! But how he perished was a mystery, and remains so till this day.'

'What happened to Susanna?'

'She lived to a good old age, as you know. If she paid for her crimes, it wasn't in this life! As you know, she had no children. But she started an orphanage and gave generously to the poor and to various schools and institutions, including a home for widows. She died peacefully in her sleep.'

'A merry widow,' I remarked. 'The Black Widow spider!'

Don't go looking for Susanna's tomb. It vanished some years ago, along with the ruins of her mansion. A smart new housing estate came up on the site, but not after several workmen and a contractor succumbed to snake bite! Occasionally, residents complain of a malignant ghost in their midst, who is given to flagging down cars, especially those driven by single men. There have been one or two mysterious disappearances. Ask anyone living along this stretch of the Delhi Ridge, and they'll tell you that's it's true.

And, after dusk, an old-fashioned horse and carriage can sometimes be seen driving through the Roshanara Gardens. Ignore it, my friend. Don't stop to answer any questions from the beautiful fair lady who smiles at you from behind lace curtains. She's still looking for a suitable husband.

The Man Who Was Kipling

I was sitting on a bench in the Indian Section of the Victoria and Albert Museum in London, when a tall, stooping, elderly gentleman sat down beside me. I gave him a quick glance, noting his swarthy features, heavy moustache and horn-rimmed spectacles. There was something familiar and disturbing about his face, and I couldn't resist looking at him again.

I noticed that he was smiling at me.

'Do you recognize me?' he asked, in a soft pleasant voice.

'Well, you do seem familiar,' I said. 'Haven't we met somewhere?'

'Perhaps. But if I seem familiar to you, that is at least something. The trouble these days is that people don't *know* me anymore—I'm a familiar, that's all. Just a name standing for a lot of outmoded ideas.'

A little perplexed, I asked, 'What is it you do?'

'I wrote books once. Poems and tales...Tell me, whose books do you read?'

'Oh, Maugham, Priestley, Thurber. And among the older lot, Bennett and Wells—.' I hesitated, groping for an important name, and I noticed a shadow, a sad shadow, pass across my companion's face.

'Oh, yes, and Kipling,' I said. 'I read a lot of Kipling.'

His face brightened up at once, and the eyes behind the thick-lensed spectacles suddenly came to life.

'I'm Kipling,' he said.

I stared at him in astonishment, and then, realizing that he might perhaps be dangerous, I smiled feebly and said, 'Oh, yes?'

'You probably don't believe me. I'm dead, of course.'

'So I thought.'

'And you don't believe in ghosts?'

'Not as a rule.'

'But you'd have no objection to talking to one, if he came along?'

'I'd have no objection. But how do I know you're Kipling? How do I know you're not an imposter?'

'Listen, then:

When my heavens were turned to blood,
When the dark had filled my day,
Furthest, but most faithful, stood
That lone star I cast away.
I had loved myself, and I
Have not lived and dare not die.'

'Once,' he said, gripping me by the arm and looking me straight in the eye. 'Once in life I watched a star; but I whistled her to go.'

'Your star hasn't fallen yet,' I said, suddenly moved, suddenly quite certain that I sat beside Kipling. 'One day, when there is a new spirit of adventure abroad, we will discover you again.'

'Why have they heaped scorn on me for so long?'

'You were too militant, I suppose—too much of an Empire man. You were too patriotic for your own good.'

He looked a little hurt. 'I was never very political,' he said. 'I wrote over six hundred poems, and you could only call a dozen of them political, I have been abused for harping on the theme of the White Man's Burden but my only aim was to show off the Empire to my audience—and I believed the Empire was a fine and noble thing. Is it wrong to believe in something? I never went deeply into political issues, that's true. You must remember, my seven years in India were very youthful years. I was in my twenties, a little immature if you like, and my interest in India was a boy's interest. Action appealed to me more than anything else. You must understand that.'

'No one has described action more vividly, or India so well. I feel at one with Kim wherever he goes along the Grand Trunk Road, in the temples at Banaras, among the Saharanpur fruit gardens, on the snow-covered Himalayas. Kim has colour and movement and poetry.'

He sighed, and a wistful look came into his eyes.

'I'm prejudiced, of course,' I continued. 'I've spent most of my life in India—not *your* India, but an India that does still have much of the colour and atmosphere that you captured. You know, Mr Kipling, you can still sit in a third-class railway carriage and meet the most wonderful assortment of people. In any village you will still find the same courtesy, dignity and courage that the Lama and Kim found on their travels.'

'And the Grand Trunk Road? Is it still a long winding procession of humanity?'

'Well, not exactly,' I said, a little ruefully. 'It's just a procession of motor vehicles now. The poor Lama would be run down by a truck if he became too dreamy on the Grand Trunk Road. Times *have* changed. There are no more Mrs Hawksbees in Shimla, for instance.'

There was a faraway look in Kipling's eyes. Perhaps he was imagining himself a boy again; perhaps he could see the hills or the red dust of Rajputana; perhaps he was having a private conversation with Privates Mulvaney and Ortheris, or perhaps he was out hunting with the Seonce wolf pack. The sound of

London's traffic came to us through the glass doors, but we heard only the creaking of bullock-cart wheels and the distant music of a flute.

He was talking to himself, repeating a passage from one of his stories. 'And the last puff of the day wind brought from the unseen villages the scent of damp woodsmoke, hot cakes, dripping undergrowth, and rotting pine cones. That is the true smell of the Himalayas, and if once it creeps into the blood of a man, that man will at the last, forgetting all else, return to the hills to die.'

A mist seemed to have risen between us—or had it come in from the streets?—and when it cleared, Kipling had gone away.

I asked the gatekeeper if he had seen a tall man with a slight stoop, wearing spectacles.

'Nope,' said the gatekeeper. 'Nobody been by for the last ten minutes.'

'Did someone like that come into the gallery a little while ago?'

'No one that I recall. What did you say the bloke's name was?'

'Kipling,' I said.

'Don't know him.'

'Didn't you ever read *The Jungle Book*?'

'Sounds familiar. Tarzan stuff, wasn't it?'

I left the museum, and wandered about the streets for a long time, but I couldn't find Kipling anywhere. Was it the boom of London's traffic that I heard, or the boom of the Sutlej river racing through the valleys?

Wilson's Bridge

The old wooden bridge has gone, and today an iron suspension bridge straddles the Bhagirathi as it rushes down the gorge below Gangotri. But villagers will tell you that you can still hear the hooves of Wilson's horse as he gallops across the bridge he had built 150 years ago. At the time people were sceptical of its safety, and so, to prove its sturdiness, he rode across it again and again. Parts of the old bridge can still be seen on the far bank of the river. And the legend of Wilson and his pretty hill bride, Gulabi, is still well known in this region.

I had joined some friends in the old forest rest house near the river. There were the Rays, recently married, and the Duttas, married many years. The younger Rays quarrelled frequently; the older Duttas looked on with more amusement than concern. I was a part of their group and yet something of an outsider. As a single man, I was a person of no importance. And as a marriage counsellor, I wouldn't have been of any use to them.

I spent most of my time wandering along the river banks or exploring the thick deodar and oak forests that covered the slopes. It was these trees that had made a fortune for Wilson and his patron, the Raja of Tehri. They had exploited the great forests to the full, floating huge logs downstream to the timber yards in the plains.

Returning to the rest house late one evening, I was halfway

across the bridge when I saw a figure at the other end, emerging from the mist. Presently I made out a woman, wearing the plain dhoti of the hills; her hair fell loose over her shoulders. She appeared not to see me, and reclined against the railing of the bridge, looking down at the rushing waters far below. And then, to my amazement and horror, she climbed over the railing and threw herself into the river.

I ran forward, calling out, but I reached the railing only to see her fall into the foaming waters below, from where she was carried swiftly downstream.

The watchman's cabin stood a little way off. The door was open. The watchman, Ram Singh, was reclining on his bed, smoking a hookah.

'Someone just jumped off the bridge,' I said breathlessly. 'She's been swept down the river!'

The watchman was unperturbed. 'Gulabi again,' he said, almost to himself; and then to me, 'Did you see her clearly?'

'Yes, a woman with long loose hair—but I didn't see her face very clearly.'

'It must have been Gulabi. Only a ghost, my dear sir. Nothing to be alarmed about. Every now and then someone sees her throw herself into the river. Sit down,' he said, gesturing towards a battered old armchair, 'be comfortable and I'll tell you all about it.'

I was far from comfortable, but I listened to Ram Singh tell me the tale of Gulabi's suicide. After making me a glass of hot sweet tea, he launched into a long, rambling account of how Wilson, a British adventurer seeking his fortune, had been hunting musk deer when he encountered Gulabi on the path from her village. The girl's grey-green eyes and peach-blossom complexion enchanted him, and he went out of his way to get to know her people. Was he in love with her, or did he simply find her beautiful and desirable? We shall never really know. In the course of his travels and adventures he had known many women, but Gulabi was different, childlike and ingenuous, and he decided he would marry her. The humble family to which she belonged had no objection. Hunting had its limitations, and Wilson found it more profitable to tap the region's great forest wealth. In a few years he had made a fortune. He built a large timbered house at Harsil, another in Dehradun and a third at Mussoorie. Gulabi had all she could have wanted, including two robust little sons. When he was away on work, she looked after their children and their large apple orchard at Harsil.

And then came the evil day when Wilson met the Englishwoman, Ruth, on the Mussoorie Mall, and decided that she should have a share of his affections and his wealth. A fine house was provided for her, too. The time he spent at Harsil with Gulabi and his children dwindled. 'Business affairs'—he was now one of the owners of a bank—kept him in the fashionable hill resort. He was a popular host and took his friends and associates on shikar parties in the Doon.

Gulabi brought up her children in village style. She heard stories of Wilson's dalliance with the Mussoorie woman and, on one of his rare visits, she confronted him and voiced her resentment, demanding that he leave the other woman. He brushed her aside and told her not to listen to idle gossip. When he turned away from her, she picked up the flintlock pistol that lay on the gun table and fired one shot at him. The bullet missed him and shattered her looking glass. Gulabi ran out of the house, through the orchard and into the forest, then down the steep path to the bridge built by Wilson only two or three years before. When he had recovered his composure, he mounted his horse and came looking for her. It was too late. She had already thrown herself off the bridge into the swirling waters far below. Her body was found a mile or two downstream, caught between some rocks.

This was the tale that Ram Singh told me, with various flourishes and interpolations of his own. I thought it would make a good story to tell my friends that evening, before the fireside in the rest house. They found the story fascinating, but when I told them I had seen Gulabi's ghost, they thought I was doing a little embroidering of my own. Mrs Dutta thought it was a tragic tale. Young Mrs Ray thought Gulabi had been very silly. 'She was a simple girl,' opined Mr Dutta. 'She responded in the only way she knew…'; 'Money can't buy happiness,' said Mr Ray. 'No,' said Mrs Dutta, 'but it can buy you a great many comforts.' Mrs Ray wanted to talk of other things, so I changed the subject. It can get a little confusing for a bachelor who must spend the evening with two married couples. There are undercurrents which he is aware of but not equipped to deal with.

I would walk across the bridge quite often after that. It was busy with traffic during the day, but after dusk there were only a few vehicles on the road and seldom any pedestrians. A mist rose from the gorge below and obscured the far end of the bridge. I preferred walking there in the evening, half expecting, half hoping to see Gulabi's ghost again. It was her face that I really wanted to see. Would she still be as beautiful as she was fabled to be?

It was on the evening before our departure that something happened that would haunt me for a long time afterwards.

There was a feeling of restiveness as our days there drew to a close. The Rays had apparently made up their differences, although they weren't talking very much. Mr Dutta was anxious to get back to his office in Delhi and Mrs Dutta's rheumatism was playing up. I was restless too, wanting to return to my writing desk in Mussoorie.

That evening I decided to take one last stroll across the bridge to enjoy the cool breeze of a summer's night in the mountains. The moon hadn't come up, and it was really quite dark, although there were lamps at either end of the bridge providing sufficient light for those who wished to cross over.

I was standing in the middle of the bridge, in the darkest part, listening to the river thundering down the gorge, when I saw the sari-draped figure emerging from the lamplight and making towards the railings.

Instinctively I called out, 'Gulabi!'

She half turned towards me, but I could not see her clearly. The wind had blown her hair across her face and all I saw was wildly staring eyes. She raised herself over the railing and threw herself off the bridge. I heard the splash as her body struck the water far below.

Once again I found myself running towards the part of the railing where she had jumped. And then someone was running towards the same spot, from the direction of the rest house. It was young Mr Ray.

'My wife!' he cried out. 'Did you see my wife?'

He rushed to the railing and stared down at the swirling waters of the river.

'Look! There she is!' He pointed at a helpless figure bobbing about in the water.

We ran down the steep bank to the river but the current had swept her on. Scrambling over rocks and bushes, we made frantic efforts to catch up with the drowning woman. But the river in that defile is a roaring torrent, and it was over an hour before we were able to retrieve poor Mrs Ray's body, caught in driftwood about a mile downstream.

She was cremated not far from where we found her and we

returned to our various homes in gloom and grief, chastened but none the wiser for the experience.

If you happen to be in that area and decide to cross the bridge late in the evening, you might see Gulabi's ghost or hear the hoofbeats of Wilson's horse as he canters across the old wooden bridge looking for her. Or you might see the ghost of Mrs Ray and hear her husband's anguished cry. Or there might be others. Who knows?

A Face Under the Pillow

'Camping in the jungle was full of danger,' I remarked. 'You must have felt much safer working in the house.'

'Well, cooking was certainly easier,' said Mehmood. 'But I don't know if it was much safer. The animals couldn't get in, true, but there were ghosts and evil spirits lurking in some of the rooms. I changed my room thrice, but there was always someone—*something*—after me. I don't know if I should tell you this, baba. You have your own small room and you may start imagining things…'

'I'm not afraid of ghosts, Mehmood.'

'That's because you haven't seen one. Although I'm not sure it was a ghost. And I did not actually see anything. But I felt it all right!'

'You can't *feel* a ghost, Mehmood. At least not in stories.'

'This wasn't a story. It was my first night in Carpet-sahib's house in the jungle. It has a big house with many rooms, and I was given a room of my own. But there was no electricity in that out-of-the way place. We used kerosene lamps or candles.

'I had brought my own razai and blanket, but the mattress was a strange one, and so was the pillow. Not a pillow, really, but an old cushion, very hard and lumpy. It was my first night in that bed, and I was very uncomfortable. The candle burnt itself out, and I was still wide awake. I could see very little, there was just a small window allowing a little moonlight into the room. I was almost asleep when I heard someone groaning beside me. Groaning loudly, as though in pain. But there was no one else in the bed, and no one beneath it.

'The groaning stopped for a time, and then, just as I was about to fall asleep, it started again. *Groan, groan, groan.* Now it seemed to come from beneath my pillow.

'I turned on my side, and slowly, carefully, I slipped my hand beneath the pillow.

'It encountered a hairy face, a gaping mouth, hollow sockets instead of eyes. Horrible to touch! Not the face of a human, baba—the face of a *rakshas*!

'I tried to pull my hand away, but it was seized by that terrible mouth. A mouth with long sharp teeth—teeth like daggers! It would have bitten my fingers off if I hadn't screamed and shouted for help.

'Carpet-sahib and his sister and the other servants came running. As they rushed into the room with torches and a lamp, these awful teeth released my hand.

'Under the pillow!' I screamed. 'Under the pillow!'

'They looked under the pillow! But there was nothing there. I showed them my fingers—they were bleeding badly.'

'A rat must have bitten you,' said Carpet-sahib's sister. But she knew it wasn't a rat. And she gave me another room to sleep in.

'And were you all right in the second room?'

'For a couple of nights, baba. And then it happened again.'

'You put your hand under the pillow again? And the face was there?'

'Not the whole face, baba. Just something soft and squishy. I thought it was a snail under my pillow. So I got up, lit my lamp, and looked under the pillow.'

'What was it, Mehmood? Tell me quickly.'

'It was an eyeball, baba. An eye that had been removed

from its socket. It was staring up at me. Just an eyeball, staring! I picked it up and threw it out of the window. I threw the pillow away too. Something terrible had happened upon that pillow, I'm sure of it.'

'So it wasn't the room?'

'It wasn't the room. It was the pillow, baba. Next day I went into town and bought a new pillow, and from then on I slept beautifully every night. Never use a strange cushion or pillow, baba. Terrible things have happened on pillows. So remember—when you return to school next month, take a new pillow, and don't use anyone else's!'

After listening to Mehmood's story, I was always careful to use my own pillow. Even now, many many years later, I carry my own pillow wherever I go. No hotel pillows for me. You never knew what might be lurking beneath them.

Some Hill Station Ghosts

Shimla has its phantom-rickshaw and Lansdowne its headless horseman. Mussoorie has its woman in white. Late at night, she can be seen sitting on the parapet wall on the winding road up to the hill station. Don't stop to offer her a lift. She will fix you with her evil eye and ruin your holiday.

The Mussoorie taxi drivers and other locals call her Bhoot Aunty. Everyone has seen her at some time or the other. To give her a lift is to court disaster. Many accidents have been attributed to her baleful presence. And when people pick themselves up from the road (or are picked up by concerned citizens), Bhoot Aunty is nowhere to be seen, although survivors swear that she was in the car with them.

Ganesh Saili, Abha and I were coming back from Dehradun late one night when we saw this woman in white sitting on the parapet by the side of the road. As our headlights fell on her, she turned her face away, Ganesh, being a thorough gentleman, slowed down and offered her a lift. She turned towards us then, and smiled a wicked smile. She seemed quite attractive except that her canines protruded slightly in vampire fashion.

'Don't stop!' screamed Abha. 'Don't even look at her! It's Aunty!'

Ganesh pressed down on the accelerator and sped past her. Next day, we heard that a tourist's car had gone off the road and the occupants had been severely injured. The accident had taken place shortly after they had stopped to pick up a woman in white who had wanted a lift. But she was not among the injured.

■

Miss Ripley-Bean, an old English lady who was my neighbour when I lived near Wynberg-Allen school, told me that her family was haunted by a malignant phantom head that always appeared before the death of one of her relatives.

She said her brother saw this apparition the night before her mother died, and both she and her sister saw it before the death of their father. The sister slept in the same room. They were both awakened one night by a curious noise in the cupboard facing their beds. One of them began getting out of bed to see if their cat was in the room, when the cupboard door suddenly opened and a luminous head appeared. It was covered with matted hair and appeared to be in an advanced stage of decomposition. Its fleshless mouth grinned at the terrified sisters. And then as they crossed themselves, it vanished. The next day they learnt that their father, who was in Lucknow, had died suddenly, at about the time that they had seen the death's head.

■

Everyone likes to hear stories about haunted houses; even sceptics will listen to a ghost story, while casting doubts on its veracity.

Rudyard Kipling wrote a number of memorable ghost stories set in India—*Imray's Return*, *The Phantom Rickshaw*, *The Mark of the Beast*, *The End of the Passage*—his favourite milieu being the haunted dak bungalow. But it was only after his return to England that he found himself actually having to live in a haunted house. He wrote about it in his autobiography, *Something of Myself*.

> The spring of '96 saw us in Torquay, where we found a house for our heads that seemed almost too good to be true. It was large and bright, with big rooms each and all open to the sun, the ground embellished with great trees and the warm land dipping southerly to the clean sea under the Mary Church cliffs. It had been inhabited for thirty years by three old maids.
>
> The revelation came in the shape of a growing depression which enveloped us both—a gathering blackness of mind and sorrow of the heart, that each put down to the new, soft climate and, without telling the other, fought against for long weeks. It was the Feng-shui—the Spirit of the house itself—that darkened the sunshine and fell upon us every time we entered, checking the very words on our lips… We paid forfeit and fled. More than thirty years later we returned down the steep little road to that house, and found, quite unchanged, the same brooding spirit of deep despondency within the rooms.

Again, thirty years later, he returned to this house in his short story, 'The House Surgeon', in which two sisters cannot come to terms with the suicide of a third sister, and brood upon the tragedy day and night until their thoughts saturate every room of the house.

Many years ago, I had a similar experience in a house in Dehradun, in which an elderly English couple had died from neglect and starvation. In 1947, when many European residents were leaving the town and emigrating to the UK, this poverty-stricken old couple, sick and friendless, had been forgotten. Too ill to go out for food or medicine, they had died in their beds, where they were discovered several days later by the landlord's munshi.

The house stood empty for several years. No one wanted to live in it. As a young man, I would sometimes roam about the neglected grounds or explore the cold, bare rooms, now stripped of furniture, doorless and windowless, and I would be assailed by a feeling of deep gloom and depression. Of course I knew what had happened there, and that may have contributed to the effect the place had on me. But when I took a friend, Jai Shankar, through the house, he told me he felt quite sick with apprehension and fear. 'Ruskin, why have you brought me to this awful house?' he said. 'I'm sure it's haunted.' And only then did I tell him about the tragedy that had taken place within its walls.

Today, the house is used as a government office. No one lives in it at night except for a Gurkha chowkidar, a man of strong nerves who sleeps in the back verandah. The atmosphere of the place doesn't bother him, but he does hear strange sounds in the night. 'Like someone crawling about on the floor above,' he tells me. 'And someone groaning. These old houses are noisy places…'

◆

A morgue is not a noisy place, as a rule. And for a morgue attendant, corpses are silent companions.

Old Mr Jacob, who lives just behind my cottage, was once a morgue attendant for the local mission hospital. In those days it was situated at Sunny Bank, about a hundred metres up the hill from here. One of the outhouses served as the morgue: Mr Jacob begs me not to identify it.

He tells me of a terrifying experience he went through when he was doing night duty at the morgue.

'The body of a young man was found floating in the Aglar River, behind Landour, and was brought to the morgue while I was on night duty. It was placed on the table and covered with a sheet.

'I was quite accustomed to seeing corpses of various kinds and did not mind sharing the same room with them, even after dark. On this occasion a friend had promised to join me, and to pass the time I strolled around the room, whistling a popular tune. I think it was "Danny Boy", if I remember right. My friend was a long time coming, and I soon got tired of whistling and sat down on the bench beside the table. The night was very still, and I began to feel uneasy. My thoughts went to the boy who had drowned and I wondered what he had been like when he was alive. Dead bodies are so impersonal...

'The morgue had no electricity, just a kerosene lamp, and after some time I noticed that the flame was very low. As I was about to turn it up, it suddenly went out. I lit the lamp again, after extending the wick. I returned to the bench, but I had not been sitting there for long when the lamp again went out, and something moved very softly and quietly past me.

'I felt quite sick and faint, and could hear my heart pounding away. The strength had gone out of my legs, otherwise I would have fled from the room. I felt quite weak and helpless, unable even to call out.

'Presently the footsteps came nearer and nearer. Something cold and icy touched one of my hands and felt its way up towards my neck and throat. It was behind me, then it was before me. Then it was *over* me. I was in the arms of the corpse!

'I must have fainted, because when I woke up I was on the floor, and my friend was trying to revive me. The corpse was back on the table.'

'It may have been a nightmare,' I suggested. 'Or you allowed your imagination to run riot.'

'No,' said Mr Jacobs. 'There were wet, slimy marks on my clothes. And the feet of the corpse matched the wet footprints on the floor.'

After this experience, Mr Jacobs refused to do any more night duty at the morgue.

◆

From Herbertpur near Paonta you can go up to Kalsi, and then up the hill road to Chakrata.

Chakrata is in a security zone, most of it off limits to tourists, which is one reason why it has remained unchanged in 150 years of its existence. This small town's population of 1,500 is the same today as it was in 1947—probably the only town in India that hasn't shown a population increase.

Courtesy a government official, I was fortunate enough to be able to stay in the forest rest house on the outskirts of the town. This is a new building, the old rest house—a little way downhill—having fallen into disuse. The chowkidar told me the old rest house was haunted, and that this was the real reason for its having been abandoned. I was a bit sceptical about this, and asked him what kind of haunting took place in it. He told me that he had himself gone through a frightening experience in the old house, when he had gone there to light a fire for some forest officers who were expected that night. After lighting the fire, he looked round and saw a large black animal, like a wild cat, sitting on the wooden floor and gazing into the fire. 'I called out to it, thinking it was someone's pet. The creature turned, and looked full at me with eyes that were human, and a face which was the face of an ugly woman. The creature snarled at me, and the snarl became an angry howl. Then it vanished!'

'And what did you do?' I asked.

'I vanished too,' said the chowkidar. I haven't been down to that house again.'

I did not volunteer to sleep in the old house but made myself comfortable in the new one, where I hoped I would not be troubled by any phantom. However, a large rat kept me company, gnawing away at the woodwork of a chest of drawers. Whenever I switched on the light it would be silent, but as soon as the light was off, it would start gnawing away again.

This reminded me of a story old Miss Kellner (of my Dehra childhood) told me, of a young man who was desperately in love with a girl who did not care for him. One day, when he was following her in the street, she turned on him and, pointing to a rat which some boys had just killed, said, 'I'd as soon marry that rat as marry you.' He took her cruel words so much to heart that he pined away and died. After his death the girl was haunted at night by a rat and occasionally she would be bitten. When the family decided to emigrate, they travelled down to Bombay in order to embark on a ship sailing for London. The ship had just left the quay, when shouts and screams were heard from the pier. The crowd scattered, and a huge rat with fiery eyes ran down to the end of the quay. It sat there, screaming with rage, then jumped into the water and disappeared. After that (according to Miss Kellner), the girl was not haunted again.

Old dak bungalows and forest rest houses have a reputation for being haunted. And most hill stations have their resident ghosts—and ghost writers! But I will not extend this catalogue of ghostly hauntings and visitations, as I do not want to discourage tourists from visiting Landour and Mussoorie. In some countries, ghosts are an added attraction for tourists. Britain boasts of hundreds of haunted castles and stately homes, and visitors to Romania seek out Transylvania and Dracula's castle. So do we promote Bhoot Aunty as a tourist attraction? Only if she reforms and stops sending vehicles off those hairpin bends that lead to Mussoorie.

Fairy Glen Palace

The old bridle path from Rajpur to Mussoorie passed through Fosterganj at a height of about five thousand feet. In the old days, before the motor road was built, this was the only road to the hill station. You could ride up on a pony, or walk, or be carried in a basket (if you were a child) or in a *doolie* (if you were a lady or an invalid). The doolie was a cross between a hammock, a stretcher, and a sedan chair, if you can imagine such a contraption. It was borne aloft by two perspiring partners. Sometimes they sat down to rest, and dropped you unceremoniously. I have a picture of my grandmother being borne uphill in a doolie, and she looks petrified. There was an incident in which a doolie, its occupant and two bearers, all went over a cliff just before Fosterganj, and perished in the fall. Sometimes you can see the ghost of this poor lady being borne uphill by two phantom bearers.

Fosterganj has its ghosts, of course. And they are something of a distraction.

Writing is my vocation, and I have always tried to follow the apostolic maxim: 'Study to be quiet and to mind your own business.' But in small-town India one is constantly drawn into other people's business, just as they are drawn towards yours. In Fosterganj it was quiet enough, there were few people; there was no excuse for shirking work. But tales of haunted houses and fairy-infested forests have always intrigued me, and when

I heard that the ruined palace halfway down to Rajpur was a place to be avoided after dark, it was natural for me to start taking my evening walks in its direction.

Fairy Glen was its name. It had been built on the lines of a Swiss or French chalet, with numerous turrets decorating its many wings—a huge, rambling building, two-storeyed, with numerous balconies, cornices and windows; a hodge-podge of architectural styles, a wedding cake of a palace, built to satisfy the whims and fancies of its late owner, the Raja of Ranipur, a small state near the Nepal border. Maintaining this ornate edifice must have been something of a nightmare; and the present heirs had quite given up on it, for bits of the roof were missing, some windows were without panes, doors had developed cracks, and what had once been a garden was now a small jungle. Apparently there was no one living there any more; no sign of a caretaker. I had walked past the wrought-iron gate several times without seeing any signs of life, apart from a large grey cat sunning itself outside a broken window.

Then one evening, walking up from Rajpur, I was caught in a storm.

A wind had sprung up, bringing with it dark, overburdened clouds. Heavy drops of rain were followed by hailstones bouncing off the stony path. Gusts of wind rushed through the oaks, and leaves and small branches were soon swirling through the air. I was still a couple of miles from the Fosterganj bazaar, and I did not fancy sheltering under a tree, as flashes of lightning were beginning to light up the darkening sky. Then I found myself outside the gate of the abandoned palace.

Outside the gate stood an old sentry box. No one had stood sentry in it for years. It was a good place in which to shelter. But I hesitated because a large bird was perched on the gate, seemingly oblivious to the rain that was still falling.

It looked like a crow or a raven, but it was much bigger than either—in fact, twice the size of a crow, but having all the features of one—and when a flash of lightning lit up the gate, it gave a squawk, opened its enormous wings and took off, flying in the direction of the oak forest. I hadn't seen such a bird before; there was something dark and malevolent and almost supernatural about it. But it had gone, and I darted into the sentry box without further delay.

I had been standing there some ten minutes, wondering when the rain was going to stop, when I heard someone running down the road. As he approached, I could see that he was just a boy, probably eleven or twelve; but in the dark I could not make out his features. He came up to the gate, lifted the latch, and was about to go in when he saw me in the sentry box.

'*Kaun?* Who are you?' he asked, first in Hindi then in English. He did not appear to be in any way anxious or alarmed.

'Just sheltering from the rain,' I said. 'I live in the bazaar.' He took a small torch from his pocket and shone it in my face.

'Yes, I have seen you there. A tourist.'

'A writer. I stay in places, I don't just pass through.'

'Do you want to come in?'

I hesitated. It was still raining and the roof of the sentry box was leaking badly.

'Do you live here?' I asked.

'Yes, I am the raja's nephew. I live here with my mother. Come in.' He took me by the hand and led me through the gate. His hand was quite rough and heavy for an eleven- or twelve-year-old. Instead of walking with me to the front steps and entrance of the old palace, he led me around to the rear of the building, where a faint light glowed in a mullioned window, and in its light I saw that he had a very fresh and pleasant face—a face as yet untouched by the trials of life.

Instead of knocking on the door, he tapped on the window. 'Only strangers knock on the door,' he said. 'When I tap on the window, my mother knows it's me.'

'That's clever of you,' I said.

He tapped again, and the door was opened by an unusually tall woman wearing a kind of loose, flowing gown that looked strange in that place, and on her. The light was behind her, and I couldn't see her face until we had entered the room. When she turned to me, I saw that she had a long reddish scar running down one side of her face. Even so, there was a certain hard beauty in her appearance.

'Make some tea—Mother,' said the boy rather brusquely. 'And something to eat. I'm hungry. Sir, will you have something?' He looked enquiringly at me. The light from a kerosene lamp fell full on his face. He was wide-eyed, full-lipped, smiling; only his voice seemed rather mature for one so young. And he spoke like someone much older, and with an almost unsettling sophistication.

'Sit down, sir.' He led me to a chair, made me comfortable. 'You are not too wet, I hope?'

'No, I took shelter before the rain came down too heavily. But you are wet, you'd better change.'

'It doesn't bother me.' And after a pause, 'Sorry there is no electricity. Bills haven't been paid for years.'

'Is this your place?'

'No, we are only caretakers. Poor relations, you might say. The palace has been in dispute for many years. The raja and his brothers keep fighting over it, and meanwhile it is slowly falling down. The lawyers are happy. Perhaps I should study and become a lawyer some day.'

'Do you go to school?'

'Sometimes.'

'How old are you?'

'Quite old, I'm not sure. Mother, how old am I?' he asked, as the tall woman returned with cups of tea and a plate full of biscuits.

She hesitated, gave him a puzzled look. 'Don't you know? It's on your certificate.'

'I've lost the certificate.'

'No, I've kept it safely.' She looked at him intently, placed a hand on his shoulder, then turned to me and said, 'He is twelve,' with a certain finality.

We finished our tea. It was still raining.

'It will rain all night,' said the boy. 'You had better stay here.'

'It will inconvenience you.'

'No, it won't. There are many rooms. If you do not mind the darkness. Come, I will show you everything. And meanwhile my mother will make some dinner. Very simple food, I hope you won't mind.'

The boy took me around the old palace, if you could still call it that. He led the way with a candle holder from which a large candle threw our exaggerated shadows on the walls.

'What's your name?' I asked, as he led me into what must have been a reception room, still crowded with ornate furniture and bric-a-brac.

'Bhim,' he said. 'But everyone calls me Lucky.'

'And are you lucky?'

He shrugged. 'Don't know...' Then he smiled up at me.

'Maybe you'll bring me luck.'

We walked further into the room. Large oil paintings hung from the walls, gathering mould. Some were portraits of royalty, kings and queens of another era, wearing decorative headgear, strange uniforms, the women wrapped in jewellery—more jewels than garments, it seemed—and sometimes accompanied by children who were also weighed down by excessive clothing. A young man sat on a throne, his lips curled in a sardonic smile.

'My grandfather,' said Bhim.

He led me into a large bedroom taken up by a four-poster bed which had probably seen several royal couples copulating upon it. It looked cold and uninviting, but Bhim produced a voluminous razai from a cupboard and assured me that it would be warm and quite luxurious, as it had been his grandfather's.

'And when did your grandfather die?' I asked.

'Oh, fifty-sixty years ago, it must have been.'

'In this bed, I suppose.'

'No, he was shot accidentally while out hunting. They said it was an accident. But he had enemies.'

'Kings have enemies.... And this was the royal bed?'

He gave me a sly smile; not so innocent after all. 'Many women slept in it. He had many queens.'

'And concubines.'

'What are concubines?'

'Unofficial queens.'

'Yes, those too.'

A worldly-wise boy of twelve.

The Haunted Bicycle

I was living at the time in a village about five miles out of Shahganj, a district in east Uttar Pradesh, and my only means of transport was a bicycle. I could of course have gone into Shahganj on any obliging farmer's bullock cart, but, in spite of bad roads and my own clumsiness as a cyclist, I found the bicycle a trifle faster. I went into Shahganj almost every day, collected my mail, bought a newspaper, drank innumerable cups of tea, and gossiped with the tradesmen. I cycled back to the village at about six in the evening, along a quiet, unfrequented forest road. During the winter months it was dark by six, and I would have to use a lamp on the bicycle.

One evening, when I had covered about half the distance to the village, I was brought to a halt by a small boy who was standing in the middle of the road. The forest at that late hour was no place for a child; wolves and hyenas were common in the district. I got down from my bicycle and approached the boy, but he didn't seem to take much notice of me.

'What are you doing here on your own?' I asked.

'I'm waiting,' he said, without looking at me.

'Waiting for whom? Your parents?'

'No, I am waiting for my sister.'

'Well, I haven't passed her on the road,' I said. 'She may be further ahead. You had better come along with me, we'll soon find her.'

The boy nodded and climbed silently on to the crossbar in front of me. I have never been able to recall his features. Already it was dark and besides, he kept his face turned away from me.

The wind was against us, and as I cycled on, I shivered with the cold, but the boy did not seem to feel it. We had not gone far when the light from my lamp fell on the figure of another child who was standing by the side of the road. This time it was a girl. She was a little older than the boy, and her hair was long and windswept, hiding most of her face.

'Here's your sister,' I said. 'Let's take her along with us.'

The girl did not respond to my smile, and she did no more than nod seriously to the boy. But she climbed up on to my back carrier, and allowed me to pedal off again. Their replies to my friendly questions were monosyllabic, and I gathered that they were wary of strangers. Well, when I got to the village, I would hand them over to the headman, and he could locate their parents. The road was level, but I felt as though I was cycling uphill. And then I noticed that the boy's head was much closer to my face, that the girl's breathing was loud and heavy, almost as though she was doing the riding. Despite the cold wind, I began to feel hot and suffocated.

'I think we'd better take rest,' I suggested.

'No!' cried the boy and girl together. 'No rest!'

I was so surprised that I rode on without any argument; and then, just as I was thinking of ignoring their demand and stopping, I noticed that the boy's hands, which were resting on the handlebar, had grown long, black and hairy.

My hands shook and the bicycle wobbled about on the road.

'Be careful!' shouted the children in unison. 'Look where you are going!'

Their tone now was menacing and far from childlike. I

took a quick glance over my shoulder and had my worst fears confirmed.

The girl's face was huge and bloated. Her legs, black and hairy, were trailing along the ground.

'Stop!' ordered the terrible children. 'Stop near the stream!'

But before I could do anything, my front wheel hit a stone and the bicycle toppled over. As I sprawled in the dust, I felt something hard, like a hoof, hit me on the hack of the head, and then there was total darkness.

When I recovered consciousness, I noticed that the moon had risen and was sparkling on the waters of a stream. The children were not to be seen anywhere. I got up from the ground and began to brush the dust from my clothes. And then, hearing the sound of splashing and churning in the stream, I looked up again.

Two small black buffaloes gazed at me from the muddy, moonlit water.

Whispering in the Dark

A wild night. Wind moaning, trees lashing themselves in a frenzy, rain beating down on the road, thunder over the mountains. Loneliness stretched ahead of me, a loneliness of the heart as well as a physical loneliness. The world was blotted out by a mist that had come up from the valley, a thick, white, clammy shroud.

I groped through the forest, groped in my mind for the memory of a mountain path, some remembered rock or ancient deodar. Then a streak of blue lightning gave me a glimpse of a barren hillside and a house cradled in mist.

It was an old-world house, built of limestone rock on the outskirts of a crumbling hill station. There was no light in its windows; probably the electricity had been disconnected long ago. But if I could get in, it would do for the night.

I had no torch, but at times the moon shone through the wild clouds, and trees loomed out of the mist like primeval giants. I reached the front door and found it locked from within. I walked round to the side and broke a windowpane, put my hand through shattered glass and found the bolt.

The window, warped by over a hundred monsoons, resisted at first. Then it yielded, and I climbed into the mustiness of a long-closed room, and the wind came in with me, scattering papers across the floor and knocking some unidentifiable object off a table. I closed the window, bolted it again, but the mist crawled through the broken glass, and the wind rattled in it like a pair of castanets.

There were matches in my pocket. I struck three before a light flared up.

I was in a large room, crowded with furniture. Pictures on the walls. Vases on the mantelpiece. A candlestand. And, strangely enough, no cobwebs. For all its external look of neglect and dilapidation, the house had been cared for by someone. But before I could notice anything else, the match burnt out.

As I stepped further into the room, the old deodar flooring creaked beneath my weight. By the light of another match I reached the mantelpiece and lit the candle, noticing at the same time that the candlestick was a genuine antique with cutglass hangings. A deserted cottage with good furniture and glass. I wondered why no one had ever broken in. And then realized that I had just done so.

I held the candlestick high and glanced round the room. The walls were hung with several watercolours and portraits in oils. There was no dust anywhere. But no one answered my call, no one responded to my hesitant knocking. It was as though the occupants of the house were in hiding, watching me obliquely from dark corners and chimneys.

I entered a bedroom and found myself facing a full-length mirror. My reflection stared back at me as though I were a stranger, as though my reflection belonged to the house, while I was only an outsider.

As I turned from the mirror, I thought I saw someone, something, some reflection other than mine, move behind me in the mirror. I caught a glimpse of whiteness, a pale oval face, burning eyes, long tresses, golden in the candlelight. But when I looked in the mirror again there was nothing to be seen but my own pallid face.

A pool of water was forming at my feet. I set the candle down on a small table, found the edge of the bed—a large old four-poster—sat down, and removed my soggy shoes and socks. Then I took off my clothes and hung them over the back of a chair.

I stood naked in the darkness, shivering a little. There was no one to see me—and yet I felt oddly exposed, almost as though I had stripped in a room full of curious people.

I got under the bedclothes—they smelt slightly of eucalyptus and lavender—but found there was no pillow. That was odd. A perfectly made bed, but no pillow! I was too tired to hunt for one. So, I blew out the candle and the darkness closed in around me, and the whispering began...

The whispering began as soon as I closed my eyes. I couldn't tell where it came from. It was all around me, mingling with the sound of the wind coughing in the chimney, the stretching of old furniture, the weeping of trees outside in the rain.

Sometimes I could hear what was being said. The words came from a distance: a distance not so much of space as of time...

'Mine, mine, he is all mine...'

'He is ours, dear, ours.'

Whispers, echoes, words hovering around me with bats' wings, saying the most inconsequential things with a logical urgency. 'You're late for supper...'

'He lost his way in the mist.'

'Do you think he has any money?'

'To kill a turtle you must first tie its legs to two posts.'

'We could tie him to the bed and pour boiling water down his throat.'

'No, it's simpler this way.'

I sat up. Most of the whispering had been distant, impersonal, but this last remark had sounded horribly near.

I relit the candle and the voices stopped. I got up and prowled around the room, vainly looking for some explanation for the voices. Once again I found myself facing the mirror, staring at my own reflection and the reflection of that other person, the girl with the golden hair and shining eyes. And this time she held a pillow in her hands. She was standing behind me.

I remembered then the stories I had heard as a boy, of two spinster sisters—one beautiful, one plain—who lured rich, elderly gentlemen into their boarding house and suffocated them in the night. The deaths had appeared quite natural, and they had got away with it for years. It was only the surviving sister's deathbed confession that had revealed the truth—and even then no one had believed her.

But that had been many, many years ago, and the house had long since fallen down...

When I turned from the mirror, there was no one behind me. I looked again, and the reflection had gone.

I crawled back into the bed and put the candle out. And I slept and dreamt (or was I awake and did it really happen?) that the woman I had seen in the mirror stood beside the bed, leant over me, looked at me with eyes flecked by orange flames. I saw people moving in those eyes. I saw myself. And then her lips touched mine, lips so cold, so dry, that a shudder ran through my body.

And then, while her face became faceless and only the eyes remained, something else continued to press down upon me, something soft, heavy, and shapeless, enclosing me in a suffocating embrace. I could not turn my head or open my mouth. I could not breathe.

I raised my hands and clutched feebly at the thing on top of me. And to my surprise it came away. It was only a pillow that had somehow fallen over my face, half suffocating me while

I dreamt of a phantom kiss.

I flung the pillow aside. I flung the bedclothes from me. I had had enough of whispering, of ownerless reflections, of pillows that fell on me in the dark. I would brave the storm outside rather than continue to seek rest in this tortured house.

I dressed quickly. The candle had almost guttered out. The house and everything in it belonged to the darkness of another time; I belonged to the light of day.

I was ready to leave. I avoided the tall mirror with its grotesque rococo design. Holding the candlestick before me, I moved cautiously into the front room. The pictures on the walls sprang to life.

One, in particular, held my attention, and I moved closer to examine it more carefully by the light of the dwindling candle. Was it just my imagination, or was the girl in the portrait the woman of my dream, the beautiful pale reflection in the mirror? Had I gone back in time, or had time caught up with me? Is it time that's passing by, or is it you and I?

I turned to leave, and the candle gave one final sputter and went out, plunging the room in darkness. I stood still for a moment, trying to collect my thoughts, to still the panic that came rushing upon me. Just then there was a knocking on the door.

'Who's there?' I called.

Silence. And then, again, the knocking, and this time a voice, low and insistent: 'Please let me in, please let me in...'

I stepped forward, unbolted the door, and flung it open.

She stood outside in the rain. Not the pale, beautiful one, but a wizened old hag with bloodless lips and flaring nostrils and—but where were the eyes? No eyes, no eyes!

She swept past me on the wind, and at the same time I took advantage of the open doorway to run outside, to run gratefully into the pouring rain, to be lost for hours among the dripping trees, to be glad for all the leeches clinging to my flesh.

And when, with the dawn, I found my way at last, I rejoiced in birdsong and the sunlight piercing and scattering the clouds.

And today if you were to ask me if the old house is still there or not, I would not be able to tell you, for the simple reason that I haven't the slightest desire to go looking for it.

The Skull

I am not normally bothered by skeletons and old bones—they are, after all, just the chalky remains of the long dead—so when my nephew Anil came back from medical college with a well-preserved skull, it was no cause for alarm. He was a second year student, at times a bit of a prankster.

'I hope you didn't take it without permission,' I said, taking the skull in my hands and admiring its symmetry but without philosophizing upon it like Hamlet.

'Oh, the college is full of them,' said Anil. 'I just borrowed it for the vacation.' He placed it on the mantelpiece, among some of the awards and mementos (cheap brassware mostly) that had accumulated over the years, and I must say it livened up the shelf a little.

Anil had placed the skull at one end of the mantelpiece, and there it stood until we'd had our dinner. He settled down with a book while I poured myself a small glass of cognac before settling into an easy chair with a notebook on my knee. It was midsummer and the window was open, so that we could hear the crickets singing in the oak trees. My cottage was on the outskirts of Mussoorie, surrounded by Himalayan oak and maple.

I had been making some notes for an article on wild flowers. When I had finished my notes and my cognac, I looked up and noticed that the skull now stood in the centre of the mantelpiece.

'Did you move the skull?' I asked.

'No,' said Anil, looking up. 'I placed it at the end of the shelf.'

'Well, it's now in the middle. How did it get there?'

'You must have moved it yourself, without noticing. That was a stiff cognac you drank, Uncle.'

I let it pass, it did not seem important.

♦

People often dropped in to see me. Schoolteachers, visitors to the hill station, students, other writers, neighbours. During that week I had a number of visitors and of course everyone noticed the skull on the mantelpiece. Some were intrigued and wanted to know whose skull it was. One or two lady teachers were frightened by it. A fellow writer thought it was in bad taste, displaying human remains in my sitting room. One visitor offered to buy it.

I would gladly have sold the wretched thing but it belonged to Anil and he intended to take it back to Meerut. But when the time came to leave he forgot about the skull, his mind no doubt taken up with other matters—such as the daily phone calls he received from a girl student in Delhi. After seeing him off at the bus stop, I came home to find that the skull was still occupying pride of place on the mantelpiece.

I ignored it for a few days, and the skull didn't seem to mind that. It was receiving plenty of attention from visitors during the day.

But it was beginning to get on my nerves. Every evening, when I sat down to enjoy a whisky or a cognac, I would feel its empty eye sockets staring at me. And on one occasion, when I tried to change its position, my hand got caught in its jawbone and it was with some difficulty that I withdrew it.

Getting fed up of its presence, I decided to lock the thing away where it wouldn't be seen.

There was a wall cupboard in the room, where I kept my manuscripts, notebooks and writing materials, and there was plenty of space there for the skull. So I shifted it to the cupboard and made sure the doors were locked.

That evening I enjoyed my drink without being watched by that remnant of a human head. The crickets were singing, a nightjar was calling and a zephyr of a wind moved softly through the trees. I finished my article and went to bed in a happy frame of mind.

In the middle of the night I woke to a loud rattling sound. At first I thought it was a loose door latch or a wobbly drainpipe, then realized the noise was coming from the wall cupboard. A rat, perhaps? But no. As soon as I opened the cupboard door, out popped the skull, landing near my feet and bouncing away right across the drawing room.

For the sake of peace and quiet, I returned it to the mantelpiece. If a skull could smile, it would probably have done so. I went back to my bed and slept like a baby. It takes more than a dancing skull to keep me from enjoying a good night's sleep.

The next morning I got to work making up a parcel. Normally, I hate making parcels, they usually fall apart. But for once I took pleasure in making a parcel. I wrapped the skull in a plastic bag, then placed it in a strong cardboard box, wrapped this in brown parcel paper, used a liberal amount of Sellotape and addressed the package to Dr Anil at his medical college. Then I walked into town and handed it over to the registration clerk at the post office.

Rubbing my hands with satisfaction, I treated myself to fish and chips and an ice cream before setting out on the walk down the hill to my cottage.

I was about halfway down the steep path that leads to one of our famous schools when I heard something rattling down the slope behind me. At first I thought it was an empty tin but then I recognized my boon companion, that wretched skull, embellished with bits of wrapping paper and Sellotape, bouncing down the hill towards me. How did the skull get out of that parcel? I shall never know. Perhaps a nosy postal clerk had opened it to check the contents. I hope he got the fright of his life. I broke into a run, making a dash for the cottage door. But it was there before me, grinning up at me from a pot full of flowering petunias.

So back it went to its favourite place on the mantelpiece. And there it remained for several weeks.

♦

The school's playing field was situated just above the path to the cottage and during the football season I could hear the boys kicking a football around.

One day a football escaped from the field and came bouncing down the hillside, landing on a flower bed. The match was over and no one bothered to come down to retrieve the ball. But it gave me an idea. I removed the bladder, stuffed the skull into the leather interior and tied it up firmly. Then I had the football delivered to the school's games master, with my compliments.

Nothing happened for a couple of days. There was no shortage of footballs. Then in the middle of the game against St George's College, a ball went out of the grounds and a spare one was required.

The replacement did not bounce quite as well as the previous one and it was inclined to spin around a lot and take off in directions opposite to those intended. Also, it squeaked whenever it received a kick and sometimes those squeaks sounded a bit like screams of protest. The goalkeepers at either end found the ball difficult to hold, it did its best to elude their grasp. And more goals were scored by accident rather than design. Finally, this eccentric ball was kicked out of play and was replaced by another.

What happens to old footballs? I expect they finally fall apart and end up in a dustbin.

In this case, the football found a new owner, for the sports master was a kind man who gave away old bats, balls and other worn-out stuff to the poor children of the locality. A boy from a village near Rajpur was the recipient of the battered football, and he and his friends carried it away with a cheer, kicking it all the way down the steep path, making so much noise that they did not hear the groans of protest that issued from the battered old football.

Well, weeks passed, months passed, without the skull making a reappearance. But then something strange began to happen. I found myself missing that troublesome skull!

It had, after all, been company of a sort for a lonely writer living on his own on the edge of the forest. And when you have lived with someone for a long time, then, no matter how much you may quarrel or get on each other's nerves, a bond is formed and the strength of that bond can only be known when it is broken.

The skull had been sharing my life for over a year and now that it was gone, seemingly forever, my life seemed rather empty.

So I began searching for the skull. I enquired among the children down in Rajpur but they had long since lost the football. I made a round of all the junk shops in Dehradun, without any luck. There were lots of old footballs lying around, but not the one I wanted. And no, they didn't buy or sell human skulls.

Young Anil, the doctor, paid me a brief visit and found me looking depressed.

'What's the trouble?' he asked. 'You look as though you've just lost a friend.'

'I have, indeed,' I said. 'I miss that skull you gave me. It was company of a sort.'

'Well, I'll get you another. No shortage of skulls in my college.'

'No, I don't want another. I want the same skull. It had a personality of its own.'

Anil looked at me as though he thought I was going off my rocker. And perhaps I was.

And then one day, as I was walking down a busy street in neighbouring Saharanpur, I noticed a fortune teller plying his trade on the pavement. I don't believe in fortune telling but everyone has to make a living and telling fortunes seems to me a harmless way of doing it. And then I noticed that he had a skull beside him and that he would consult it before handing his customer a slip of paper with words of advice or encouragement written on it. It looked a bit like my skull but I couldn't be sure. All the kicking and manhandling it had received had possibly altered its appearance.

But, anyway, I gave the fortune teller some money and asked him for a prediction. He chanted something, then extracted a slip of paper from beneath the skull and handed it to me with a flourish.

I read the words printed neatly on the paper.

'Ullu ka patha', went the message, followed by 'Gadhe ka baccha!'

It was definitely my skull! Only an old friend could abuse me like that.

So I pleaded and haggled with the fortune teller, paid him a hundred rupees for the skull and carried it home in triumph.

And there it is today, decorating my mantelpiece, a little the worse for wear and with a silly grin on its skeletal face. To improve its looks I have placed an old cricket cap on its head.

Sometimes we don't value our friends until we lose them.

The Ghost and the Idiot

In a village near Agra there lived a family who was under the special protection of a *munjia*, a ghost who lived in a peepul tree. The ghost had attached himself to this particular family and showed his fondness for its members by throwing stones, bones, night-soil and other rubbish at them, and making hideous noises, terrifying them at every opportunity. Under his patronage, the family dwindled away. One by one they died, the only survivor being an idiot boy, whom the ghost did not bother because he felt it beneath his dignity to do so.

But in an Indian village, marriage (like birth and death) must come to all, and it was not long before the neighbours began to make plans for the marriage of the idiot.

After a meeting of the village elders it was decided, first, that the idiot should be married; and second, that he should be married to a shrew of a girl who had passed the age of twenty without finding a suitor!

The shrew and the idiot were soon married off, then left to manage for themselves. The poor idiot had no means of earning a living and had to resort to begging. He had barely been able to support himself before, and now his wife was an additional burden. The first thing she did when she entered the house was to give him a box on the ear and send him out to bring something home for dinner.

The poor fellow went from door to door, but nobody gave

him anything, because the same people who had arranged the marriage were annoyed that he had not given them a wedding feast. In the evening, when he returned home empty-handed, his wife cried out: 'Are you back, you lazy idiot? Why have you been so long, and what have you brought for me?'

When she found he hadn't even a paisa, she flew into a rage and, removing his head-cloth, tossed it into the peepul tree. Then, taking up her broom, she belaboured her husband until he fled from the house.

But the shrew's anger had not yet been assuaged. Seeing her husband's head-cloth in the peepul tree, she began venting her rage on the tree-trunk, accompanying her blows with the most shocking abuse. The ghost who lived in the tree was sensitive to both her blows and her language. Alarmed that her terrible curses might put an end to him, he took to his heels and left the tree in which he had lived for so many years.

Riding on a whirlwind, the ghost soon caught up with the idiot who was still fleeing down the road away from the village. 'Not so fast, brother!' cried the ghost. 'Desert your wife, by all means, but don't abandon your old family ghost! That shrew has driven me out of the peepul tree. What powerful arms she has—and what a vile tongue! She has made brothers of us—brothers in misfortune. And so we must seek our fortunes together! But first promise me you will not return to your wife.'

The idiot made this promise very willingly, and together they journeyed until they reached a large city.

Before they entered the city, the ghost said, 'Now listen, brother. If you follow my advice, your fortune is made. In this city there are two very beautiful girls, one the daughter of a king and the other the daughter of a rich moneylender. I will go and possess the daughter of the king, and when he finds her possessed by a spirit he will try every sort of remedy but with no effect. Meanwhile you must walk daily through the streets in the dress of a sadhu—one who has renounced the world—and when the king comes and asks you if you can cure his daughter, undertake to do so and make your own terms. As soon as I see you, I shall leave the girl. Then I shall go and possess the daughter of the moneylender. But do not go near her, because I am in love with the girl and do not intend giving her up! If you come near her, I shall break your neck.'

The ghost went off on his whirlwind, while the idiot entered the city on his own and found a bed at the local inn for pilgrims. The following day everyone in the city was agog with the news that the king's daughter was dangerously ill. Physicians of all sorts came and went, and all pronounced the girl incurable. The king was on the verge of a nervous breakdown. He offered half his fortune to anyone who could cure his beautiful and only child. The idiot, having smeared himself with dust and ashes like a sadhu, began walking the streets, reciting religious verses.

The people were struck by the idiot's appearance. They took him for a wise and holy man, and reported him to the king, who immediately came into the city, prostrated himself before the idiot, and begged him to cure his daughter. After a show of modesty and reluctance, the idiot was persuaded to accompany the king back to the palace, and the girl was brought before him. Her hair was dishevelled, her teeth were chattering, and her eyes almost starting from their sockets. She howled and cursed and tore at her clothes. The idiot confronted her and recited a few meaningless spells. And the ghost, recognizing him, cried out in terror; 'I'm going, I'm going! I'm on my way!'

'Give me a sign that you have gone,' demanded the idiot.

'As soon as I leave the girl,' said the ghost, 'you will see that mango tree uprooted. That is the sign I'll give.'

A few minutes later the mango tree came crashing down.

The girl recovered from her fit and seemed unaware of what had happened. The news of her miraculous cure spread through the city, and the idiot became an object of veneration and wonder. The king kept his word and gave him half his fortune; and so began a period of happiness and prosperity for the idiot.

A few weeks later the ghost took possession of the moneylender's daughter, with whom he was in love. Seeing his daughter take leave of her senses, the money-lender sent for the highly respected idiot and offered him a great sum of money to cure his daughter. But remembering the ghost's warning, the idiot refused. The moneylender was enraged and sent his henchmen to bring the idiot to him by force; and the idiot was dragged along to the rich man's house.

As soon as the ghost saw his old companion, he cried out in a rage: 'Idiot, why have you broken our agreement and come here? Now I will have to break your neck!'

But the idiot, whose reputation for wisdom had actually helped to make his wiser, said, 'Brother ghost, I have not come to trouble you but to tell you a terrible piece of news. Old friend and protector, we must leave this city soon. *She* has come here—my dreaded wife!—to torment us both, and to drag us back to the village. She is on her way and will be here any minute!'

When the ghost heard this, he cried out, 'Oh no, oh no! If *she* has come, then we must go!'

And breaking down the walls and doors of the house, the ghost gathered himself up into a little whirlwind and went scurrying out of the city to look for a vacant peepul tree. The moneylender, delighted that his daughter had been freed of the evil influence, embraced the idiot and showered presents on him. And in due course the idiot married the moneylender's beautiful daughter, inherited his wealth and debtors, and became the richest and most successful moneylender in the city.

The Overcoat

It was clear, frosty weather, and as the moon came up over the Himalayan peaks, I could see that patches of snow still lay on the roads of the hill station. I would have been quite happy in bed, with a book and a hot-water bottle at my side, but I'd promised the Kapadias that I'd go to their party and I felt it would be churlish of me to stay away. I put on two sweaters, an old football scarf, and an overcoat and set off down the moonlit road.

It was a walk of just over a mile to the Kapadias' house and I had covered about half the distance when I saw a girl standing in the middle of the road.

She must have been sixteen or seventeen. She looked rather old-fashioned—long hair, hanging to her waist, and a sequined dress, pink and lavender, that reminded me of the photos in my grandmother's family album. When I went closer, I noticed that she had lovely eyes and a winning smile.

'Good evening,' I said. 'It's a cold night to be out.'

'Are you going to the party?' she asked.

'That's right. And I can see from your lovely dress that you're going, too. Come along, we're nearly there.'

She fell into step beside me and we soon saw lights from the Kapadias' house shining brightly through the deodars. The girl told me her name was Julie. I hadn't seen her before but then I'd only been in the hill station a few months.

There was quite a crowd at the party but no one seemed to know Julie. Everyone thought she was a friend of mine. I did not deny it. Obviously she was someone who was feeling lonely and wanted to be friendly with people. And she was certainly enjoying herself. I did not see her do much eating or drinking, but she flitted about from one group to another, talking, listening, laughing; and when the music began, she was dancing almost continuously, alone or with partners, it didn't matter which, she was completely wrapped up in the music.

It was almost midnight when I got up to go. I had drunk a fair amount of punch, and I was ready for bed. As I was saying goodnight to my hosts and wishing everyone a merry Christmas, Julie slipped her arm into mine and said she'd be going home, too.

When we were outside, I said, 'Where do you live, Julie?'

'At Wolfsburn,' she said. 'At the top of the hill.'

'There's a cold wind,' I said. 'And although your dress is beautiful, it doesn't look very warm. Here, you'd better wear my overcoat. I've plenty of protection.'

She did not protest and allowed me to slip my overcoat over her shoulders. Then we started out on the walk home. But I did not have to escort her all the way. At about the spot where we had met, she said, 'There's a shortcut from here. I'll just scramble up the hillside.'

'Do you know it well?' I asked. 'It's a very narrow path.'

'Oh, I know every stone on the path. I use it all the time. And besides, it's a really bright night.'

'Well, keep the coat on,' I said. 'I can collect it tomorrow.'

She hesitated for a moment, then smiled and nodded at me. She then disappeared up the hill, and I went home alone.

The next day, I walked up to Wolfsburn. I crossed a little brook, from which the house had probably got its name, and entered an open iron gate. But of the house itself little remained. Just a roofless ruin, a pile of stones, a shattered chimney, a few Doric pillars where a verandah had once stood.

Had Julie played a joke on me? Or had I found the wrong house?

I walked around the hill to the mission house where the Taylors lived, and asked old Mrs Taylor if she knew a girl called Julie.

'No, I don't think so,' she said. 'Where does she live?'

'At Wolfsburn, I was told. But the house is just a ruin.'

'Nobody has lived at Wolfsburn for over forty years. The Mackinnons lived there. One of the old families who settled here. But when their girl died...' She stopped and gave me a queer look. 'I think her name was Julie.... Anyway, when she died, they sold the house and went away. No one ever lived in it again, and it fell into decay. But it couldn't be the same Julie you're looking for. She died of consumption—there wasn't much you could do about it in those days. Her grave is in the cemetery, just down the road.'

I thanked Mrs Taylor and walked slowly down the road to the cemetery: not really wanting to know any more, but propelled forward almost against my will.

It was a small cemetery under the deodars. You could see the eternal snows of the Himalaya standing out against the pristine blue of the sky. Here lay the bones of forgotten Empire-builders—soldiers, merchants, adventurers, their wives and children. It did not take me long to find Julie's grave. It had a simple headstone with her name clearly outlined on it:

Julie Mackinnon
1923–39
With us one moment,

Taken the next
Gone to her Maker,
Gone to her rest.

Although many monsoons had swept across the cemetery wearing down the stones, they had not touched this little tombstone.

I was turning to leave when I caught a glimpse of something familiar behind the headstone. I walked around to where it lay.

Neatly folded on the grass was my overcoat.

Bhoot Aunty
(An extract from Mr Oliver's diary)

A ghost on the main highway past our school. She's known as Bhoot Aunty—a spectral apparition who appears to motorists on their way to Sanjauli. She waves down passing cars and asks for a lift; and if you give her one, you are liable to have an accident.

This lady in white is said to be the revenant of a young woman who was killed in a car accident not far from here, a few months ago. Several motorists claim to have seen her. Oddly enough, pedestrians don't come across her.

Miss Ramola, Miss D'Costa and I are the exceptions.

I had accompanied some of the staff and boys to the girls' school to see a hockey match, and afterwards the ladies asked me to accompany them back as it was getting dark and they had heard there was a panther about.

'The only panther is Mr Oliver,' remarked Miss D'Costa, who was spending the weekend with Anjali Ramola.

'Such a harmless panther,' said Anjali.

I wanted to say that panthers always attack women who wore outsize earrings (such as Miss D'Costa's) but my gentlemanly upbringing prevented a rude response.

As we turned the corner near our school gate, Miss D'Costa cried out, 'Oh, do you see that strange woman sitting on the parapet wall?'

Sure enough, a figure clothed in white was resting against the wall, its face turned away from us.

'Could it—could it be—Bhoot Aunty?' stammered Miss D'Costa.

The two ladies stood petrified in the middle of the road. I stepped forward and asked, 'Who are you, and what can we do for you?'

The ghostly apparition raised its arms, got up suddenly and rushed past me. Miss D'Costa let out a shriek. Anjali turned and fled. The figure in white flapped about, then tripped over its own winding-cloth, and fell in front of me.

As it got to its feet, the white sheet fell away and revealed—Mirchi!

'You wicked boy!' I shouted. 'Just what do you think you are up to?'

'Sorry, sir,' he gasped. 'It's just a joke. Bhoot Aunty, sir!' And he fled the scene.

When the ladies had recovered, I saw them home and promised to deal severely with Mirchi. But on second thoughts I decided to overlook his prank. Miss D'Costa deserved getting a bit of a fright for calling me a panther.

I had picked up Mirchi's bedsheet from the road, and after supper I carried it into the dormitory and placed it on his bed without any comment. He was about to get into bed, and looked up at me in some apprehension.

'Er—thank you, sir,' he said.

'An enjoyable performance,' I told him. 'Next time, make it more convincing.'

After making sure that all the dormitory and corridor lights were out, I went for a quiet walk on my own. I am not averse to a little solitude. I have no objection to my own company. This is different from loneliness, which can assail you even when you are among people. Being a misfit in a group of boisterous party-goers can be a lonely experience. But being alone as a matter of choice is one of life's pleasures.

As I passed the same spot where Mirchi had got up to mischief, I was surprised to see a woman sitting by herself on the low parapet wall. *Another lover of solitude*, I thought. I gave her no more than a glance. She was looking the other way. A pale woman, dressed very simply. I had gone some distance when a thought suddenly came to me. Had I just passed Bhoot Aunty? The real bhoot? The pale woman in white had seemed rather ethereal.

I stopped, turned, and looked again.

The lady had vanished.

From the Primaeval Past

I discovered the pool near Rajpur on a hot summer's day, some fifteen years ago. It was shaded by close-growing sal trees, and looked cool and inviting. I took off my clothes and dived in.

The water was colder than I had expected. It was icy, glacial cold. The sun never touched it for long, I supposed. Striking out vigorously, I swam to the other end of the pool and pulled myself up on the rocks, shivering.

But I wanted to swim. So I dived in again and did a gentle breast-stroke towards the middle of the pool. Something slid between my legs. Something slimy, pulpy. I could see no one, hear nothing. I swam away, but the floating, slippery thing followed me. I did not like it. Something curled around my leg. Not an underwater plant. Something that sucked at my foot. A long tongue licking at my calf. I struck out wildly, thrust myself away from whatever it was that sought my company. Something lonely, lurking in the shadows. Kicking up spray, I swam like a frightened porpoise fleeing from some terror of the deep.

Safely out of the water, I looked for a warm, sunny rock, and stood there looking down at the water.

Nothing stirred. The surface of the pool was now calm and undisturbed. Just a few fallen leaves floating around. Not a frog, not a fish, not a water-bird in sight. And that in itself seemed strange, for you would have expected some sort of pond life to have been in evidence.

But something lived in the pool, of that I was sure. Something very cold-blooded; colder and wetter than the water. Could it have been a corpse trapped in the weeds? I did not want to know; so I dressed and hurried away.

A few days later I left for Delhi, where I went to work in an ad agency, telling people how to beat the summer heat by drinking fizzy drinks that made you thirstier. The pool in the forest was forgotten. And it was ten years before I visited Rajpur again.

Leaving the small hotel where I was staying, I found myself walking through the same old sal forest, drawn almost irresistibly towards the pool where I had not been able to finish my swim. I was not over-eager to swim there again, but I was curious to know if the pool still existed.

Well, it was there all right, although the surroundings had changed and a number of new houses and buildings had come up where formerly there had only been wilderness. And there was a fair amount of activity in the vicinity of the pool.

A number of labourers were busy with buckets and rubber pipes, doing their best to empty the pool. They had also dammed off and diverted the little stream that fed it.

Overseeing this operation was a well-dressed man in a white safari suit. I thought at first that he was an honorary forest warden, but it turned out that he was the owner of a new school that had come up nearby.

'Do you live in Rajpur?' he asked.

'I used to...once upon a time...Why are you draining the pool?'

'It's become a hazard,' he said. 'Two of my boys were drowned here recently. Both senior students. Of course they weren't supposed to be swimming here without permission, the pool is off limits. But you know what boys are like. Make a rule and they feel duty-bound to break it.'

He told me his name, Kapoor, and led me back to his house, a newly-built bungalow with a wide, cool verandah. His servant brought us glasses of cool sherbet. We sat in cane chairs overlooking the pool and the forest. Across a clearing, a gravelled road led to the school buildings, newly white-washed and glistening in the sun.

'Were the boys there at the same time?' I asked.

'Yes, they were friends. And they must have been attacked by fiends. Limbs twisted and broken, faces disfigured. But death was due to drowning—that was the verdict of the medical examiner.'

We gazed down at the shallows of the pool, where a couple of men were still at work, the others having gone for their mid-day meal.

'Perhaps it would be better to leave the place alone,' I said. 'Put a barbed-wire fence around it. Keep your boys away. Thousands of years ago this valley was an inland sea. A few small pools and streams are all that is left of it.'

'I want to fill it in and build something there. An open-air theatre, maybe. We can always create an artificial pond somewhere else.'

Presently only one man remained at the pool, knee-deep in muddy, churned-up water. Kapoor and I both saw what happened next.

Something rose out of the bottom of the pool. It looked like a giant snail, but its head was part human, its body and limbs part squid or octopus. An enormous succubus. It stood taller than the man in the pool. A creature soft and slimy, a survivor from our primaeval past.

With a great sucking motion it enveloped the man completely, so that only his arms and legs could be seen thrashing about wildly and futilely. The succubus dragged him down under the water.

Kapoor and I left the verandah and ran to the edge of the pool. Bubbles rose from the green scum near the surface. All was still and silent. And then, like bubblegum issuing from the mouth of a child, the mangled body of the man shot out of the water and came spinning towards us.

Dead and drowned and sucked dry of its fluids.

Naturally no more work was done at the pool. A labourer had slipped and fallen to his death on the rocks, that was the story that was put out. Kapoor swore me to secrecy. His school would have to close down if there were too many strange drownings and accidents in its vicinity. But he walled the place off from his property and made it practically inaccessible. The jungle's undergrowth now hides the approach.

The monsoon rains came and the pool filled up again. I can tell you how to get there, if you'd like to see it. But I wouldn't advise you to go for a swim.

A Traveller's Tale

Gopalpur-on-sea!
A name to conjure with... And as a boy I'd heard it mentioned, by my father and others, and described as a quaint little seaside resort with a small port on the Orissa coast. The years passed, and I went from boyhood to manhood and eventually old age (is seventy-six old age? I wouldn't know) and still it was only a place I'd heard about and dreamt about but never visited.

Until last month, when I was a guest of KiiT International School in Bhubaneswar, and someone asked me where I'd like to go, and I asked, 'Is Gopalpur very far?'

And off I went, along a plam-fringed highway, through busy little market-towns with names Rhamba and Humma, past the enormous Chilka Lake which opens into the sea through paddy fields and keora plantations, and finally on to Gopalpur's beach road, with the sun glinting like gold on the great waves of the ocean, and the fishermen counting their catch, and the children sprinting into the sea, tumbling about in the shallows.

But the seafront wore a neglected look. The hotels were empty, the cafés deserted. A cheeky crow greeted me with a disconsolate caw from its perch on a weathered old wall. Some of the buildings were recent, but around us there were also the shells of older buildings that had fallen into ruin. And no one was going to preserve these relics of a colonial past. A small house called Brighton Villa still survived.

But away from the seafront a tree-lined road took us past some well-maintained bungalows, a school, an old cemetery, and finally a PWD rest house where we were to spend the night.

It was growing dark when we arrived, and in the twilight I could just make out the shapes of the trees that surround the old bungalow—a hoary old banyan, a jackfruit and several mango trees. The light from the bungalow's verandah fell on some oleander bushes. A hawk moth landed on my shirt-front and appeared reluctant to leave. I took it between my fingers and deposited it on the oleander bush.

It was almost midnight when I went to bed. The rest house staff—the caretaker and the gardener—went to some trouble to arrange a meal, but it was a long time coming. The gardener told me the house had once been the residence of an Englishman who had left the country at the time of Independence, some sixty years or more ago. Some changes had been carried out, but the basic structure remained—high-ceilinged rooms with skylights, a long verandah and enormous bathrooms. The bathroom was so large you could have held a party in it. But there was just one potty and a basin. You could sit on the potty and meditate, fixing your thoughts (or absence of thought) on the distant basin.

I closed all doors and windows, switched off all lights (I find it impossible to sleep with a light on), and went to bed.

It was a comfortable bed, and I soon fell asleep. Only to be awakened by a light tapping on the window near my bed.

Probably a branch of the oleander bush, I thought, and fell asleep again. But there was more tapping, louder this time, and then I was fully awake.

I sat up in bed and drew aside the curtains.

There was a face at the window.

In the half-light from the verandah I could not make out

the features, but it was definitely a human face.

Obviously someone wanted to come in, the caretaker perhaps, or the chowkidar. But then, why not knock on the door? Perhaps he had. The door was at the other end of the room, and I may not have heard the knocking.

I am not in the habit of opening my doors to strangers in the night, but somehow I did not feel threatened or uneasy, so I got up, unlatched the door, and opened it for my midnight visitor.

Standing on the threshold was an imposing figure.

A tall dark man, turbaned, and dressed all in white. He wore some sort of uniform—the kind worn by those immaculate doormen at five-star hotels; but a rare sight in Gopalpur-on-sea.

'What is it you want?' I asked. 'Are you staying here?'

He did not reply but looked past me, possibly through me, and then walked silently into the room. I stood there, bewildered and awestruck, as he strode across to my bed, smoothed out the sheets and patted down my pillow. He then walked over to the next room and came back with a glass and a jug of water, which he placed on the bedside table. As if that were not enough, he picked up my day clothes, folded them neatly and placed them on a vacant chair. Then, just as unobtrusively and without so much as a glance in my direction, he left the room and walked out into the night.

Early next morning, as the sun came up like thunder over the Bay of Bengal, I went down to the sea again, picking my way over the puddles of human excreta that decorated parts of the beach. Well, you can't have everything. The world might be more beautiful without the human presence; but then, who would appreciate it?

Back at the rest house for breakfast, I was reminded of my visitor of the previous night.

'Who was the tall gentleman who came to my room last night?' I asked. 'He looked like a butler. Smartly dressed, very dignified.'

The caretaker and the gardener exchanged meaningful glances.

'You tell him,' said the caretaker to his companion.

'It must have been Hazoor Ali,' said the gardener, nodding. 'He was the orderly, the personal servant of Mr Robbins, the port commissioner—the Englishman who lived here.'

'But that was over sixty years ago,' I said. 'They must all be dead.'

'Yes, all are dead, sir. But sometimes the ghost of Hazoor Ali appears, especially if one of our guests reminds him of his old master. He was quite devoted to him, sir. In fact, he received this bungalow as a parting gift when Mr Robbins left the country. But unable to maintain it, he sold it to the government and returned to his home in Cuttack. He died many years ago, but revisits this place sometimes. Do not feel alarmed, sir. He means no harm. And he does not appear to everyone—you are the lucky one this year! I have but seen him twice. Once, when I took service here twenty years ago, and then, last year, the night before the cyclone. He came to warn us, I think. Went to every door and window and made sure they were secured. Never said a word. Just vanished into the night.'

'And it's time for me to vanish by day,' I said, getting my things ready. I had to be in Bhubaneswar by late afternoon, to board the plane for Delhi. I was sorry it had been such a short stay. I would have liked to spend a few days in Gopalpur, wandering about its backwaters, old roads, mango groves, fishing villages, sandy inlets... Another time perhaps. In this life, if I am so lucky. Or the next, if I am luckier still.

A Traveller's Tale

At the airport in Bhubaneswar, the security asked me for my photo-identity. 'Driving licence, PAN card, passport? Anything with your picture on it will do, since you have an e-ticket,' he explained.

I do not have a driving licence and have never felt the need to carry my PAN card with me. Luckily, I always carry my passport on my travels. I looked for it in my little travel-bag and then in my suitcase, but couldn't find it. I was feeling awkward fumbling in all my pockets, when another senior officer came to my rescue. 'It's all right. Let him in. I know Mr Ruskin Bond,' he called out, and beckoned me inside. I thanked him and hurried into the check-in area.

All the time in the flight, I was trying to recollect where I might have kept my passport. Possibly tucked away somewhere inside the suitcase, I thought. Now that my baggage was sealed at the airport, I decided to look for it when I reached home.

A day later I was back in my home in the hills, tired after a long road journey from Delhi. I like travelling by road, there is so much to see, but the ever-increasing volume of traffic turns it into an obstacle race most of the time. To add to my woes, my passport was still missing. I looked for it everywhere—my suitcase, travel-bag, in all my pockets.

I gave up the search. Either I had dropped it somewhere, or I had left it at Gopalpur. I decided to ring up and check with the rest house staff the next day.

It was a frosty night, bitingly cold, so I went to bed early, well covered with razai and blanket. Only two nights previously I had been sleeping under a fan!

It was a windy night, the windows were rattling; and the old tin roof was groaning, a loose sheet flapping about and making a frightful din.

I slept only fitfully.

When the wind abated, I heard someone knocking on my front door.

'Who's there?' I called, but there was no answer.

The knocking continued, insistent, growing louder all the time.

'Who's there? *Kaun hai?*' I called again.

Only that knocking.

Someone in distress, I thought. I'd better see who it is. I got up shivering, and walked barefoot to the front door. Opened it slowly, opened it wider, someone stepped out of the shadows.

Hazoor Ali salaamed, entered the room, and as in Gopalpur, he walked silently into the room. It was lying in disarray because of my frantic search for my passport. He arranged the room, removed my garments from my travel-bag, folded them and placed them neatly upon the cupboard shelves. Then, he did a salaam again and waited at the door.

Strange, I thought. If he did the entire room why did he not set the travel-bag in its right place? Why did he leave it lying on the floor? Possibly he didn't know where to keep it; he left the last bit of work for me. I picked up the bag to place it on the top shelf. And there, from its front pocket my passport fell out, on to the floor.

I turned to look at Hazoor Ali, but he had already walked out into the cold darkness.

The Chakrata Cat

Chakrata is a small hill station. I would roughly trek from one hill station to another, sometimes alone, sometimes in company. It would take me about five days to cover the distance. I am a leisurely walker. You couldn't enjoy a hike if you felt you had to catch a train at the end of it.

At Chakrata there was an old forest rest house where I would sometimes spend the night. Don't go looking for it now. It has fallen into disuse and been replaced by a new building closer to the tour.

Towards sunset, late that summer, I trudged up to the rest house and called out for the chowkidar. I forget his name. He was a grizzled old man, uncommunicative. If you told him you had just been chased by a bear, he would simply nod and say, 'You'd better rest, then. You must be tired.' Nothing about the bear!

Anyway, he opened up one of the bedrooms for me, prepared a modest meal (which I enjoyed, having eaten little all day) and offered to make a fire in the old fireplace.

Chakrata can be cold, even in September, and I offered to pay for the firewood if he would fetch some. He switched on the bedroom and verandah lights and then walked to the rear of the building to fetch some wood.

That was when I saw the cat.

It was a large black cat, and it was sitting before the fireplace, almost as though expecting a fire to be lit. I hadn't noticed it entering the room, and it did not pay much attention to me, just kept staring into the fireplace. Then, when it heard the chowkidar returning, it got up and left the room.

'You have a cat?' I asked, trying to make conversation while he lit the fire.

He shook his head. 'Cats come for rats,' he said, which left me no wiser. And he took off, promising to bring me a cup of tea early next morning. There was a small bookshelf in a corner of the room, and I found an old favourite, *A Warning to the Curious* by M.R. James. These haunting stories of ghosts in old colleges kept me awake for a couple of hours; then I put out the light and got into bed.

I had forgotten about the cat.

Now I heard a soft purring as the cat jumped on to the bed and curled up near my feet. I am not particularly fond of cats and my first impulse was to kick it off the bed. Then I thought, well, it's probably used to sleeping in this room, especially with the fire lit. I'll let it be, as long as it doesn't start chasing rats in the middle of the night! And all it did was come a little closer to me, advancing from my feet to my knees, and purring loudly, as though quite satisfied with the situation.

I fell asleep and slept soundly. In fact, I must have slept for a couple of hours before I awoke to a feeling of wetness under my armpit. My vest was wet and something was sucking away at my flesh.

It was with a feeling of horror that I realized that the cat had crawled into bed with me, that it was now stretched out beside me and that it was licking away at my armpit with a certain amount of relish. For the purring was louder than ever.

I sat up in bed, flung the cat from me and made a dash for the light switch. As the light came on, I saw the cat standing at the foot of the bed, tail erect and hair on end. It was very angry. And then, for the space of five seconds at the most, its appearance changed and its head was that of a human—a woman, black-browed with flaring nostrils and large crooked ears, her lips full and drenched with blood—my blood!

The moment passed and it was a cat's head once again. She let out a howl, sprang from the bed and disappeared through the bathroom door.

My shirt and vest were soaked with blood. For over an hour the cat had been licking and sucking at my fragile skin, wearing it away until the blood oozed out. Cat or vampire or witches revenant? Or a combination of all three.

I went to the bathroom. The cat had taken off through an open window. I closed the window, bathed my wound and examined myself in the mirror.

I had not been bitten. There were no teeth marks, no scratches. The tongue, and constant licking, had done the damage.

I found some cotton-wool in my haversack and used it to stop the trickle of blood from my armpit. Then I changed my vest and shirt and sat down on an easy chair to wait for dawn. It was three in the morning. I felt weak and fell asleep in my chair, to be awakened by the chowkidar knocking on my door with a cup of tea.

Chakrata is a lovely place, prettier than most hill stations, but I had no desire to stay there any longer. There was a bus to Dehradun at eight o'clock. I decided to cut my trek short and take the bus.

'Where's that cat of yours?' I asked the chowkidar before I left. He knew nothing about a cat. He did not care for cats. They were unlucky, the companions of evil spirits, creatures of the world of dead.

I did not stop to argue, but thanked him for his hospitality and took my leave.

The wound, if you can call it that, took some time to heal. The skin beneath my armpit was all crinkly for a few weeks, but the body heals itself, if given a chance to do so.

But what remains on my skin is a bright red mark, the size and shape of a cat's tongue. It's been there all these years and won't go away. I'll show it to you the next time you come to see me.

A Dreadful Gurgle

Have you ever woken up in the night to find someone in your bed who wasn't supposed to be there? Well, it happened to me when I was at boarding school in Shimla, many years ago.

I was sleeping in the senior dormitory, along with some twenty other boys, and my bed was positioned in a corner of the long room, at some distance from the others. There was no shortage of pranksters in our dormitory, and one had to look out for the introduction of stinging-nettle or pebbles or possibly even a small lizard under the bedsheets. But I wasn't prepared for a body in my bed.

At first I thought a sleep-walker had mistakenly got into my bed, and I tried to push him out, muttering, 'Devinder, get back into your own bed. There isn't room for two of us.' Devinder was a notorious sleep-walker, who had even ended up on the roof on one occasion.

But it wasn't Devinder.

Devinder was a short boy, and this fellow was a tall, lanky person. His feet stuck out of the blanket at the foot of the bed. *It must be Ranjit*, I thought. Ranjit had huge feet.

'Ranjit,' I hissed. 'Stop playing the fool, and get back to your own bed.'

No response.

I tried pushing, but without success. The body was heavy

and inert. It was also very cold.

I lay there wondering who it could be, and then it began to dawn on me that the person beside me wasn't breathing, and the horrible realization came to me that there was a corpse in my bed. How did it get there, and what was I to do about it?

'Vishal,' I called out to a boy who was sleeping a short distance away. 'Vishal, wake up, there's a corpse in the bed!'

Vishal did wake up. 'You're dreaming, Bond. Go to sleep and stop disturbing everyone.'

Just then there was a groan followed by a dreadful gurgle, from the body beside me. I shot out of the bed, shouting at the top of my voice, waking up the entire dormitory.

Lights came on. There was total confusion. The housemaster came running. I told him and everyone else what had happened. They came to my bed and had a good look at it. But there was no one there.

On my insistence, I was moved to the other end of the dormitory. The house prefect, Johnson, took over my former bed. Two nights passed without further excitement, and a couple of boys started calling me a funk and a scaredy cat. My response was to punch one of them on the nose.

Then, on the third night, we were all woken by several ear-splitting shrieks, and Johnson came charging across the dormitory, screaming that two icy hands had taken him by the throat and tried to squeeze the life out of him. Lights came on, and the poor old housemaster came dashing in again. We calmed Johnson down and put him in a spare bed. The housemaster shone his torch on the boy's face and neck, and sure enough, we saw several bruises on his flesh and the outline of a large hand.

Next day, the offending bed was removed from the dormitory, but it was a few days before Johnson recovered from the shock.

He was kept in the infirmary until the bruises disappeared. But for the rest of the year he was a nervous wreck.

Our nursing sister, who had looked after the infirmary for many years, recalled that some twenty years earlier, a boy called Tomkins had died suddenly in the dormitory. He was very tall for his age, but apparently suffered from a heart problem. That day he had taken part in a football match, and had gone to bed looking pale and exhausted. Early next morning, when the bell rang for morning gym, he was found stiff and cold, having died during the night.

'He died peacefully, poor boy,' recalled our nursing sister.

But I'm not so sure. I can still hear that dreadful gurgle from the body in my bed. And there was the struggle with Johnson. No, there was nothing peaceful about that death. Tomkins had gone most unwillingly...

The White Pigeon

About fifty years ago in Dehradun, there lived a very happily married couple—an English colonel and his wife. They were both enthusiastic gardeners and their beautiful bungalow was covered with bougainvillea, while in the garden, the fragrance of the jasmine challenged the sweet fragrance of the honeysuckle. They had lived together many years when the wife suddenly became very ill. Nothing could be done for her. As she lay dying, she told her family and her servants that she would return to the garden in the form of a white pigeon, so that she could be near her husband and the place she had loved so dearly.

Years passed, but no white pigeon appeared. The colonel was lonely; and when he met an attractive widow, a few years younger to him, he married her and brought her home to his beautiful house. But as he was carrying his new bride through the porch and up the verandah steps, a white pigeon came fluttering into the garden and perched on a jasmine bush. There it remained for a long time, cooing and murmuring in a sad, subdued manner.

Afterwards, it entered the garden everyday and alighted on the jasmine bush, where it would call sadly and persistently. The servants became upset and frightened. They remembered the dying promise of their former mistress, and they were convinced that her spirit dwelt in the white pigeon.

When she heard the story, the colonel's new wife was very upset. When the colonel saw how troubled she was, he decided to do something about it. So when the pigeon appeared the next day, he took his gun and slipped out of the house, stealthily making his way down the verandah steps. When he saw the pigeon on the jasmine bush, he raised his gun and fired.

There was a woman's high-pitched scream. And then the pigeon flew away, its white breast dark with blood.

That same night the colonel died in his sleep. No one ever knew the reason for his sudden death. When I looked up the cause of death in the local burial register, I saw that it had been given as 'respiratory failure'. In other words, he had just stopped breathing!

The colonel's widow left Dehradun, and the beautiful bungalow fell into ruin. You can still see the ruins on the banks of the Bindal watercourse. The garden has become a jungle, and jackals slink through the roofless rooms.

The colonel was buried in the grounds of his estate, and the gravestone is still there, although the inscription has long since disappeared.

Few people pass that way. But those who do say that they have often seen a white pigeon resting on the grave, and that on its white breast a crimson stain could be noticed.

The Trouble with Djinns

My friend Jimmy has only one arm. He lost the other when he was a young man of twenty-five. The story of how he lost his good right arm is a little difficult to believe, but I swear that it is absolutely true.

To begin with, Jimmy was (and presumably still is) a djinn. Now a djinn isn't really a human like us. A djinn is a spirit creature from another world who has assumed, for a lifetime, the physical aspect of a human being. Jimmy was a true djinn and he had the djinn's gift of being able to elongate his arm at will. Most djinns can stretch their arms to a distance of twenty or thirty feet. Jimmy could attain forty feet. His arm would move through space or up walls or along the ground like a beautiful gliding serpent. I have seen him stretched out beneath a mango tree, helping himself to ripe mangoes from the top of the tree. He loved mangoes. He was a natural glutton and it was probably his gluttony that first led him to misuse his peculiar gifts.

We were at school together at a hill station in northern India. Jimmy was particularly good at basketball. He was clever enough not to lengthen his arm too much because he did not want anyone to know that he was a djinn. In the boxing ring, he generally won his fights. His opponents never seemed to get past his amazing reach. He just kept tapping them on the nose until they retired from the ring, bloody and bewildered.

It was during the half-term examinations that I stumbled on Jimmy's secret. We had been set a particularly difficult algebra paper, but I had managed to cover a couple of sheets with correct answers and was about to forge ahead on another sheet when I noticed someone's hand on my desk. At first I thought it was the invigilator's. But when I looked up there was no one beside me.

Could it be the boy sitting directly behind? No, he was engrossed in his question paper and had his hands to himself. Meanwhile, the hand on my desk had grasped my answer sheets and was cautiously moving off. Following its descent, I found that it was attached to an arm of amazing length and pliability. This moved stealthily down the desk and slithered across the floor, shrinking all the while, until it was restored to its normal length. Its owner was of course one who had never been any good at algebra.

I had to write out my answers a second time but after the exam, I went straight up to Jimmy, told him I didn't like his game and threatened to expose him. He begged me not to let anyone know, assured me that he couldn't really help himself and offered to be of service to me whenever I wished. It was tempting to have Jimmy as my friend, for with his long reach he would obviously be useful. I agreed to overlook the matter of the pilfered papers and we became the best of pals.

It did not take me long to discover that Jimmy's gift was more of a nuisance than a constructive aid. That was because Jimmy had a second-rate mind and did not know how to make proper use of his powers. He seldom rose above the trivial. He used his long arm in the tuck shop, in the classroom, in the dormitory. And when we were allowed out to the cinema, he used it in the dark of the hall.

Now the trouble with all djinns is that they have a weakness for women with long black hair. The longer and blacker the hair, the better for djinns. And should a djinn manage to take possession of the woman he desires, she goes into a decline and her beauty decays. Everything about her is destroyed except for the beautiful long black hair.

Jimmy was still too young to be able to take possession in this way, but he couldn't resist touching and stroking long black hair. The cinema was the best place for the indulgence of his whims. His arm would start stretching, his fingers would feel their way along the rows of seats, and his lengthening limb would slowly work its way along the aisle until it reached the back of the seat in which sat the object of his admiration. His hand would stroke the long black hair with great tenderness and if the girl felt anything and looked round, Jimmy's hand would disappear behind the seat and lie there poised like the hood of a snake, ready to strike again.

At college two or three years later, Jimmy's first real victim succumbed to his attentions. She was a lecturer in economics, not very good looking, but her hair, black and lustrous, reached almost to her knees. She usually kept it in plaits but Jimmy saw her one morning just after she had taken a head bath, and her hair lay spread out on the cot on which she was reclining. Jimmy could no longer control himself. His spirit, the very essence of his personality, entered the woman's body and the next day she was distraught, feverish and excited. She would not eat, went into a coma and in a few days dwindled to a mere skeleton. When she died, she was nothing but skin and bone but her hair had lost none of its loveliness.

I took pains to avoid Jimmy after this tragic event. I could not prove that he was the cause of the lady's sad demise but in my own heart, I was quite certain of it. For since meeting Jimmy, I had read a good deal about djinns and knew their ways.

We did not see each other for a few years. And then, holidaying in the hills last year, I found we were staying at the same hotel. I could not very well ignore him and after we had drunk a few beers together I began to feel that I had perhaps misjudged Jimmy and that he was not the irresponsible djinn I had taken him for. Perhaps the college lecturer had died of some mysterious malady that attacks only college lecturers and Jimmy had nothing at all to do with it.

We had decided to take our lunch and a few bottles of beer to a grassy knoll just below the main motor road. It was late afternoon and I had been sleeping off the effects of the beer when I woke to find Jimmy looking rather agitated.

'What's wrong?' I asked.

'Up there, under the pine trees,' he said. 'Just above the road. Don't you see them?'

'I see two girls,' I said. 'So what?'

'The one on the left. Haven't you noticed her hair?'

'Yes, it is very long and beautiful and—now look, Jimmy, you'd better get a grip on yourself!' But already his hand was out of sight, his arm snaking up the hillside and across the road.

Presently I saw the hand emerge from some bushes near the girls and then cautiously make its way to the girl with the black tresses. So absorbed was Jimmy in the pursuit of his favourite pastime that he failed to hear the blowing of a horn. Around the bend of the road came a speeding Mercedes Benz truck.

Jimmy saw the truck but there wasn't time for him to shrink his arm back to normal. It lay right across the entire width of the road and when the truck had passed over it, it writhed and twisted like a mortally wounded python.

By the time the truck driver and I could fetch a doctor, the arm (or what was left of it) had shrunk to its ordinary size. We took Jimmy to hospital where the doctors found it necessary to amputate. The truck driver, who kept insisting that the arm he ran over was at least thirty feet long, was arrested on a charge of drunken driving.

Some weeks later I asked Jimmy, 'Why are you so depressed? You still have one arm. Isn't it gifted in the same way?'

'I never tried to find out,' he said, 'and I'm not going to try now.'

He is, of course, still a djinn at heart and whenever he sees a girl with long black hair he must be terribly tempted to try out his one good arm and stroke her beautiful tresses. But he has learnt his lesson. It is better to be a human without any gifts than a djinn or a genius with one too many.

Pistols at Twenty Paces:
A Duel at Poona

Duels among British officers serving in India were fairly common in the early part of the nineteenth century, but we do not come across many accounts of them, as the penalties for duelling were severe. Such incidents were usually hushed up. And many of the 'resignations' and sudden deaths from 'cholera' were, in fact, the result of duels.

Perhaps the most tragic of these was the duel that was fought at Poona in June 1842. In that year, the 27th Foot (Inniskillings), a North of Ireland regiment, whose officers were all Irish Protestants, was quartered at Poona. It had been some three months since an Irishman named Sarsfield, a mere boy of nineteen, belonging to an old and distinguished Catholic family, had been posted to the regiment. One of his ancestors had been James II's general at the Siege of Londonderry and such ancestry and religion told against him in a Protestant regiment. His advent was looked upon as an insult to the regiment and it was decided to make his life so intolerable that he would either resign or ask for a transfer to another regiment.

One night at the mess, Sarsfield, who had been drinking with the others, questioned a statement made by another officer and, on being asked by the latter if he thought it was a lie, replied that he did. Immediately the other officer rose, bowed ceremoniously to Sarsfield, and left the mess room in company with the paymaster. The others followed, leaving Sarsfield, who had a few more drinks before leaving and going home to bed.

At about four in the morning he was aroused by the paymaster, who brought him a challenge or a demand for an apology. Not realizing what he was doing, the young man dazedly signed the document the paymaster gave him, which was an abject apology. The next morning at six he appeared on parade, and, having but the faintest recollection of what had happened, walked up to the group of officers waiting for the parade to be formed. To his cheery good morning they returned a blank and contemptuous stare, and then, each turning on his heel, walked away. To give an apology was considered a most cowardly action.

For the next three months Sarsfield's life was miserable, for he was cut dead by everyone in the garrison. None spoke to him except on a matter of duty, and when he entered the mess, a dead silence fell over the company. The end came after three months, and there can be no doubt that the unfortunate young man was by now half demented.

One night he entered the mess room, and, as usual, conversation ceased abruptly. There was a vacant seat immediately opposite the paymaster and this Sarsfield took. By this time the conversation had been resumed, not the slightest notice being taken of him either by word or glance. He was waited upon by the servants just as the others were and it was only as the table was being cleared for the second course that Sarsfield spoke.

'Will you take wine with me?' he said to the paymaster.

'I do not take wine with a coward,' was the blunt reply.

'But will you take this?' was Sarsfield's rejoinder, as he dashed his wine glass and its contents into the paymaster's face.

In a moment all were on their feet, and amidst a roar of voices Sarsfield was pulled out of the mess room by the doctor.

'You will have to fight now, my boy,' said the doctor, more

sorrowfully than might have been expected.

'I know,' said Sarsfield. 'I came for that purpose.'

The whole party now proceeded to a garden on the outskirts of the cantonment where such affairs were usually settled. All the preliminaries were quickly arranged, the captain acting as Sarsfield's second. It was a bright moonlit night, and the result was never for a moment in doubt for the paymaster, at the first exchange of shots, put a bullet through Sarsfield's heart. Sarsfield did not fire. He had made no attempt to discharge his pistol.

The next issue of the *Poona Gazette* contained the following announcement:

'Suddenly, of cholera, in the officers' line of Her Majesty's 27th Foot, Ensign J. S. Sarsfield.'

When an account of the circumstances reached Sarsfield's friends and relatives, a brother arrived at Poona and tried to ascertain the truth. But he could gain nothing more than what the doctor's certificate stated—'death by cholera'—for there was a mutual conspiracy of silence.

Phantom Lover

Night unto night
When the world's asleep,
You come to me,
Our tryst to keep,
Held captive, in thrall,
As the stars look down,
Body and soul
From night unto dawn.
Silent you come
And softly you go,
Ours is a love
That none must know.

Do You Believe in Ghosts?

'Do you believe in ghosts?'
Asked the passenger
On platform number three.
'I'm a rational man,' said I,
'I believe in what I can see—
Your hands, your feet, your beard!'
'Then look again,' said he,
And promptly disappeared!

Whistling in the Dark

The moon was almost at the full. Bright moonlight flooded the road. But I was stalked by the shadows of the trees, by the crooked oak branches reaching out towards me—some threateningly, others as though they needed companionship. Once I dreamt that the trees could walk. That on moonlit nights like this they would uproot themselves for a while, visit each other, talk about old times—for they had seen many men and happenings, especially the older ones. And then, before dawn, they would return to the places where they had been condemned to grow. Lonely sentinels of the night. And this was a good night for them to walk. They appeared eager to do so: a restless rustling of leaves, the creaking of branches—these were sounds that came from within them in the silence of the night...

Occasionally other strollers passed me in the dark. It was still quite early, just eight o'clock, and some people were on their way home. Others were walking into town for a taste of the bright lights, shops and restaurants. On the unlit road I could not recognize them. They did not notice me. I was reminded of an old song from my childhood. Softly, I began humming the tune, and soon the words came back to me:

We three,
We're not a crowd;
We're not even company—

My echo,
My shadow,
And me...

I looked down at my shadow, moving silently beside me. We take our shadows for granted, don't we? There they are, the uncomplaining companions of a lifetime, mute and helpless witnesses to our every act of commission or omission. On this bright moonlit night I could not help noticing you, Shadow, and I was sorry that you had to see so much that I was ashamed of; but glad, too, that you were around when I had my small triumphs. And what of my echo? I thought of calling out to see if my call came back to me; but I refrained from doing so, as I did not wish to disturb the perfect stillness of the mountains or the conversations of the trees.

The road wound up the hill and levelled out at the top, where it became a ribbon of moonlight entwined between tall deodars. A flying squirrel glided across the road, leaving one tree for another. A nightjar called. The rest was silence.

The old cemetery loomed up before me. There were many old graves—some large and monumental—and there were a few recent graves too, for the cemetery was still in use. I could see flowers scattered on one of them—a few late dahlias and scarlet salvia. Further on near the boundary wall, part of the cemetery's retaining wall had collapsed in the heavy monsoon rains. Some of the tombstones had come down with the wall. One grave lay exposed. A rotting coffin and a few scattered bones were the only relics of someone who had lived and loved like you and me.

Part of the tombstone lay beside the road, but the lettering had worn away. I am not normally a morbid person, but something made me stoop and pick up a smooth round shard of bone, probably part of a skull. When my hand closed over it, the bone crumbled into fragments. I let them fall to the grass. Dust to dust.

And from somewhere, not too far away, came the sound of someone whistling.

At first I thought it was another late-evening stroller, whistling to himself much as I had been humming my old song. But the whistler approached quite rapidly; the, whistling was loud and cheerful. A boy on a bicycle sped past. I had only a glimpse of him, before his cycle went weaving through the shadows on the road.

But he was back again in a few minutes. And this time he stopped a few feet away from me, and gave me a quizzical half-smile. A slim dusky boy of fourteen or fifteen. He wore a school blazer and a yellow scarf. His eyes were pools of liquid moonlight.

'You don't have a bell on your cycle,' I said.

He said nothing, just smiled at me with his head a little to one side. I put out my hand, and I thought he was going to take it. But then, quite suddenly, he was off again, whistling cheerfully though rather tunelessly. A whistling schoolboy. A bit late for him to be out but he seemed an independent sort.

The whistling grew fainter, then faded away altogether. A deep sound-denying silence fell upon the forest. My shadow and I walked home.

Next morning I woke to a different kind of whistling—the song of the thrush outside my window.

It was a wonderful day, the sunshine warm and sensuous, and I longed to be out in the open. But there was work to be done, proofs to be corrected, letters to be written. And it was several days before I could walk to the top of the hill, to that lonely tranquil resting place under the deodars. It seemed to me ironic that those who had the best view of the glistening snow-capped peaks were all buried several feet underground.

Some repair work was going on. The retaining wall of the cemetery was being shored up, but the overseer told me that there was no money to restore the damaged grave. With the help of the chowkidar, I returned the scattered bones to a little hollow under the collapsed masonry, and left some money with him so that he could have the open grave bricked up. The name on the gravestone had worn away, but I could make out a date—20 November 1950—some fifty years ago, but not too long ago as gravestones go...

I found the burial register in the church vestry and turned back the yellowing pages to 1950, when I was just a schoolboy myself. I found the name there—Michael Dutta, aged fifteen—and the cause of death: road accident.

Well, I could only make guesses. And to turn conjecture into certainty, I would have to find an old resident who might remember the boy or the accident.

There was old Miss Marley at Pine Top. A retired teacher from Woodstock, she had a wonderful memory, and had lived in the hill station for more than half a century.

White-haired and smooth-cheeked, her bright blue eyes full of curiosity, she gazed benignly at me through her old-fashioned pince-nez.

'Michael was a charming boy—full of exuberance, always ready to oblige. I had only to mention that I needed a newspaper or an Aspirin, and he'd be off on his bicycle, swooping down these steep roads with great abandon. But these hills roads, with their sudden corners, weren't meant for racing around on a bicycle. They were widening our roads for motor traffic, and a truck was coming uphill, loaded with rubble, when Michael came round a bend and smashed headlong into it. He was rushed to the hospital, and the doctors did their best, but he did not recover consciousness. Of course, you must have seen his grave. That's why you're here. His parents? They left shortly afterwards. Went abroad, I think... A charming boy, Michael, but just a bit too reckless. You'd have liked him, I think.'

I did not see the phantom bicycle rider again for some time, although I felt his presence on more than one occasion. And when, on a cold winter's evening, I walked past that lonely cemetery, I thought I heard him whistling far away. But he did not manifest himself. Perhaps it was only the echo of a whistle, in communion with my insubstantial shadow.

It was several months before I saw that smiling face again. And then it came at me out of the mist as I was walking home in drenching monsoon rain. I had been to a dinner party at the old community centre, and I was returning home along a very narrow, precipitous path known as the Eyebrow. A storm had been threatening all evening. A heavy mist had settled on the hillside. It was so thick that the light from my torch simply bounced off it. The sky blossomed with sheet lightning and thunder rolled over the mountains. The rain became heavier. I moved forward slowly, carefully, hugging the hillside. There was a clap of thunder, and then I saw him emerge from the mist and stand in my way—the same slim dark youth who had materialized near the cemetery. He did not smile. Instead he put up his hand and waved at me. I hesitated, stood still. The mist lifted a little, and I saw that the path had disappeared. There was a gaping emptiness a few feet in front of me. And then a drop of over a hundred feet to the rocks below.

As I stepped back, clinging to a thorn bush for support, the boy vanished, I stumbled back to the community centre and spent the night on a chair in the library.

I did not see him again.

But weeks later, when I was down with a severe bout of flu, I heard him from my sickbed, whistling beneath my window. Was he calling to me to join him, I wondered, or was he just trying to reassure me that all was well? I got out of bed and looked out, but I saw no one. From time to time I heard his whistling; but as I got better, it grew fainter until it ceased altogether.

Fully recovered, I renewed my old walks to the top of the hill. But although I lingered near the cemetery until it grew dark, and paced up and down the deserted road, I did not see or hear the whistler again. I felt lonely, in need of a friend, even if it was only a phantom bicycle rider. But there were only the trees.

And so every evening I walk home in the darkness, singing the old refrain:

We three,
We're not alone,
We're not even company—
My echo,
My shadow,
And me...

The Skeleton in the Cupboard

Yes, there was a skeleton in the cupboard, and although I never saw it, I played a small part in the events that followed its discovery.

I was fifteen that year, and back in my boarding school in Shimla after spending the long winter holidays in Dehradun. My mother was still managing the old Green's Hotel in Dehra—a hotel that was soon to disappear and become part of Dehra's unrecorded history. It was called Green's not because it purported to spread any greenery (its neglected garden was choked with lantana), but because it had been started by an Englishman, Mr Green, back in 1920, just after the Great War had ended in Europe. Mr Green had died at the outset of World War II. He had just sold the hotel and was on his way back to England when the ship on which he was travelling was torpedoed by a German submarine. Mr Green went down with the ship.

The hotel had already been in decline, and the new owner, a Sikh businessman from Ludhiana, had done his best to keep it going. But in the wake of the War and India's newly won Independence, Dehra was going through a lean period. My stepfather's motor workshop was also going through a lean period—a crisis, in fact—and my mother was glad to take the job of running the small hotel, while he took a job in Delhi.

She wrote to me about once a month, giving me news of the hotel, some of its more interesting guests, and the pictures that were showing in town.

'I know you're interested in detective stories,' she wrote during the summer term,

> and that you fancy yourself a Sherlock Holmes or Ellery Queen. So what do you make of this strange happening? Last week we decided to clear out an old storeroom that hadn't been opened for years. The keys were missing, so we had to break open the lock. Inside there was a lot of old furniture, rotting carpets, dusty files, broken flowerpots, even a mounted tiger's head. There were two or three locked cupboards which had to be forced open. Nothing much in the first two, but the third cupboard gave everyone a fright. As Tirloki, our billiard marker, pulled open the door, a skeleton tumbled out! I mean a complete human skeleton! It must have been there for twenty years or more. How did it get there, and why? If you were here, you could do some detective work, but you'll have to wait for the winter holidays. Of course, we had to inform the police, and they took the skeleton away, saying they'd have it examined. But I doubt if they'll do much about it. It's obviously someone who died long ago—perhaps a hotel guest!—and someone here decided to hush it up. Suicide? Murder? Accident? Probably we'll never know...

Well, boy-detective that I fancied myself, I wrote back to my mother and said, 'I'll solve the case when I come home. But was it a man's skeleton, or a woman's? And did you find anything else in the cupboard?'

A week later my mother wrote back:

> I didn't look too closely at the skeleton—I like bones to be fully-fleshed if possible—but the police did say it was

a woman. Not an old woman, and not too young either. There was nothing else in the cupboard except for some chipped or cracked plates and dishes, which have now been thrown away. The shelves were covered with sheets of old newspapers. I've kept those for you.

The newspapers excited me, and I wrote and asked my mother for some details.
She wrote back:

I hope you're preparing for your exams. After all, there's not much we can do about a skeleton that's been hidden away for fifteen or twenty years. Anyway, there were two newspapers in the cupboard. The *Daily Chronicle*, published from Delhi on 18 January 1930, is complete. That was four years before you were born. The main headline refers to the 'Bareilly Train Disaster' in which thirteen passengers were killed and nineteen seriously injured. There are also two pages of book reviews, including a review of *The Glenlitten Murder* by E. Phillips Oppenheim. I think you may have read some of his books. He wrote that story 'Crooks in the Sunshine', if you remember.

The other book is about the spirit world, and the possibility of communicating with those who have passed from this material world. Perhaps we can summon up the spirit of the person who inhabited the skeleton? She could tell us how she met her end. Old Miss Kellner holds séances and table-rappings. But how would she summon up a spirit if she doesn't know who it was in the first place?

The second newspaper—incomplete—is *The Civil and Military Gazette* of 2 March 1930. This was published from Lahore, and as you know, Mr Kipling worked on it a few years earlier. The front page is missing, but page

5 carries an ad for a film called *The Awakening of Love* starring Vilma Bank. Vilma was a popular heroine when I was a girl. Nothing much else of interest except for a small item under the headline, 'Elder Murder Sequel':

Patna, Feb. 28: The Chief Justice and Mr Justice Scroope have dismissed the appeal of O. W. Harrison, who was charged with the murder of Mr W. P. Elder in July and confirmed the sentence of death passed on him by the Sessions Judge of Manbhum.

Nothing to do with our skeleton, of course, because Mr Elder was buried at Jamshedpur, while Harrison occupies an unknown grave. And in any case our skeleton is a woman's. But I remember the case. Harrison was having an affair with Mr Elder's wife. When confronted by the outraged husband, Harrison took out his revolver and shot the poor man. All very sordid. No mystery there for you. Concentrate on your studies. Second-term exams must be near. I am sending you a parcel of socks. I know they don't last very long on you.

Two weeks later I wrote:

Dear Mum,

Thanks for the socks. But I wish you had sent me a food parcel instead. How about some guava cheese? And some mango pickle. They don't give us pickle in school. Headmaster's wife says it heats the blood.

About that skeleton. If a dead body was hidden in that cupboard after 1930—must have been, if the newspapers of that year were under the skeleton—it must have been someone who disappeared around that time or a little later. Must have been before Tirloki joined the hotel, or he'd remember. What about the hotel registers—would they give us a clue?

I soon received a parcel containing guava cheese, strawberry jam, and mango pickle. Headmaster confiscated the pickle. Maybe he needed it to heat his blood.

A note enclosed with the parcel read:

> Old hotel registers missing. Must have been thrown out. Or perhaps Mr Green took them away when he left. Tirloki says a German spy stayed in the hotel just before the War broke out. The spy used to visit the Gurkha lines and the armaments factory. He was passing information on to a dentist who visited Germany every year. When the War broke out, the dentist was kept in a prisoner-of-war camp. The spy disappeared—some say to Tibet. Could the spy have been silenced and put away in the cupboard? But I keep forgetting it was a woman's skeleton. Tirloki says the spy was a man. But a clever spy may have been a woman dressed as a man. What do you think?

It was the football season, and I wasn't doing much thinking. Chasing a football in the monsoon mist and slush called for single-minded endurance, especially when we were being beaten 5–0 by the Shimla Youngs, a team of junior clerks from the government offices. Not the ideal training for a boy-detective. The winter holidays were still four months distant, and the case of the unidentified skeleton appeared to be resolving itself with a little help from my mother and her friends.

'Well, I went to see Miss Kellner,' wrote my mother a few weeks later,

> You know, the crippled old lady who used to be your Granny's tenant. She had me over for tea, and we talked

about the old days, and what a good place Green's Hotel used to be, famous for its food and service and flower garden. Mr Green was a great one for the ladies. Very dapper and handsome. Women couldn't resist his charm, his polished manner, and he could dance! A great dancer, like Fred Astaire. Ballroom dancing, of course. None of your rumbas or sambas or jitterbugging.

And what of Mrs Green,' I asked. 'He was married, wasn't he?'

'Poor Mrs Green,' said Miss Kellner, 'she had to put up with his amours and affairs. A quiet person, she came from a good English family. He'd married her for her money, of course. Her father owned hotels in Brighton. Green talked him into financing a couple of hotels in India. One in Poona, one in Dehra. This was a promising place, then. Europeans wanted to settle here. But once married, Green neglected his wife. He fancied himself a Don Juan, and carried on with several women.'

'So did she leave him?' I asked.

'No one really knew what happened,' said Miss Kellner. 'Mrs Green just disappeared. It was all a great mystery, and of course there were all sorts of rumours. You see, if she'd just walked out on him she'd have told someone, confided in a friend. She did have a few friends. I like to think I was one of them. We were all expecting her to leave Green, but no one knew where she went or when. There were no letters, no postcards. Green gave out that she'd gone to stay with friends in Bombay, but after a six-month absence, speculation was rife. And no one believed she'd taken off with another man—she wasn't the sort.

'And what about her father,' I asked Miss Kellner. 'Didn't he come looking for her?'

'Indeed, he did,' said Miss Kellner. 'She hadn't been in touch with him, and she hadn't returned to England as far as he knew.'

Apparently, he made enquiries all over India—no one had seen her or heard from her. So he spoke to the few friends she had in Dehra, including Miss Kellner. They only confirmed his suspicions, that she had been done away with—but how and where? He reported her disappearance to the police, but there was little they could do except question Mr Green, who maintained that he was just as mystified as anyone else and offered a large reward to anyone who could locate her! By then, of course, everyone was convinced that she was dead, and that Green had done away with her—or paid someone to do the dirty work.

Several years passed, and then Green sold up and went away. 'And deserved to go down with the ship,' added Miss Kellner. 'That was the general opinion.'

When I told Miss Kellner about the skeleton in the cupboard, she was certain that it was Mrs Green's.

He must have strangled her or poisoned her, and then locked the body in that cupboard in the storeroom. Only he had the key to the stores.

I've spoken to Padre Dutt and one or two others who were here at the time, and they are all convinced that the skeleton is Mrs Green's. What can we do about it now? So many years have passed, and her old father is long dead. She did not have any children. If there were distant relatives it would be almost impossible to trace them after all this time. Padre Dutt thinks we should give the skeleton a Christian burial, on the strong assumption that it's Mrs Green.

The mystery of the skeleton in the cupboard appeared to have been solved without the assistance of boy-detective Ruskin. I tried to forget it and concentrate on chemistry and mathematics, but I'm afraid I was spending more and more time perusing the works of Agatha Christie, Rex Stout, and Raymond Chandler—and trying to write a detective story in which our Headmaster was found bludgeoned to death in the science lab.

My mother brought me up to date on events in Dehra.

> Padre Dutt managed to retrieve the skeleton from police custody, and it was interred in a corner of the cemetery, not far from your grandfather's grave. I attended the funeral with two or three other old-timers who had known the Greens. Miss Kellner is bedridden now and could not come. Padre Dutt is getting on too, and is a little absent-minded.
>
> It was raining heavily during the funeral service and by mistake he read out the 'Burial at Sea'. Not that anyone seemed to notice. Anyway, he had arranged for a decent coffin, and there's to be a tombstone too, paid for out of church funds and with a contribution from our Sardar-ji, the present owner of the hotel. So poor Mrs Green has found a final resting place. May she rest in peace!

And there the matter rested until the school term ended and I came home for my holidays.

◆

My mother was still managing Green's, even though its days were numbered. The day after my return I joined her in the small office, where she sat behind her overlarge desk, telephone on her right, a tin of Gold Flake (her favourite cigarette) on her left, and the latest paperback western before her, ready to be taken up when nothing much was happening—which was fairly often. My mother enjoyed reading westerns—particularly Luke Short, Max Brand, and Clarence E. Mulford—much in the same way that I enjoyed detective fiction. Both genres were freely available in cheap Collins White Circle editions published during and just after the War.

We discussed the affair of the skeleton in the cupboard, but as there was no longer any mystery about it, there was nothing for me to investigate. However, armed with the keys to the storeroom, I went down to the basement on my own and made a thorough search of all the old furniture, on the off-chance that another skeleton might tumble out of a cupboard or be found jammed into a drawer or trunk. I did find some old tennis rackets, back numbers of *Punch*, a cracked china chamberpot, some old postcards of Darjeeling and Shimla, and a framed photograph of King Edward VII. I took the copies of *Punch* to my room, and read the reviews of all the plays that had been running in London between 1926 and 1930, thus becoming an authority on the theatre in England of that period.

'No more skeletons,' I remarked to my mother in the office, two or three days later.

'How disappointing,' she said. 'And the one we did find is not only dead, it's buried. Why don't you join a cricket team?'

'Snooker is more exciting. Tirloki is teaching me.'

'I hope he isn't teaching you to smoke and drink.'

'When did you start smoking, Mum?'

'None of your business.'

Someone was standing in the doorway. An elderly woman, very fluffy, very pink. Her cheeks were pink, her dress was pink, her hair was bunched up and white. She was straight out of Agatha Christie.

'Miss Marple!' I exclaimed.

'May I come in?' asked the pink lady.

'Please come in,' said my mother. 'Do sit down. Do you require a room?'

'Not today, thank you. I'm staying with Padre Dutt. He insisted on putting me up. But I may want a room for a day or two—just for old times' sake.'

'You've stayed here before?'

'A long time ago. I'm Mrs Green, you know. The missing Mrs Green. The one for whom you put up that handsome tombstone in the cemetery. I was very touched by it. And I'm glad you didn't add "Beloved Wife of Henry Green", because I didn't love him any more than he loved me.'

'Then—then—you aren't the skeleton?' stammered my mother.

'Do I look like a skeleton?'

'No!' we said together.

'But we heard you disappeared,' I said, 'and when we found that skeleton—'

'You put two and two together.'

'Well, it was Miss Kellner who convinced us,' said my mother. 'And you did disappear mysteriously. You were missing for years. And everyone knew Mr Green was a philanderer.'

'Couldn't wait to get away from him,' said the pink lady. 'Couldn't stand him any more. He was a ladykiller, but not a *real* killer.'

'But your father came looking for you. Didn't you get in touch with him?'

'My father and I were never very close. Mother died when I was very young, and the only relative I had was a cousin in West Africa. So that's where I went—Sierra Leone!'

'How romantic!' said my mother.

'It's hot and steamy in Sierra Leone,' said Mrs Green. 'But the climate does wonders for your libido. I lived in sin with a wonderful black man for several years.'

'What happened to him?' I asked, conjuring up a picture of a small pink woman and a large black man having sex together. At fifteen, the imagination is swamped by erotic images.

'He was killed in a tribal war,' said Mrs Green without any show of emotion. 'It was a long time ago.'

'And that skeleton,' I asked. 'What about the skeleton in the cupboard? Did you know about it?'

'Yes, I knew about it. But I have no idea whose skeleton it was. You see, back in the 1920s, when Green took over this hotel, he had one of his sudden enthusiasms and was convinced this town needed a medical school or college, and he set about preparing the ground for one. He was ready to finance the project, or part of it. And of course medical students need a skeleton. So he acquired one from the Lady Hardinge Medical College in New Delhi. It was a medical-school skeleton you found. And if you'd looked closely, you'd have noticed that it was *varnished*.'

'Why was it varnished?' I asked.

'To help preserve it, of course. It was also articulated.'

'Articulated?'

'That means the joints were connected up, so that the whole thing wouldn't fall apart. Want to be a doctor, young man?'

'No,' I said. 'A detective.'

'Well, you didn't solve this case.'

'I wasn't here. And now we'll never be able to identify the skeleton.'

'Some poor woman of the streets, no doubt. Unclaimed, unwanted. But in the end you gave her a decent burial—even if she wasn't a Christian. Padre Dutt is a bit embarrassed, but

I've told him I don't mind my name on the tombstone. I'll be returning to Africa shortly, and when I die I shall have another tombstone there. Not everyone is lucky enough to have two tombstones!'

And with that she made a graceful exit from our lives.

Hill of the Fairies

Fairy Hill, or Pari Tibba as the paharis call it, is a lonely uninhabited hill, almost a mountain, lying to the east of Mussoorie, at a height of about 6,000 feet. Some nights I have seen a greenish light zigzagging about the hill. Is this 'fairy light' what gives the hill its name? No one has been able to explain it satisfactorily to me; but often from my window I see this strange light.

I have visited Pari Tibba occasionally, scrambling up its rocky slopes where the only paths are the narrow tracks made by goats and the small hill cattle. Rhododendrons and a few stunted oaks are the only trees on the hillsides, but at the summit is a small, grassy plateau ringed by pine trees.

It may have been on this plateau that the early settlers tried building their houses. All their attempts met with failure. The area seemed to attract the worst of any thunderstorm, and several dwellings were struck by lightning and burnt to the ground. People then confined themselves to the adjacent Landour hill, where a flourishing hill station soon grew up.

Why Pari Tibba should be struck so often by lightning has always been something of a mystery to me. Its soil and rock seem no different from the soil or rock of any other mountain in the vicinity. Perhaps a geologist can explain the phenomenon; or perhaps it has something to do with the fairies.

'Why do they call it the Hill of the Fairies?' I asked an old resident, a retired schoolteacher. 'Is the place haunted?'

'So they say,' he said.

'Who say?'

'Oh, people who have heard it's haunted. Some years after the site was abandoned by the settlers, two young runaway lovers took shelter for the night in one of the ruins. There was a bad storm and they were struck by lightning. Their charred bodies were found a few days later. They came from different communities and were buried far from each other, but their spirits hold a tryst every night under the pine trees. You might see them if you're on Pari Tibba after sunset.'

There are no ruins on Pari Tibba, and I can only presume that the building materials were taken away for use elsewhere. And I did not stay on the hill till after sunset. Had I tried climbing downhill in the dark, I would probably have ended up as the third ghost on the mountain. The lovers might have resented my intrusion; or, who knows, they might have welcomed a change. After a hundred years together on a windswept mountain-top, even the most ardent of lovers must tire of each other.

Who could have been seeing ghosts on Pari Tibba after sunset? The nearest resident is a woodcutter who makes charcoal at the bottom of the hill. Terraced fields and a small village straddle the next hill. But the only inhabitants of Pari Tibba are the langurs. They feed on oak leaves and rhododendron buds. The rhododendrons contain intoxicating nectar, and after dining—or wining—to excess, the young monkeys tumble about on the grass in high spirits.

The black bulbuls also feed on the nectar of the rhododendron flower, and perhaps this accounts for the cheekiness of these birds. They are aggressive, disreputable little creatures, who go about in rowdy gangs. The song of most bulbuls consists of several pleasant tinkling notes; but that of the Himalayan black bulbul is as musical as the bray of an ass. Men of science, in their wisdom, have given this bird the sibilant name of *Hypsipetes Psaroides*. But the hillmen, in their greater wisdom, call the species the *ban bakra*, which means the 'jungle goat'.

Perhaps the flowers have something to do with the fairy legend. In April and May, Pari Tibba is covered with the dazzling yellow flowers of St. John's Wort (wort meaning herb). The paharis call the flower a wild rose, and it does resemble one. In Ireland it is called the Rose of Sharon. In Europe this flower is reputed to possess certain magical and curative properties. It is believed to drive away all evil and protect you from witches.

Can St. John's Wort be connected with the fairy legend of Pari Tibba? It is said that most flowers, when they die, become fairies. This might be especially true of St. John's Wort.

There is yet another legend connected with the mountain. A shepherd boy, playing on his flute, discovered a beautiful silver snake basking on a rock. The snake spoke to the boy, saying, 'I was a princess once, but a jealous witch cast a spell over me and turned me into a snake. This spell can only be broken if someone who is pure in heart kisses me thrice. Many years have passed, and I have not been able to find one who is pure in heart.' Then the shepherd boy took the snake in his arms, and he put his lips to its mouth, and at the third kiss he discovered that he was holding a beautiful princess in his arms. What happened afterwards is anybody's guess.

There are snakes on Pari Tibba, and though they are probably harmless, I have never tried taking one of them in my arms. Once, near a spring, I came upon a checkered water snake. Its body was a series of bulges. I used a stick to exert pressure along the snake's length, and it disgorged five frogs. They came out one after the other, and, to my astonishment, hopped off, little the worse for their harrowing experience. Perhaps they, too, were enchanted. Perhaps shepherd boys, when they kiss the snake-princess, are turned into frogs and remain inside the snake's belly until a writer comes along with a magic stick and releases them from bondage.

Biologists probably have their own explanation for the frogs, but I'm all for perpetuating the fairy legends of Pari Tibba.

Reunion at the Regal

If you want to see a ghost, just stand outside New Delhi's Regal Cinema for twenty minutes or so. The approach to the grand old cinema hall is a great place for them. Sooner or later you'll see a familiar face in the crowd. Before you have time to recall who it was or who it may be, it will have disappeared and you will be left wondering if it really was so-and-so…because surely so-and-so died several years ago…

The Regal was very posh in the early '40s when, in the company of my father, I saw my first film there. The Connaught Place cinemas still had a new look about them, and they showed the latest offerings from Hollywood and Britain. To see a Hindi film, you had to travel all the way to Kashmere Gate or Chandni Chowk.

Over the years, I was in and out of the Regal quite a few times, and so I became used to meeting old acquaintances or glimpsing familiar faces in the foyer or on the steps outside.

On one occasion, I was mistaken for a ghost.

I was about thirty at the time. I was standing on the steps of the arcade, waiting for someone, when a young Indian male came up to me and said something in German or what sounded like German.

'I'm sorry,' I said. 'I don't understand. You may speak to me in English or Hindi.'

'Aren't you Hans? We met in Frankfurt last year. You look

exactly like Hans.'

'Maybe I'm his double. Or maybe I'm his ghost!'

My facetious remark did not amuse the young man. He looked confused and stepped back, a look of horror spreading over his face. 'No, no,' he stammered. 'Hans is alive, you can't be his ghost!'

'I was only joking.'

But he had turned away, hurrying off through the crowd. He seemed agitated. I shrugged philosophically. So I had a double called Hans, I reflected; perhaps I'd run into him some day.

I mention this incident only to show that most of us have lookalikes, and that sometimes we see what we want to see, or are looking for, even if on looking closer, the resemblance isn't all that striking.

But there was no mistaking Kishen when he approached me. I hadn't seen him for five or six years, but he looked much the same. Bushy eyebrows, offset by gentle eyes; a determined chin, offset by a charming smile. The girls had always liked him, and he knew it; and he was content to let them do the pursuing.

We saw a film—I think it was *The Wind Cannot Read*—and then we strolled across to the old Standard Restaurant, ordered dinner and talked about old times, while the small band played sentimental tunes from the 1950s.

Yes, we talked about old times—growing up in Dehra, where we lived next door to each other, exploring our neighbours' litchi orchards, cycling about the town in the days before the scooter had been invented, kicking a football around on the maidan, or just sitting on the compound wall doing nothing. I had just finished school, and an entire year stretched before me until it was time to go abroad. Kishen's father, a civil engineer, was under transfer orders, so Kishen, too, temporarily did not have to go to school.

He was an easygoing boy, quite content to be at a loose end in my company—I was to describe a couple of our escapades in my first novel, *The Room on the Roof*. I had literary pretensions; he was apparently without ambition although, as he grew older, he was to surprise me by his wide reading and erudition.

One day, while we were cycling along the bank of the Rajpur canal, he skidded off the path and fell into the canal with his cycle. The water was only waist-deep; but it was quite swift, and I had to jump in to help him. There was no real danger, but we had some difficulty getting the cycle out of the canal.

Later, he learnt to swim.

But that was after I'd gone away...

Convinced that my prospects would be better in England, my mother packed me off to her relatives in Jersey, and it was to be four long years before I could return to the land I truly cared for. In that time, many of my Dehra friends had left the town; it wasn't a place where you could do much after finishing school. Kishen wrote to me from Calcutta, where he was at an engineering college. Then he was off to 'study abroad'. I heard from him from time to time. He seemed happy. He had an equable temperament and got on quite well with most people. He had a girlfriend too, he told me.

'But,' he wrote, 'you're my oldest and best friend. Wherever I go, I'll always come back to see you.'

And, of course, he did. We met several times while I was living in Delhi, and once we revisited Dehra together and walked down Rajpur Road and ate tikkis and golgappas behind the clock tower. But the old familiar faces were missing. The streets were overbuilt and overcrowded, and the litchi gardens were fast disappearing. After we got back to Delhi, Kishen accepted a job in Mumbai. We kept in touch in desultory fashion, but our paths and our lives had taken different directions. He was busy nurturing his career with an engineering firm; I had retreated to the hills with radically different goals—to write and be free of the burden of a 9-to-5 desk job.

Time went by and I lost track of Kishen.

About a year ago, I was standing in the lobby of the India International Centre, when an attractive young woman in her mid-thirties came up to me and said, 'Hello, Rusty, don't you remember me? I'm Manju. I lived next to you and Kishen and Ranbir when we were children.'

I recognized her then, for she had always been a pretty girl, the 'belle' of Dehra's Astley Hall.

We sat down and talked about old times and new times, and I told her that I hadn't heard from Kishen for a few years. 'Didn't you know?' she asked. 'He died about two years ago.'

'What happened?' I was dismayed, even angry, that I hadn't heard about it. 'He couldn't have been more than thirty-eight.'

'It was an accident on a beach in Goa. A child had got into difficulties and Kishen swam out to save her. He did rescue the little girl, but when he swam ashore he had a heart attack. He died right there on the beach. It seems he had always had a weak heart. The exertion must have been too much for him.'

I was silent. I knew he'd become a fairly good swimmer, but I did not know about the heart.

'Was he married?' I asked.

'No, he was always the eligible bachelor boy.'

It had been good to see Manju again, even though she had given me sad news. She told me she was happily married, with a small son. We promised to keep in touch.

And that's the end of this tale, apart from my brief visit to Delhi last November.

I had taken a taxi to Connaught Place and decided to get down at the Regal. I stood there a while, undecided about what to do or where to go. It was almost time for a show to start, and there were a lot of people milling around.

I thought someone called my name. I looked around, and there was Kishen in the crowd.

'Kishen!' I called, and started after him.

But a stout lady climbing out of a scooter rickshaw got in my way, and by the time I had a clear view again, my old friend had disappeared.

Had I seen his lookalike, a double? Or had he kept his promise to come back to see me once more?

The Monkeys

I couldn't be sure, next morning, if I had been dreaming or if I had really heard dogs barking in the night and had seen them scampering about on the hillside below the cottage. There had been a golden cocker, a retriever, a peke, a dachshund, a black labrador and one or two nondescripts. They had woken me with their barking shortly after midnight and had made so much noise that I had got out of bed and looked out of the open window. I saw them quite plainly in the moonlight, five or six dogs rushing excitedly through the bracket and long monsoon grass.

It was only because there had been so many breeds among the dogs that I felt a little confused. I had been in the cottage only a week, and I was already on nodding or speaking terms with most of my neighbours. Colonel Fanshawe, retired from the Indian army, was my immediate neighbour. He did keep a cocker, but it was black. The elderly Anglo-Indian spinsters who lived beyond the deodars kept only cats. (Though why cats should be the prerogative of spinsters, I have never been able to understand.) The milkman kept a couple of mongrels. And the Punjabi industrialist who had bought a former prince's palace—without ever occupying it—left the property in charge of a watchman who kept a huge Tibetan mastiff.

None of these dogs looked like the ones I had seen in the night.

'Does anyone here keep a retriever?' I asked Colonel Fanshawe, when I met him taking his evening walk.

'No one that I know of,' he said and gave me a swift, penetrating look from under his bushy eyebrows. 'Why, have you seen one around?'

'No, I just wondered. There are a lot of dogs in the area, aren't there?'

'Oh, yes. Nearly everyone keeps a dog here. Of course, every now and then a panther carries one off. Lost a lovely little terrier myself only last winter.'

Colonel Fanshawe, tall and red-faced, seemed to be waiting for me to tell him something more—or was he just taking time to recover his breath after a stiff uphill climb?

That night I heard the dogs again. I went to the window and looked out. The moon was at the full, silvering the leaves of the oak trees.

The dogs were looking up into the trees and barking. But I could see nothing in the trees, not even an owl.

I gave a shout, and the dogs disappeared into the forest.

Colonel Fanshawe looked at me expectantly when I met him the following day. He knew something about those dogs, of that I was certain; but he was waiting to hear what I had to say. I decided to oblige him.

'I saw at least six dogs in the middle of the night,' I said. 'A cocker, a retriever, a peke, a dachshund and two mongrels. Now, Colonel, I'm sure you must know whose they are.'

The Colonel was delighted. I could tell by the way his eyes glinted that he was going to enjoy himself at my expense. 'You've been seeing Miss Fairchild's dogs,' he said with smug satisfaction.

'Oh, and where does she live?'

'She doesn't, my boy. Died fifteen years ago.'

'Then what are her dogs doing here?'

'Looking for monkeys,' said the Colonel. And he stood back to watch my reaction.

'I'm afraid I don't understand,' I said.

'Let me put it this way,' said the Colonel. 'Do you believe in ghosts?'

'I've never seen any,' I said.

'But you have, my boy, you have. Miss Fairchild's dogs died years ago—a cocker, a retriever, a dachshund, a peke and two mongrels. They were buried on a little knoll under the oaks. Nothing odd about their deaths, mind you. They were all quite old, and didn't survive their mistress very long. Neighbours looked after them until they died.'

'And Miss Fairchild lived in the cottage where I stay? Was she young?'

'She was in her mid-forties, an athletic sort of woman, fond of the outdoors. Didn't care much for men. I thought you knew about her.'

'No, I haven't been here very long, you know. But what was it you said about monkeys? Why were the dogs looking for monkeys?'

'Ah, that's the interesting part of the story. Have you seen the langur monkeys that sometimes come to eat oak leaves?'

'No.'

'You will, sooner or later. There has always been a band of them roaming these forests. They're quite harmless really, except that they'll ruin a garden if given half a chance... Well, Miss Fairchild fairly loathed those monkeys. She was very keen on her dahlias—grew some prize specimens—but the monkeys would come at night, dig up the plants and eat the dahlia bulbs. Apparently they found the bulbs much to their liking. Miss Fairchild would be furious. People who are passionately fond of gardening often go off balance when their best plants are ruined—that's only human, I suppose. Miss Fairchild set her dogs on the monkeys whenever she could, even if it was in the middle of the night. But the monkeys simply took to the trees and left the dogs barking.

'Then one day—or rather one night—Miss Fairchild took desperate measures. She borrowed a shotgun and sat up near a window. And when the monkeys arrived, she shot one of them dead.'

The Colonel paused and looked out over the oak trees which were shimmering in the warm afternoon sun.

'She shouldn't have done that,' he said.

'Never shoot a monkey. It's not only that they're sacred to Hindus—but they are rather human, you know. Well, I must be getting on. Good day!' And the Colonel, having ended his story rather abruptly, set off at a brisk pace through the deodars.

I didn't hear the dogs that night. But the next day I saw the monkeys—the real ones, not ghosts. There were about twenty of them, young and old, sitting in the trees munching oak leaves. They didn't pay much attention to me, and I watched them for some time.

They were handsome creatures, their fur a silver-grey, their tails long and sinuous. They leapt gracefully from tree to tree and were very polite and dignified in their behaviour towards each other—unlike the bold, rather crude red monkeys of the plains. Some of the younger ones scampered about on the hillside, playing and wrestling with each other like schoolboys.

There were no dogs to molest them—and no dahlias to tempt them into the garden.

But that night, I heard the dogs again. They were barking more furiously than ever.

'Well, I'm not getting up for them this time,' I mumbled, and pulled the blanket over my ears.

But the barking grew louder and was joined by other sounds, a squealing and a scuffling.

Then suddenly, the piercing shriek of a woman rang through the forest. It was an unearthly sound, and it made my hair stand up.

I leapt out of bed and dashed to the window.

A woman was lying on the ground, three or four huge monkeys were on top of her, biting her arms and pulling at her throat. The dogs were yelping and trying to drag the monkeys off, but they were being harried from behind by others. The woman gave another bloodcurdling shriek, and I dashed back into the room, grabbed hold of a small axe and ran into the garden.

But everyone—dogs, monkeys and shrieking woman—had disappeared, and I stood alone on the hillside in my pyjamas, clutching an axe and feeling very foolish.

The Colonel greeted me effusively the following day.

'Still seeing those dogs?' he asked in a bantering tone.

'I've seen the monkeys too,' I said.

'Oh, yes, they've come around again. But they're real enough, and quite harmless.'

'I know—but I saw them last night with the dogs.'

'Oh, did you really? That's strange, very strange.' The Colonel tried to avoid my eye, but I hadn't quite finished with him.

'Colonel,' I said. 'You never did get around to telling me how Miss Fairchild died.'

'Oh, didn't I? Must have slipped my memory. I'm getting old, don't remember people as well as I used to. But, of course, I remember about Miss Fairchild, poor lady. The monkeys killed her. Didn't you know? They simply tore her to pieces...'

His voice trailed off, and he looked thoughtfully at a caterpillar that was making its way up his walking stick. 'She shouldn't have shot one of them,' he said. 'Never shoot a monkey—they're rather human, you know...'

TALES OF MYSTERY

He Who Rides a Tiger

To the boatmen of the Hooghly and the woodcutters and honey-gatherers of the Sunderbans, 'Gazi Saheb' is a name that is still invoked in times of storm or stress. Stories of the magical powers of this wonderful fakir have come down to us in song and legend.

In the south of Calcutta where the town of Baruipur now stands, there was once a dense, impenetrable jungle laced with crocodile-infested creeks. Into this wasteland came a fakir, Mobrah Gazi by name, to take up his residence at a place called Basra. He so overawed the wild animals that they became his servants, and 'Gazi Saheb' (as he came to be known) was often seen riding about on a tiger.

It is said that the zamindar of the pargana in which Basra was situated was placed under arrest because he was unable to pay the annual revenue to the emperor at Delhi. The zamindar's mother, fearing for her son's life, sought the assistance of the great Gazi. The fakir promised his aid.

After sending the woman home, he dismounted from his royal Bengal tiger and sat down in deep meditation. So great were his powers that his thoughts were telegraphed over the many hundred miles separating his jungle from Delhi and he gave the emperor a dream in which he, Gazi Saheb, appeared surrounded by wild beasts, saying that he was the proprietor of the Basra jungles and that the zamindar's dues would be paid from his own treasures buried in the forest. He told the emperor to have the zamindar released, threatening him with every misfortune if he disobeyed.

The emperor awoke late the next morning and, overtaken by the business of his court, forgot the dream. The following morning when he ascended his throne, instead of seeing the usual courtiers and attendants, he found himself surrounded by wild animals. He immediately remembered the dream and in great haste ordered the release of the zamindar. The animals vanished. A few weeks later, the revenue arrived, paid out of the Gazi's treasure.

In gratitude for the Gazi's aid, the zamindar erected a mosque in the jungles of Basra as a residence for the saint but Gazi Saheb, who had no use for material possessions and used his mysterious treasure only to assist others, said that he preferred the shelter of the forests in the sunshine and rain and desired neither a mosque nor house. The zamindar then ordered that every village in his zamindari should erect an altar dedicated to Gazi Saheb, 'King of the Sunderbans and of the Wild Beasts,' and warned his tenants that if they failed to make an offering before going into the jungle, they would almost certainly be devoured by tigers or crocodiles.

And so, even today, between Calcutta and the sea, Gazi Saheb is recognized as a saint in many of the villages of the Sunderbans and his name is held in reverence by both Hindus and Muslims.

There is no record of Gazi Saheb ever having taken a wife, yet there are a number of fakirs who call themselves his descendants, gaining a livelihood from the offerings of boatmen and woodcutters. That they do not have the powers of the original Gazi have been proved more than once, for it is usually the fakirs and not the village folk who are carried off by tigers or crocodiles.

Many people have tried to ascertain the whereabouts of the tomb of Gazi Saheb. Some declare it lies near Baruipur where the saint first took up his abode. Others say that it is to be found in the jungles of Sagar Island by the creek that runs into the sea. And there are some who feel sure that there is no tomb and that Gazi Saheb left this earth in no ordinary way but was taken to paradise, riding on the back of a royal Bengal tiger.

He Said It with Arsenic

Is there such a person as a born murderer—in the sense that there are born writers and musicians, born winners and losers? One can't be sure. The urge to do away with troublesome people is common to most of us but only a few succumb to it.

If ever there was a born murderer, he must surely have been William Jones. The thing came so naturally to him. No extreme violence, no messy shootings or hacking or throttling. Just the right amount of poison, administered with skill and discretion.

A gentle, civilized sort of person was Mr Jones. He collected butterflies and arranged them systematically in glass cases. His ether bottle was quick and painless. He never stuck pins into the beautiful creatures.

Have you ever heard of the Agra Double Murder? It happened, of course, a great many years ago, when Agra was a far-flung outpost of the British Empire. In those days, William Jones was a male nurse in one of the city's hospitals. The patients—especially terminal cases—spoke highly of the care and consideration he showed them. While most nurses, both male and female, preferred to attend to the more hopeful cases, Nurse William was always prepared to stand duty over a dying patient.

He felt a certain empathy for the dying. He liked to see them on their way. It was just his good nature, of course.

On a visit to nearby Meerut, he met and fell in love with

Mrs Browning, the wife of the local stationmaster. Impassioned love letters were soon putting a strain on the Agra–Meerut postal service. The envelopes grew heavier—not so much because the letters were growing longer but because they contained little packets of a powdery white substance, accompanied by detailed instructions as to its correct administration.

Mr Browning, an unassuming and trustful man—one of the world's born losers, in fact—was not the sort to read his wife's correspondence. Even when he was seized by frequent attacks of colic, he put them down to an impure water supply. He recovered from one bout of vomitting and diarrhoea only to be racked by another.

He was hospitalized on a diagnosis of gastroenteritis. And, thus freed from his wife's ministrations, soon got better. But on returning home and drinking a glass of nimbu-pani brought to him by the solicitous Mrs Browning, he had a relapse from which he did not recover.

Those were the days when deaths from cholera and related diseases were only too common in India and death certificates were easier to obtain than dog licences.

After a short interval of mourning (it was the hot weather and you couldn't wear black for long) Mrs Browning moved to Agra where she rented a house next door to William Jones.

I forgot to mention that Mr Jones was also married. His wife was an insignificant creature, no match for a genius like William. Before the hot weather was over, the dreaded cholera had taken her too. The way was clear for the lovers to unite in holy matrimony.

But Dame Gossip lived in Agra, too, and it was not long before tongues were wagging and anonymous letters were being received by the superintendent of police. Inquiries were instituted. Like most infatuated lovers, Mrs Browning had hung on to her beloved's letters and *billet doux*, and these soon came to light. The silly woman had kept them in a box beneath her bed.

Exhumations were ordered in both Agra and Meerut. Arsenic keeps well, even in the hottest of weather, and there was no dearth of it in the remains of both victims.

Mr Jones and Mrs Browning were arrested and charged with murder.

'Is Uncle Bill really a murderer?' I asked from the drawing-room sofa in my grandmother's house in Dehra. (It's time I told you that William Jones was my uncle, my mother's half-brother.)

I was eight or nine at the time. Uncle Bill had spent the previous summer with us in Dehra and had stuffed me with bazaar sweets and pastries, all of which I had consumed without suffering any ill effects.

'Who told you that about Uncle Bill?' asked Grandmother.

'I heard it in school. All the boys are asking me the same question—"Is your uncle a murderer?" They say he poisoned both his wives.'

'He had only one wife,' snapped Aunt Mabel.

'Did he poison her?'

'No, of course not. How can you say such a thing!'

'Then why is Uncle Bill in gaol?'

'Who says he's in gaol?'

'The boys at school. They heard it from their parents. Uncle Bill is to go on trial in the Agra fort.'

There was a pregnant silence in the drawing room, then Aunt Mabel burst out: 'It was all that awful woman's fault.'

'Do you mean Mrs Browning?' asked Grandmother.

'Yes, of course. She must have put him up to it. Bill couldn't have thought of anything so—so diabolical!'

'But he sent her the powders, dear. And don't forget—Mrs Browning has since…'

Grandmother stopped in mid-sentence and both she and Aunt Mabel glanced surreptitiously at me.

'Committed suicide,' I filled in. 'There were still some powders with her.'

Aunt Mabel's eyes rolled heavenwards. 'This boy is impossible. I don't know what he will be like when he grows up.'

'At least I won't be like Uncle Bill,' I said. 'Fancy poisoning people! If I kill anyone, it will be in a fair fight. I suppose they'll hang uncle?'

'Oh, I hope not!'

Grandmother was silent. Uncle Bill was her stepson but she did have a soft spot for him. Aunt Mabel, his sister, thought he was wonderful. I had always considered him to be a bit soft but had to admit that he was generous. I tried to imagine him dangling at the end of a hangman's rope but somehow he didn't fit the picture.

As things turned out, he didn't hang. White people in India seldom got the death sentence, although the hangman was pretty busy disposing of dacoits and political terrorists. Uncle Bill was given a life sentence and settled down to a sedentary job in the prison library at Naini, near Allahabad. His gifts as a male nurse went unappreciated. They did not trust him in the hospital.

He was released after seven or eight years, shortly after the country became an independent republic. He came out of jail to find that the British were leaving, either for England or the remaining colonies. Grandmother was dead. Aunt Mabel and her husband had settled in South Africa. Uncle Bill realized that there was little future for him in India and followed his sister out to Johannesburg. I was in my last year at boarding school. After my father's death, my mother had married an Indian and now my future lay in India.

I did not see Uncle Bill after his release from prison and

no one dreamt that he would ever turn up again in India.

In fact fifteen years were to pass before he came back, and by then I was in my early thirties, the author of a book that had become something of a bestseller. The previous fifteen years had been a struggle—the sort of struggle that every young freelance writer experiences—but at last the hard work was paying off and the royalties were beginning to come in.

I was living in a small cottage on the outskirts of the hill station of Fosterganj, working on another book, when I received an unexpected visitor.

He was a thin, stooped, grey-haired man in his late fifties with a straggling moustache and discoloured teeth. He looked feeble and harmless but for his eyes which were a pale cold blue. There was something slightly familiar about him.

'Don't you remember me?' he asked. 'Not that I really expect you to, after all these years...'

'Wait a minute. Did you teach me at school?'

'No—but you're getting warm.' He put his suitcase down and I glimpsed his name on the airlines label. I looked up in astonishment. 'You're not—you couldn't be...'

'Your Uncle Bill,' he said with a grin and extended his hand. 'None other!' And he sauntered into the house.

I must admit that I had mixed feelings about his arrival. While I had never felt any dislike for him, I didn't exactly approve of what he had done. Poisoning, I felt, was a particularly reprehensible way of getting rid of inconvenient people. Not that I could think of any commendable ways of getting rid of them! Still, it had happened a long time ago, he'd been punished, and presumably he was a reformed character.

'And what have you been doing all these years?' he asked me, easing himself into the only comfortable chair in the room.

'Oh, just writing,' I said.

'Yes, I heard about your last book. It's quite a success, isn't it?'
'It's doing quite well. Have you read it?'
'I don't do much reading.'
'And what have you been doing all these years, Uncle Bill?'
'Oh, knocking about here and there. Worked for a soft drink company for some time. And then with a drug firm. My knowledge of chemicals was useful.'
'Weren't you with Aunt Mabel in South Africa?'
'I saw quite a lot of her until she died a couple of years ago. Didn't you know?'
'No. I've been out of touch with relatives.' I hoped he'd take that as a hint. 'And what about her husband?'
'Died too, not long after. Not many of us left, my boy. That's why, when I saw something about you in the papers, I thought—why not go and see my only nephew again?'
'You're welcome to stay a few days,' I said quickly. 'Then I have to go to Bombay.' (This was a lie but I did not relish the prospect of looking after Uncle Bill for the rest of his days.)
'Oh, I won't be staying long,' he said. 'I've got a bit of money put by in Johannesburg. It's just that—so far as I know—you're my only living relative and I thought it would be nice to see you again.'

Feeling relieved, I set about trying to make Uncle Bill as comfortable as possible. I gave him my bedroom and turned the window seat into a bed for myself. I was a hopeless cook but, using all my ingenuity, I scrambled some eggs for supper. He waved aside my apologies. He'd always been a frugal eater, he said. Eight years in jail had given him a cast-iron stomach.

He did not get in my way but left me to my writing and my lonely walks. He seemed content to sit in the spring sunshine and smoke his pipe.

It was during our third evening together that he said, 'Oh,

I almost forgot. There's a bottle of sherry in my suitcase. I brought it especially for you.'

'That was very thoughtful of you, Uncle Bill. How did you know I was fond of sherry?'

'Just my intuition. You do like it, don't you?'

'There's nothing like a good sherry.'

He went to his bedroom and came back with an unopened bottle of South African sherry.

'Now you just relax near the fire,' he said agreeably. 'I'll open the bottle and fetch glasses.'

He went to the kitchen while I remained near the electric fire, flipping through some journals. It seemed to me that Uncle Bill was taking rather a long time. Intuition must be a family trait because it came to me quite suddenly—the thought that Uncle Bill might be intending to poison me.

After all, I thought, here he is after nearly fifteen years, apparently for purely sentimental reasons. But I had just published a bestseller. And I was his nearest relative. If I was to die Uncle Bill could lay claim to my estate and probably live comfortably on my royalties for the next five or six years!

What had really happened to Aunt Mabel and her husband, I wondered. And where did Uncle Bill get the money for an air ticket to India?

Before I could ask myself any more questions, he reappeared with the glasses on a tray. He set the tray on a small table that stood between us. The glasses had been filled. The sherry sparkled.

I stared at the glass nearest me, trying to make out if the liquid in it was cloudier than that in the other glass. But there appeared to be no difference.

I decided I would not take any chances. It was a round tray, made of smooth Kashmiri walnut wood. I turned it round with my index finger, so that the glasses changed places.

'Why did you do that?' asked Uncle Bill.

'It's a custom in these parts. You turn the tray with the sun, a complete revolution. It brings good luck.'

Uncle Bill looked thoughtful for a few moments, then said, 'Well, let's have some more luck,' and turned the tray around again.

'Now you've spoilt it,' I said. 'You're not supposed to keep revolving it! That's bad luck. I'll have to turn it about again to cancel out the bad luck.'

The tray swung round once more and Uncle Bill had the glass that was meant for me.

'Cheers!' I said and drank from my glass.

It was good sherry.

Uncle Bill hesitated. Then he shrugged, said 'Cheers' and drained his glass quickly.

But he did not offer to fill the glasses again.

Early next morning he was taken violently ill. I heard him retching in his room and I got up and went to see if there was anything I could do. He was groaning, his head hanging over the side of the bed. I brought him a basin and a jug of water.

'Would you like me to fetch a doctor?' I asked.

He shook his head. 'No, I'll be all right. It must be something I ate.'

'It's probably the water. It's not too good at this time of the year. Many people come down with gastric trouble during their first few days in Fosterganj.'

'Ah, that must be it,' he said and doubled up as a fresh spasm of pain and nausea swept over him.

He was better by evening—whatever had gone into the glass must have been by way of the preliminary dose and a day later he was well enough to pack his suitcase and announce his departure. The climate of Fosterganj did not agree with him, he told me.

Just before he left, I said: 'Tell me, Uncle, why did you drink it?'

'Drink what? The water?'

'No, the glass of sherry into which you'd slipped one of your famous powders.'

He gaped at me, then gave a nervous whinnying laugh. 'You will have your little joke, won't you?'

'No, I mean it,' I said. 'Why did you drink the stuff? It was meant for me, of course.'

He looked down at his shoes, then gave a little shrug and turned away.

'In the circumstances,' he said, 'it seemed the only decent thing to do.'

I'll say this for Uncle Bill: he was always the perfect gentleman.

A Job Well Done

Dhuki, the gardener, was clearing up the weeds that grew in profusion around the old disused well. He was an old man, skinny and bent and spindly-legged; but he had always been like that; his strength lay in his wrists and in his long, tendril-like fingers. He looked as frail as a petunia, but he had the tenacity of a vine.

'Are you going to cover the well?' I asked. I was eight, a great favourite of Dhuki. He had been the gardener long before my birth; had worked for my father, until my father died, and now worked for my mother and stepfather.

'I must cover it, I suppose,' said Dhuki. 'That's what the Major sahib wants. He'll be back any day, and if he finds the well still uncovered, he'll get into one of his raging fits and I'll be looking for another job!'

The 'Major sahib' was my stepfather, Major Summerskill. A tall, hearty, back-slapping man, who liked polo and pig-sticking. He was quite unlike my father. My father had always given me books to read. The Major said I would become a dreamer if I read too much, and took the books away. I hated him and did not think much of my mother for marrying him.

'The boy's too soft,' I heard him tell my mother. 'I must see that he gets riding lessons.'

But before the riding lessons could be arranged, the Major's regiment was ordered to Peshawar. Trouble was expected from some of the frontier tribes. He was away for about two months. Before leaving, he had left strict instructions for Dhuki to cover up the old well.

'Too damned dangerous having an open well in the middle of the garden,' my stepfather had said. 'Make sure that it's completely covered by the time I get back.'

Dhuki was loath to cover up the old well. It had been there for over fifty years, long before the house had been built. In its walls lived a colony of pigeons. Their soft cooing filled the garden with a lovely sound. And during the hot, dry, summer months, when taps ran dry, the well was always a dependable source of water. The bhisti still used it, filling his goatskin bag with the cool clear water and sprinkling the paths around the house to keep the dust down.

Dhuki pleaded with my mother to let him leave the well uncovered.

'What will happen to the pigeons?' he asked.

'Oh, surely they can find another well,' said my mother. 'Do close it up soon, Dhuki. I don't want the sahib to come back and find that you haven't done anything about it.'

My mother seemed just a little bit afraid of the Major. How can we be afraid of those we love? It was a question that puzzled me then, and puzzles me still.

The Major's absence made life pleasant again. I returned to my books, spent long hours in my favourite banyan tree, ate buckets of mangoes, and dawdled in the garden talking to Dhuki.

Neither he nor I were looking forward to the Major's return. Dhuki had stayed on after my mother's second marriage only out of loyalty to her and affection for me; he had really been my father's man. But my mother had always appeared deceptively frail and helpless, and most men, Major Summerskill included, felt protective towards her. She liked people who did things for her.

'Your father liked this well,' said Dhuki. 'He would often sit here in the evenings, with a book in which he made drawings of birds and flowers and insects.'

I remembered those drawings, and I remembered how they had all been thrown away by the Major when he had moved into the house. Dhuki knew about it, too. I didn't keep much from him.

'It's a sad business closing this well,' said Dhuki again. 'Only a fool or a drunkard is likely to fall into it.'

But he had made his preparations. Planks of sal wood, bricks and cement were neatly piled up around the well.

'Tomorrow,' said Dhuki. 'Tomorrow I will do it. Not today. Let the birds remain for one more day. In the morning, baba, you can help me drive the birds from the well.

On the day my stepfather was expected back, my mother hired a tonga and went to the bazaar to do some shopping. Only a few people had cars in those days. Even colonels went about in tongas. Now, a clerk finds it beneath his dignity to sit in one.

As the Major was not expected before evening, I decided I would make full use of my last free morning. I took all my favourite books and stored them away in an outhouse where I could come for them from time to time. Then, my pockets bursting with mangoes, I climbed into the banyan tree. It was the darkest and coolest place on a hot day in June.

From behind the screen of leaves that concealed me, I could see Dhuki moving about near the well. He appeared to be most unwilling to get on with the job of covering it up.

'Baba!' he called, several times; but I did not feel like stirring from the banyan tree. Dhuki grasped a long plank of wood and placed it across one end of the well. He started hammering. From my vantage point in the banyan tree, he looked very bent and old.

A jingle of tonga bells and the squeak of unoiled wheels told me that a tonga was coming in at the gate. It was too early for my mother to be back. I peered through the thick, waxy leaves of the tree, and nearly fell off my branch in surprise. It was my stepfather, the Major! He had arrived earlier than expected.

I did not come down from the tree. I had no intention of confronting my stepfather until my mother returned.

The Major had climbed down from the tonga and was watching his luggage being carried on to the verandah. He was red in the face and the ends of his handlebar moustache were stiff with brilliantine. Dhuki approached with a half-hearted salaam.

'Ah, so there you are, you old scoundrel!' exclaimed the Major, trying to sound friendly and jocular. 'More jungle than garden, from what I can see. You're getting too old for this sort of work, Dhuki. Time to retire! And where's the memsahib?'

'Gone to the bazaar,' said Dhuki.

'And the boy?'

Dhuki shrugged. 'I have not seen the boy, today, Sahib.'

'Damn!' said the Major. 'A fine homecoming, this is. Well, wake up the cook-boy and tell him to get some sodas.'

'Cook-boy's gone away,' said Dhuki.

'Well, I'll be double-damned,' said the Major.

The tonga went away, and the Major started pacing up and down the garden path. Then he saw Dhuki's unfinished work at the well. He grew purple in the face, strode across to the well, and started ranting at the old gardener.

Dhuki began making excuses. He said something about a shortage of bricks; the sickness of a niece; unsatisfactory cement; unfavourable weather; unfavourable gods. When none of this seemed to satisfy the Major, Dhuki began mumbling about something bubbling up from the bottom of the well, and pointed down into its depths. The Major stepped on to the low parapet and looked down. Dhuki kept pointing. The Major leant over a little.

Dhuki's hands moved swiftly, like a conjurer's making a pass. He did not actually push the Major. He appeared merely to tap him once on the bottom. I caught a glimpse of my stepfather's boots as he disappeared into the well. I couldn't help thinking of *Alice in Wonderland*, of Alice disappearing down the rabbit hole.

There was a tremendous splash, and the pigeons flew up, circling the well thrice before settling on the roof of the bungalow.

By lunch time—or tiffin, as we called it then—Dhuki had the well covered over with the wooden planks.

'The Major will be pleased,' said my mother, when she came home. 'It will be quite ready by evening, won't it, Dhuki?'

By evening, the well had been completely bricked over. It was the fastest bit of work Dhuki had ever done.

Over the next few weeks, my mother's concern changed to anxiety, her anxiety to melancholy, and her melancholy to resignation. By being gay and high-spirited myself, I hope I did something to cheer her up. She had written to the colonel of the regiment, and had been informed that the Major had gone home on leave a fortnight previously. Somewhere, in the vastness of India, the Major had disappeared.

It was easy enough to disappear and never be found. After several months had passed without the Major turning up, it was presumed that one of the two things must have happened. Either he had been murdered on the train, and his corpse flung into a river; or, he had run away with a tribal girl and was living in some remote corner of the country.

Life had to carry on for the rest of us. The rains were over, and the guava season was approaching.

My mother was receiving visits from a colonel of His Majesty's 32nd Foot. He was an elderly, easy-going, seemingly absent-minded man, who didn't get in the way at all, but left slabs of chocolate lying around the house.

'A *good* Sahib,' observed Dhuki, as I stood beside him behind the bougainvillaea, watching the colonel saunter up the verandah steps. 'See how well he wears his sola-topee! It covers his head completely.'

'He's bald underneath,' I said.

'No matter. I think he will be all right.'

'And if he isn't,' I said, 'we can always open up the well again.'

Dhuki dropped the nozzle of the hosepipe, and water gushed out over our feet. But he recovered quickly, and taking me by the hand, led me across to the old well, now surmounted by a three-tiered cement platform which looked rather like a wedding cake.

'We must not forget our old well,' he said. 'Let us make it beautiful, baba. Some flower pots, perhaps.'

And together we fetched pots, and decorated the covered well with ferns and geraniums. Everyone congratulated Dhuki on the fine job he'd done. My only regret was that the pigeons had gone away.

The Wicked Guru

A certain king of the South had a beautiful daughter. When she had reached a marriageable age, the king spoke to his Guru (spiritual teacher) and said: 'Tell me, O Guru, by the stars the auspicious day for my daughter's marriage.'

But the Guru had become enamoured of the girl's beauty, and he answered with guile, 'It will be wrong to celebrate your daughter's marriage at this time. It will bring evil on both of you. Instead, adorn her with thirty-six ornaments and clothe her in the finest of her garments, cover her with flowers and sprinkle her with perfumes, and then set her in a spacious box afloat on the waters of the ocean.'

It was the time of Dwapara Yuga—the third age of the world—and the Guru had to be obeyed. So they did as he said, to the great sorrow of the king and all his subjects. The king asked the Guru to stay and comfort them, but he said he had to return at once to his sacred seat, and left for his own home some three days distant.

As soon as he reached his house, the Guru stocked it with gold and pearl and silver and coral and the finest of fabrics that women delight in, and called his three hundred and sixty disciples and said: 'My children, go and search the ocean, and whoever finds floating on it a large box, bring it here, and do not come to me again until I summon you.'

They all scattered to do as they had been told.

Meanwhile, the king of a neighbouring country had gone hunting on the sea-shore, where he had wounded a bear in the leg. The wounded bear limped about and gave vent to short savage grunts. As the king looked out to sea, he saw a box floating on the crests of the waves. He was quite a young man, and, being an expert swimmer, he soon brought the box ashore. Great was his surprise and joy to find that it contained a beautiful girl adorned as a bride.

He put the lame bear into the box and set it afloat once again. Then he hurried home with his prize. The girl was only too glad to marry her deliverer, and a great wedding took place.

All this time the Guru's disciples were searching for the box, and when one of them found it floating near the shore he duly brought it to the Guru, and then disappeared as he had been told. The Guru was delighted. He prepared sweets and fruits and flowers and scents. He closed all the doors of his chamber. He could hardly contain himself as he opened the box.

As soon as the box was open, out jumped the bear, savage and hungry and at war with all human beings because of the treatment he had received. He seized the Guru in a bear-hug and then tore out his throat.

Feeling his life ebbing, the Guru dipped his finger in his own blood and wrote this Sloka:

Man's desires are not fulfilled.
The God's desires prevail.
The king's daughter is in the king's palace.
The bear has eaten the priest.

When the Guru failed to send for his disciples, they went together to his house, where, on breaking open his chamber door, they found his body. The Guru's murder appeared to be a mystery, until the king, who had been sent for, found the verses on the wall and had them translated by his scholars. One scholar proved that the bear could have escaped by means of a large drain that was found in the building.

Now it happened that this king was related to the neighbouring king who had found and married the princess in the box, and went to visit him.

'How remarkably like my daughter,' he remarked, on seeing his hostess.

'Yes, the same daughter who was set afloat in a box,' said the queen. But they were overjoyed to see each other again; and the king was especially pleased, because he had all along hoped that his daughter would marry the king-next-door.

A Hill Station's Vintage Murders

There is less crime in the hills than in the plains, and so the few murders that do take place from time to time stand out as landmarks in the annals of a hill station.

Among the gravestones in the Mussoorie cemetery there is one which bears the inscription: 'Murdered by the hand he befriended.' This is the grave of Mr James Reginald Clapp, a chemist's assistant, who was brutally done to death on the night of 31 August 1909.

Miss Ripley-Bean, who has spent most of her eighty-seven years in this hill station, remembers the case clearly, though she was only a girl at the time. From the details she has given me, and from a brief account in *A Mussoorie Miscellany*, now out of print, I am able to reconstruct this interesting case and a couple of others which were the sensations of their respective 'seasons'.

Mr Clapp was an assistant in the chemist's shop of Messrs. J.B. & E. Samuel (no longer in existence), situated in one of the busiest sections of the Mall. At that time the adjoining cantonment of Landour was an important convalescent centre for British soldiers. Mr Clapp was popular with the soldiers, and he had befriended some of them when they had run short of money. He was a steady worker and sent most of his savings home, to his mother in Birmingham; she was planning to use the money to buy the house in which she lived.

At the time of the murder, Clapp was particularly friendly

with a Corporal Allen, who was eventually to be hanged at the Naini Jail. The murder was brutal, the initial attack being launched with a soda-water bottle on the victim's head. Clapp's throat was then cut from ear to ear with his own razor, which was left behind in the room. The body was discovered on the floor of the shop the next morning by the proprietor, Mr Samuel, who did not live on the premises.

Suspicion immediately fell on Corporal Allen because he had left Mussoorie that same night, arriving at Rajpur, in the foothills (a seven-mile walk by the bridle path) many hours later than he was expected at a Rajpur boarding-house. According to some, Clapp had last been seen in the corporal's company.

There was other circumstantial evidence pointing to Allen's guilt. On the day of the murder, Mr Clapp had received his salary, and this sum, in sovereigns and notes, was never traced. Allen was alleged to have made a payment in sovereigns at Rajpur. Someone had given Allen a biscuit tin packed with sandwiches for his journey down, and it was thought that perhaps the tin had been used by the murderer as a safe for the money. But no tin was found, and Allen denied having had one with him.

Allen was arrested at Rajpur and brought back to Mussoorie under escort. He was taken immediately to the victim's bedside, where the body still lay, the police hoping that he might confess his guilt when confronted with the body of the victim; but Allen was unmoved, and protested his innocence.

Meanwhile, other soldiers from among Mr Clapp's friends had collected on the Mall. They had removed their belts and were ready to lynch Allen as soon as he was brought out of the shop. The situation was tense, but further mishap was averted by the resourcefulness of Mr Rust, a photographer, who, being of the same build as the corporal, put on an army coat with a turned-up collar, and arranged to be handcuffed between two policemen. He remained with them inside the shop, in partial view of the mob, while the rest of the police party escorted the corporal out by a back entrance. Mr Rust did not abandon his disguise or leave the shop until word arrived that Allen was secure in the police station.

Corporal Allen was eventually found guilty, and was hanged. But there were many who felt that he had never really been proved guilty, and that he had been convicted on purely circumstantial evidence; and looking back on the case from this distance in time one cannot help feeling that the soldier may have been a victim of circumstances, and perhaps of local prejudice, for he was not liked by his fellows. Allen himself hinted that he was not in the vicinity of the crime that night but in the company of a lady whose integrity he was determined to shield. If this was true, it was a pity that the lady prized her virtue more than her friend's life, for she did not come forward to save him. The chaplain who administered to Allen during his last days in the 'condemned cell' was prepared to absolve the corporal and could not accept that he was a murderer.

One of the hill station's most sensational crimes was committed on 25 July 1927, at the height of the 'season' and in the heart of the town, in Zephyr Hall, then a boarding-house. It provided a good deal of excitement for the residents of the boarding-house.

Soon after midday, Zephyr Hall residents were startled into brisk activity when a woman screamed and a shot rang out from one of the rooms. Other shots followed in rapid succession.

Those boarders who happened to be in the public lounge or verandah dived for the safety of their rooms; but one unhappy resident, taking the precaution of coming around a corner with his hands held well above his head, ran straight into a levelled pistol. And the man with the gun, who had just killed his wife and wounded his daughter, was still able to see some humour in the situation, for he burst into laughter! The boarder escaped unhurt. But the murderer, Mr Owen, did not savour the situation for long. He shot himself long before the police arrived.

Ten years earlier, on 24 November 1917, another husband had shot his wife.

Mrs Fennimore, the wife of a schoolmaster, had got herself inextricably enmeshed in a defamation law suit, each hearing of which was more distasteful to Mr Fennimore than the previous one. Finally he determined on his own solution. Late at night he armed himself with a loaded revolver, moved to his wife's bedside, and, finding her lying asleep on her side, shot her through the back of the head. For no accountable reason he put the weapon under her pillow, and then completed his plan. Going to the lavatory, three rooms beyond his wife's bedroom, he leaned over his loaded rifle and shot himself.

Strychnine in the Cognac

Sick was she on Thursday,
Dead was she on Friday,
Glad was Tom on Saturday night
To bury his wife on Sunday.

Miss Bean was reclining in a cane chair in a corner of the hotel's Beer Garden, reciting old nursery rhymes to herself, when Mr Lobo, the resident pianist, walked over and placed a glass of lemon juice beside her.

'Oranges and lemons,' he said, sitting down beside her. 'Which do you prefer?'

'Both,' she said. 'Oranges for the complexion, lemons for the digestion.'

'Words of wisdom. But that nursery rhyme sounded a bit wicked. I can only remember the innocent ones like Jack and Jill.'

'Not so innocent. "Jack fell down and broke his crown"—he wouldn't have survived a broken head. Maybe Jill pushed him over a cliff—and went tumbling after!'

'Like the judge who fell into the Kempty Waterfall. Was he pushed, or did he fall?'

'We shall never know. No witnesses. But here come the Roys—what a handsome couple!'

The Roys were, indeed, a handsome couple, as you would expect them to be. Dilip Roy was in his mid-forties, but still a name to be reckoned with in Bollywood. He was greying a little at the temples, just below the edges of his wig; but he remained lean and athletic looking, and the meaty romantic roles still came his way. His wife, Rosie Roy, was two or three years younger than him, but inclined to plumpness. When she was in her late twenties and early thirties she had starred in several very popular films—two of them opposite Dilip Roy, whom she had married while on location with him in Kashmir—but of late she had been having some difficulty in getting parts to her liking. She hadn't been feeling very well and had taken to sleeping late in the mornings. Her doctor had suspected diabetes and had advised a complete check-up, but she kept putting off the necessary tests.

'You need change,' said Dilip, always concerned about her health. 'A change from Bombay. A fortnight in the hills will do wonders for you. I'll spend a few days with you too, before I start shooting in Switzerland. Where would you like to go—Shimla, Mussoorie, Darjeeling, Ooty?'

'Why not Switzerland?'

Dilip laughed uneasily. 'It wouldn't be much of a holiday. I'd be shooting all the time and you'd be pestered by hangers-on and loads of admirers.'

'Former admirers.'

'Well, better an old admirer than none at all. And I'm still jealous.'

They settled on Mussoorie—partly because Dilip Roy's father was an old friend of Nandu, the owner of the hotel, and partly because Rosie had spent an idyllic summer there as a girl, staying with an aunt in Barlowganj. When the couple arrived at the hotel, the first person they encountered was Miss Bean, watering the potted aspidistras in the porch of the hotel.

'Hello,' said Rosie, smiling curiously at Miss Bean. 'Are you the new gardener?'

'I'm the old gardener,' said Miss Bean. 'A long-time resident, actually. But the gardener never waters these aspidistras—he thinks they are hardy enough to go without. But plants are like humans—they need a little attention from time to time, otherwise they die of neglect. I've seen you somewhere, haven't I?'

'Only if you go to the movies,' said Rosie. And added, 'Old movies.'

'You're Rosie Roy,' said Miss Bean. 'I saw you in *Cobra Lady*.'

'Wasn't it terrible?'

'It was so bad that I enjoyed every moment of it. And this must be the great Dilip Roy,' observed Miss Bean, as the well-known actor joined them, followed by room boys loaded with luggage. 'The hero of *Love in Kathmandu*,' said Miss Bean, but the hero ignored her.

Dilip Roy did not stop to gossip, but continued up the steps to the lobby, followed by his wife and the room boys. Miss Bean gave her attention to the aspidistras.

'Friendly heroine but not so friendly hero,' she said to the nearest potted plant. The aspidistra appeared to agree.

♦

The couple settled in, and over the next few days Miss Bean saw quite a lot of them although she took care not to intrude in any way, for it was obvious that the Roys were not looking for company.

In the evenings Dilip Roy would plant himself on a bar stool, and work his way through several whiskies, occasionally answering polite questions from the bartender or a casual customer, but always rather morosely, his mind obviously elsewhere. In the background, Mr Lobo, the hotel pianist, would play popular numbers but without receiving any encouragement or applause.

Rosie did not join her husband at the bar. But occasionally

a martini was served to her in her room—sometimes two martinis—it was obvious that she liked a gin and vermouth cocktail now and then. Nandu presented her with a bottle of cognac, and she kept it on her dresser, intending to open it only when her husband was in the mood to drink with her.

They went out for quiet walks together, avoiding the Mall where they would quickly be recognized by both locals and tourists. Sometimes they passed Miss Bean, who was herself a great walker. As they were fellow residents of the hotel they would stop to exchange comments on the weather, the view, the hotel, the town, sometimes even the country and the rest of the world. But from the quiet of the mountains the rest of the world can seem very far away.

Rosie Roy liked the look of Miss Bean and was always ready to stop and talk. Dilip Roy was polite but brusque. The local gossip did not interest him, and he thought Miss Bean a rather quaint and rather foolish bit of flotsam surviving from the days of the British Raj. But then (as Rosie argued) the hotel, the cottages, the winding footpaths, the hill station itself, were all survivors of the Raj, and if their old-world atmosphere did not please you, it might have been better to holiday in Goa—and soak up the Portuguese atmosphere!

India would always be haunted by its history...

◆

One day the Roys had a violent quarrel. Miss Bean was no eavesdropper but she couldn't help overhearing every word that was spoken. Her favourite place was a bench situated behind a tall hibiscus hedge. It looked out upon the snows, and Miss Bean liked to spend a half hour there with a book while Fluff, her little terrier, investigated the hillside, looking for rats' holes. You couldn't see the bench from the Beer Garden, and it was in the Beer Garden that Rosie and Dilip Roy were confronting each other.

'You're off because of that woman in Bandra.' Rosie's voice was quite shrill. 'A week away from her and you're beginning to look like a real Majnu—all pale and melancholy.'

'Don't make up things.' Dilip Roy sounded impatient rather than melancholy. 'You know they start shooting on the new film next week. And it's in Switzerland, not Bandra.'

'You're not the star. They can do without you. You've been getting too fat for leading roles. And you're drinking too much.'

'I'll end up an alcoholic if I stay here much longer. The doctors advised rest for you, not for me. You've given yourself ulcers and you won't get any better if you worry over trifles.'

Here the couple were interrupted by a group of youngsters seeking autographs, and Miss Bean took advantage of the diversion to slip away, taking a roundabout path to her room. Fluff enjoyed the extended walk.

That evening Dilip Roy opened the bottle of cognac. He was leaving the next morning, and he was in a mood to celebrate. But he was not particularly fond of cognac, and did most of his celebrating with his favourite Scotch. Rosie poured herself a glass of cognac, then put the bottle away on the dresser in their room. There it remained all night.

Dilip Roy breakfasted alone in the dining room, then sent for a taxi to take him down to Dehradun. Rosie did not see him off.

'She's sleeping late,' explained Dilip. 'She has a headache. Don't disturb her.'

'Enjoy yourself in Switzerland,' said Nandu, the affable proprietor.

'Look after Rosie,' said Dilip Roy. 'Let her get plenty of rest.'

And everyone did their best to make Rosie comfortable and

welcome, because she was much the more gracious of the two. The manager and staff fussed over her, and Mr Lobo played her favourite tunes, especially the one she always requested:

The future is hard to see,
Whatever will be will be...

Even Miss Bean was drawn towards Rosie and joined her on an inspection of the garden, for they were both fond of flowers, and in late summer the grounds were awash with bright yellow marigolds, petunias, larkspur and climbing roses. They had coffee together and Rosie recalled her parents and happy childhood days spent in Mussoorie; she did not talk about her marriage.

As evening came on, Rosie would retire to her room and send for a martini; it would be followed by a second. She would have a light supper in her room—usually a chicken or mushroom soup with toast—followed by a few sips of cognac as a nightcap...and then to bed.

This routine continued for three or four days, and the cognac bottle was still half full because Rosie preferred martinis. Dilip Roy made a couple of calls from Bombay—the crew would be off to Switzerland any day, and meanwhile they were shooting some scenes in Lonavala.

He had been away for almost a week when Rosie suddenly fell ill. At about ten o'clock after her dinner she rang her bell. A room boy answered her summons, found her on her bed, still dressed, and having a fit of sorts. He ran for the manager. The manager hurried to the room, followed by a concerned Mr Lobo. They found her still having convulsions.

'I'll go get Dr Bisht,' said Lobo, and hurried from the room. Minutes later they heard the splutter of his scooter as he took the winding driveway down to the Mall. Dr Bisht had a scooter too—it was the Age of the Scooter—and he arrived in time to give Rosie some basic first aid and arrange for her to be taken to the local hospital. He was cautious in his diagnosis. 'Looks like food poisoning,' he said, and then his eye fell on the open bottle of cognac, of which about half remained. There was still some liquor in a glass, and he sniffed at it and made a face. 'Or something else.... We'd better have this bottle examined.' But that would take time.

A call was put through to Dilip Roy's studio in Bombay; but the actor was in Switzerland, and air flights were not very frequent those days. It would be two or three days before he could return.

Miss Bean visited Rosie Roy every day, and so, occasionally, did Nandu and Mr Lobo. To everyone's relief and amazement, Rosie made a good recovery. There were crystals of strychnine at the bottom of that bottle, but they had only just begun to dissolve. Another evening's drinking and Rosie would have reached the fatal dose lying in wait for her. For it was obvious that someone had placed the poison in the bottle, and that someone could only have been Dilip Roy, before he had left Mussoorie. Far away at the time of his wife's expiry, he would have the perfect alibi.

Of course, nothing could be proven—all was surmise and conjecture—but Rosie was certain in her own mind that her husband had intended to do away with her in absentia, so to speak—and had very nearly succeeded.

She and Miss Bean had become fast friends, and Rosie found herself confiding all her fears and suspicions to the older person, and turning to her for advice and guidance.

◆

They sat together on the lawns of the Savoy, Rosie reclining in an easy chair, Miss Bean quite at ease on a wooden bench.

From indoors came the tinkle of a piano as Mr Lobo played 'September Song'. Miss Bean sang the words softly, almost to herself:

> But it's a long time from May to December,
> And the days grown short when we reach September.

'That's a pretty song,' said Rosie. 'A little sad, though.'

'September is a sad month,' said Miss Bean musingly. 'The end of summer, the end of all those lovely picnics. Holding hands and paddling in mountain streams. Hot sunny days. And then all that rain—weeks of endless rain and mist. September brings back the sunshine if only for a short time, and then those icy winds will start coming down from the snows.'

'How romantic!' exclaimed Rosie. 'You are lucky to have lived here most of your life. Well, perhaps I'll come and join you when I've finished with that wretched husband of mine in Bombay.'

'What do you intend to do, my dear? Put arsenic in his vodka?'

'Arsenic is too slow. But if he eats enough of those chocolate-coated hazelnuts of which he is so fond, he could well come to a sticky end.'

'What do you mean, dear?'

'This is only for your ears, Auntie May.'

She addressed Miss Bean by her first name whenever she became trustful and confiding. 'I know you won't give me away—just in case something happens.'

'What could happen now?'

'Well, during the last two years I've been so miserable that I've always kept a little cyanide pill with me, just so that I can put an end to my life if it becomes too unbearable.'

'Oh, dear. Do throw it away. Don't even think of doing away with yourself.'

'Well, actually I did throw it away—got rid of it. I took the pill and gave it a nice coating of chocolate and then mixed it up with all the little hazelnut chocolates in the tin that Dilip always carries around.'

'Oh, but that was wicked of you. Quite diabolical! Understandable though, when you think of what he tried to do to you. But he could get to that chocolate pill any day. Pop it into his mouth, and then—'

'Pop off?' added Rosie, a glint in her hazel eyes.

'But it's been some time, hasn't it? Almost three weeks since he left. Someone else might have helped himself or herself to a chocolate—'

Just then they saw Nandu advancing across the lawn. It wasn't his usual amble, he looked very purposeful.

'Bad news,' he said, when he reached their sunny corner. 'I've just had a call from Dilip's manager. Your husband died last night. Suicide, it appears. Cyanide. He must have been feeling very guilty about what happened to you. I'm sorry for your loss, Rosie...'

◆

That evening Miss Bean dined with Rosie in the old ballroom. It was the end of the season, and only a few tables were occupied. Mr Lobo was at the piano, playing nostalgic numbers.

'What will you have, Auntie May? You're my special guest today. It's not that I want to celebrate or anything like that—'

'I quite understand, my dear.'

'So you must have a decent wine, instead of that dreadful crème-de-menthe you make in your room. Here's the wine list.'

Miss Bean ran her eye down the wine list. She was no blackmailer, but she couldn't help feeling a little surge of power as she made her choice. And it was such a long time since she'd enjoyed a really good wine. So she plumped for the most expensive wine on the list, and sat back in anticipation.

A Case for Inspector Lal

I met Inspector Keemat Lal about two years ago, while I was living in the hot, dusty town of Shahpur in the plains of northern India.

Keemat Lal had charge of the local police station. He was a heavily built man, slow and rather ponderous, and inclined to be lazy; but, like most lazy people, he was intelligent. He was also a failure. He had remained an inspector for a number of years, and had given up all hope of further promotion. His luck was against him, he said. He should never have been a policeman. He had been born under the sign of Capricorn and should really have gone into the restaurant business, but now it was too late to do anything about it.

The inspector and I had little in common. He was nearing forty, and I was twenty-five. But both of us spoke English, and in Shahpur there were very few people who did. In addition, we were both fond of beer. There were no places of entertainment in Shahpur. The searing heat, the dust that came whirling up from the east, the mosquitoes (almost as numerous as the flies), and the general monotony gave one a thirst for something more substantial than stale lemonade.

My house was on the outskirts of the town, where we were not often disturbed. On two or three evenings in the week, just as the sun was going down and making it possible for one to emerge from the khas-cooled confines of a dark, high-ceilinged bedroom, Inspector Keemat Lal would appear on the verandah steps, mopping the sweat from his face with a small towel, which he used instead of a handkerchief. My only servant, excited at the prospect of serving an inspector of police, would hurry out with glasses, a bucket of ice and several bottles of the best Indian beer.

One evening, after we had overtaken our fourth bottle, I said, 'You must have had some interesting cases in your career, Inspector.'

'Most of them were rather dull,' he said. 'At least the successful ones were. The sensational cases usually went unsolved—otherwise I might have been a superintendent by now. I suppose you are talking of murder cases. Do you remember the shooting of the minister of the interior? I was on that one, but it was a political murder and we never solved it.'

'Tell me about a case you solved,' I said. 'An interesting one.' When I saw him looking uncomfortable, I added, 'You don't have to worry, Inspector. I'm a very discreet person, in spite of all the beer I consume.'

'But how can you be discreet? You are a writer.'

I protested: 'Writers are usually very discreet. They always change the names of people and places.'

He gave me one of his rare smiles. 'And how would you describe me, if you were to put me into a story?'

'Oh, I'd leave you as you are. No one would believe in you, anyway.'

He laughed indulgently and poured out more beer. 'I suppose I can change names, too... I will tell you of a very interesting case. The victim was an unusual person, and so was the killer. But you must promise not to write this story.'

'I promise,' I lied.

'Do you know Panauli?'

'In the hills? Yes, I have been there once or twice.'

'Good, then you will follow me without my having to be too descriptive. This happened about three years ago, shortly after I had been stationed at Panauli. Nothing much ever happened there. There were a few cases of theft and cheating, and an occasional fight during the summer. A murder took place about once every ten years. It was therefore quite an event when the Rani of —— was found dead in her sitting room, her head split open with an axe. I knew that I would have to solve the case if I wanted to stay in Panauli.

'The trouble was, anyone could have killed the Rani, and there were some who made no secret of their satisfaction that she was dead. She had been an unpopular woman. Her husband was dead, her children were scattered, and her money—for she had never been a very wealthy rani—had been dwindling away. She lived alone in an old house on the outskirts of the town, ruling the locality with the stern authority of a matriarch. She had a servant, and he was the man who found the body and came to the police, dithering and tongue-tied. I arrested him at once, of course. I knew he was probably innocent, but a basic rule is to grab the first man on the scene of crime, especially if he happens to be a servant. But we let him go after a beating. There was nothing much he could tell us, and he had a sound alibi.

'The axe with which the Rani had been killed must have been a small woodcutter's axe—so we deduced from the wound. We couldn't find the weapon. It might have been used by a man or a woman, and there were several of both sexes who had a grudge against the Rani. There were bazaar rumours that she had been supplementing her income by trafficking in young women: she had the necessary connections. There were also rumours that she possessed vast wealth, and that it was stored away in her godowns. We did not find any treasure. There were so many rumours darting about like battered shuttlecocks that I decided to stop wasting my time in trying to follow them up. Instead, I restricted my inquiries to those people who had been close to the Rani—either in their personal relationships or in actual physical proximity.

'To begin with, there was Mr Kapur, a wealthy businessman from Bombay who had a house in Panauli. He was supposed to be an old admirer of the Rani's. I discovered that he had occasionally lent her money, and that, in spite of his professed friendship for her, had charged a high rate of interest.

'Then there were her immediate neighbours—an American missionary and his wife, who had been trying to convert the Rani to Christianity; an English spinster of seventy, who made no secret of the fact that she and the Rani had hated each other with great enthusiasm; a local councillor and his family, who did not get on well with their aristocratic neighbour; and a tailor, who kept his shop close by. None of these people had any powerful motive for killing the Rani—or none that I could discover. But the tailor's daughter interested me.

'Her name was Kusum. She was twelve or thirteen years old—a thin, dark girl, with lovely black eyes and a swift, disarming smile. While I was making my routine inquiries in the vicinity of the Rani's house, I noticed that the girl always tried to avoid me. When I questioned her about the Rani, and about her own movements on the day of the crime, she pretended to be very vague and stupid.

'But I could see she was not stupid, and I became convinced that she knew something unusual about the Rani. She might even know something about the murder. She could have been protecting someone, and was afraid to tell me what she knew. Often, when I spoke to her of the violence of the Rani's death, I saw fear in her eyes. I began to think the girl's life might be in danger, and I had a close watch kept on her. I liked her. I liked her youth and freshness, and the innocence and wonder in her eyes. I spoke to her whenever I could, kindly and paternally, and though I knew she rather liked me and found me amusing—the ups and downs of Panauli always left me panting for breath—and though I could see that she *wanted* to tell me something, she always held back at the last moment.

'Then, one afternoon, while I was in the Rani's house going through her effects, I saw something glistening in a narrow crack near the doorstep. I would not have noticed it if the sun had not been pouring through the window, glinting off the little object. I stooped and picked up a piece of glass. It was part of a broken bangle.

'I turned the fragment over in my hand. There was something familiar about its colour and design. Didn't Kusum wear similar glass bangles? I went to look for the girl but she was not in her father's shop. I was told that she had gone down the hill, to gather firewood.

'I decided to take the narrow path down the hill. It went round some rocks and cacti, and then disappeared into a forest of oak trees. I found Kusum sitting at the edge of the forest, a bundle of twigs beside her.

'"You are always wandering about alone," I said. "Don't you feel afraid?"

'"It is safer when I am alone," she replied. "Nobody comes here."

'I glanced quickly at the bangles on her wrist, and noticed that their colour matched that of the broken piece. I held out the bit of broken glass and said, "I found it in the Rani's house. It must have fallen..."

'She did not wait for me to finish what I was saying. With

a look of terror, she sprang up from the grass and fled into the forest.

'I was completely taken aback. I had not expected such a reaction. Of what significance was the broken bangle? I hurried after the girl, slipping on the smooth pine needles that covered the slopes. I was searching among the trees when I heard someone sobbing behind me. When I turned round, I saw the girl standing on a boulder, facing me with an axe in her hands.

'When Kusum saw me staring at her, she raised the axe and rushed down the slope towards me.

'I was too bewildered to be able to do anything but stare with open mouth as she rushed at me with the axe. The impetus of her run would have brought her right up against me, and the axe, coming down, would probably have crushed my skull, thick though it is. But while she was still six feet from me, the axe flew out of her hands. It sprang into the air as though it had a life of its own and came curving towards me.

'In spite of my weight, I moved swiftly aside. The axe grazed my shoulder and sank into the soft bark of the tree behind me. And Kusum dropped at my feet weeping hysterically.'

Inspector Keemat Lal paused in order to replenish his glass. He took a long pull at the beer, and the froth glistened on his moustache.

'And then what happened?' I prompted him.

'Perhaps it could only have happened in India—and to a person like me,' he said. 'This sudden compassion for the person you are supposed to destroy. Instead of being furious and outraged, instead of seizing the girl and marching her off to the police station, I stroked her head and said silly comforting things.'

'And she told you that she had killed the Rani?'

'She told me how the Rani had called her to her house

and given her tea and sweets. Mr Kapur had been there. After some time he began stroking Kusum's arms and squeezing her knees. She had drawn away, but Kapur kept pawing her. The Rani was telling Kusum not to be afraid, that no harm would come to her. Kusum slipped away from the man and made a rush for the door. The Rani caught her by the shoulders and pushed her back into the room. The Rani was getting angry. Kusum saw the axe lying in a corner of the room. She seized it, raised it above her head and threatened Kapur. The man realized that he had gone too far, and valuing his neck, backed away. But the Rani, in a great rage, sprang at the girl. And Kusum, in desperation and panic, brought the axe down upon the Rani's head.

'The Rani fell to the ground. Without waiting to see what Kapur might do, Kusum fled from the house. Her bangle must have broken when she stumbled against the door. She ran into the forest, and after concealing the axe among some tall ferns, lay weeping on the grass until it grew dark. But such was her nature, and such the resilience of youth, that she recovered sufficiently to be able to return home looking her normal self. And during the following days, she managed to remain silent about the whole business.'

'What did you do about it?' I asked.

Keemat Lal looked me straight in my beery eye.

'Nothing,' he said. 'I did absolutely nothing. I couldn't have the girl put away in a remand home. It would have crushed her spirit.'

'And what about Kapur?'

'Oh, he had his own reasons for remaining quiet, as you may guess. No, the case was closed—or perhaps I should say the file was put in my pending tray. My promotion, too, went into the pending tray.'

'It didn't turn out very well for you,' I said.

'No. Here I am in Shahpur, and still an inspector. But, tell me, what would you have done if you had been in my place?'

I considered his question carefully for a moment or two, then said, 'I suppose it would have depended on how much sympathy the girl evoked in me. She had killed in innocence...'

'Then, you would have put your personal feeling above your duty to uphold the law?'

'Yes. But I would not have made a very good policeman.'

'Exactly.'

'Still, it's a pity that Kapur got off so easily.'

'There was no alternative if I was to let the girl go. But he didn't get off altogether. He found himself in trouble later on for swindling some manufacturing concern, and went to jail for a couple of years.'

'And the girl—did you see her again?'

'Well, before I was transferred from Panauli, I saw her occasionally on the road. She was usually on her way to school. She would greet me with folded hands, and call me uncle.'

The beer bottles were all empty, and Inspector Keemat Lal got up to leave. His final words to me were, 'I should never have been a policeman.'

In a Crystal Ball:
A Mussoorie Mystery

Conan Doyle, the creator of Sherlock Holmes, had a lifelong interest in unusual criminal cases, and his friends often passed on to him interesting accounts of crime and detection from around the world. It was in this way that he learnt of the strange death of Miss Frances Garnett-Orme in the Indian hill station of Mussoorie. Here was a murder combining the weird borders of the occult with a crime mystery as inexplicable as any devised by Doyle himself.

In April 1912 (shortly before the *Titanic* went down), Conan Doyle received a letter from his Sussex neighbour Rudyard Kipling:

> Dear Doyle,
> There has been a murder in India. A murder by suggestion at Mussoorie, which is one of the most curious things in its line on record.
> Everything that is improbable and on the face of it impossible is in this case.

Kipling had received details of the case from a friend working in the Allahabad *Pioneer*, a paper for which, as a young man, he had worked in the 1880s. Urging Doyle to pursue the story, Kipling concluded: 'The psychology alone is beyond description.'

Doyle was indeed interested to hear more, for India had furnished him with material in the past, as in *The Sign of Four* and several short stories. Kipling, too, had turned to crime and detection in his early stories of Strickland of the Indian Police. The two writers got together and discussed the case, which was indeed a fascinating affair.

The scene was set in Mussoorie, a popular hill station in the foothills of the Himalayas. It wasn't as grand as Shimla (where the Viceroy and his entourage went) but it was a charming and convivial place, with a number of hotels and boarding houses, a small military cantonment, and several private schools for European children.

It was during the summer 'season' of 1911 that Miss Frances Garnett-Orme came to stay in Mussoorie, taking a suite at the Savoy, a popular resort hotel. On 28 July she celebrated her forty-ninth birthday. She was the daughter of George Garnett-Orme, of Skipton-in-Craven in Yorkshire, a district registrar of the Country Court. It was a family important enough to be counted among the landed gentry. Her father had died in 1892.

She came out to India in 1893 with the intention of marrying Jack Grant of the United Provinces Police. But he died in 1894 and she went back to England. Upset by his death following so soon after her father's, she turned to spiritualism in the hope of communicating with him. We must remember that spiritualism was all the rage in the early years of the century, seances and table-rappings being part of the social scene both in England and India. Madam Blavatsky, the chief exponent of spiritualism, was probably at the height of her popularity around this time; she spent her 'seasons' in neighbouring Shimla, where she had many followers.

Miss Garnett-Orme's life was unsettled. She was drawn back to India, returning in 1901 to live in Lucknow, the regional capital of the United Provinces. She was still in contact with Jack

Grant's family and saw his brother occasionally. The summer of 1907 was spent at Nainital, a hill station popular with Lucknow residents. It was here that she met Miss Eva Mountstephen, who was working as a governess.

Eva Mountstephen, too, had an interest in spiritualism. It appears that she had actually told several of her friends about this time that she had learnt (in the course of a seance) that in 1911 she would come into a great deal of money.

We are told that there was something sinister about Miss Mountstephen. She specialized in crystal-gazing, and what she saw in the glass often took a violent form. Her 'control', that is her connection in the spirit world, was a dead friend named Mrs Winter.

As a result of their common interest in the occult, Miss Garnett-Orme took on the younger woman as a companion when she returned to Lucknow in the winter. There they settled down together. But the summers were spent at one of the various hill stations. Was there a latent lesbianism in their relationship? It was a restless, rootless life, but they were held together by the strong and heady influence of the seance table and the crystal ball. Miss Garnett-Orme's indifferent health also made her dependent on the younger woman.

In the summer of 1911, the couple went up to Mussoorie, probably the most frivolous of hill stations, where 'seasonal' love affairs were almost the order of the day. They took rooms in the Savoy. Electricity had yet to reach Mussoorie, and it was still the age of candelabras and gas-lit streets. Every house had a grand piano. If you didn't go out to a ball, you sang or danced at home. But Miss Garnett-Orme's spiritual pursuits took precedence over these more mundane entertainments. Towards the end of the 'season', on 12 September, Miss Mountstephen returned to Lucknow to pack up their household for a move to Jhansi, where they planned to spend the winter.

On the morning of 19 September, while Miss Mountstephen was still away, Miss Garnett-Orme was found dead in her bed. The door was locked from the inside. On her bedside table was a glass. She was positioned on the bed as though laid out by a nurse or undertaker.

Because of these puzzling circumstances, Major Birdwood of the Indian Medical Service (who was the civil surgeon in Mussoorie) was called in. He decided to hold an autopsy. It was discovered that Miss Garnett-Orme had been poisoned with prussic acid.

Prussic acid is a quick-acting poison, and would have killed too quickly for the victim to have composed herself in the way she was found. An ayah told the police that she had seen someone (she could not tell whether it was a man or a woman) slipping away through a large skylight and escaping over the roof.

Hill stations are hotbeds of rumour and intrigue, and of course the gossips had a field day. Miss Garnett-Orme suffered from dyspepsia and was always dosing herself from a large bottle of sodium bicarbonate, which was regularly refilled. It was alleged that the bottle had been tampered with, that an unknown white powder had been added. Her doctor was questioned thoroughly. They even questioned a touring mind reader, Mr Alfred Capper, who claimed that Miss Mountstephen had hurried from a room rather than have her mind read!

After several weeks the police arrested Miss Mountstephen. Although she had a convincing alibi (due to her absence in Jhansi) the police sought to prove that some kind of sinister influence had been exerted on Miss Garnett-Orme to take her medicine at a particular time. Thus, through suggestion, the murderer could kill and yet be away at the time of death. In Agatha Christie's first novel, *The Mysterious Affair at Styles*

(1920), the poisoner was in a distant place by the time her victim reached the fatal dose, the poison having precipitated to the bottom of the mixture. Perhaps Miss Christie read accounts of the Garnett-Orme case in the British press. Even the motive was similar.

But there was no Hercule Poirot in Mussoorie, and in court this theory could never be made convincing. The police case was never strong (they would have done better to have followed the ayah's lead), and it appears that they only acted because there was considerable ill feeling in Mussoorie against Miss Mountstephen.

When the trial came up at Allahabad in March 1912, it caused a sensation. Murder by remote control was something new in the annals of crime. But after hearing many days of evidence about the ladies' way of life, about crystal-gazing and premonitions of death, the court found Miss Mountstephen innocent. The Chief Justice, in delivering his verdict, remarked that the true circumstances of Miss Garnett-Orme's death would probably never be known. And he was right.

Miss Mountstephen applied for probate of her friend's will. But the Garnett-Orme family in England sent out her brother, Mr Hunter Garnett-Orme, to contest it. The case went in favour of Mr Garnett-Orme. The District Judge (W. D. Burkitt) turned down Miss Mountstephen's application on grounds of 'fraud and undue influence in connection with spiritualism and crystal-gazing'. She went in appeal to the Allahabad High Court, but the lower court's decision was upheld.

Miss Mountstephen returned to England. We do not know her state of mind, but if she was innocent, she must have been a deeply embittered woman. Miss Garnett-Orme's doctor lost his flourishing practice in Mussoorie and left the country too. There were rumours that he and Miss Mountstephen had conspired to get hold of Miss Garnett-Orme's considerable fortune.

There was one more puzzling feature of the case. Mr Charles Jackson, a painter friend of many of those involved, had died suddenly, apparently of cholera, two months after Miss Garnett-Orme's mysterious death. The police took an interest in his sudden demise. When he was exhumed on 23 December, the body was found to be in a perfect state of preservation. He had died of arsenic poisoning.

Murder or suicide? This puzzle, too, was never resolved. Was there a connection with Miss Garnett-Orme's death? That too we shall never know. Had Conan Doyle taken up Kipling's suggestion and involved himself in the case (as he had done in so many others in England), perhaps the outcome would have been different.

As it is, we can only make our own conjectures.

Death of a Familiar

When I learnt from a mutual acquaintance that my friend Sunil had been killed, I could not help feeling a little surprised, even shocked. Had Sunil killed somebody, it would not have surprised me in the least; he did not greatly value the lives of others. But for him to have been the victim was a sad reflection of his rapid decline.

He was twenty-one at the time of his death. Two friends of his had killed him, stabbing him several times with their knives. Their motive was said to have been revenge. Apparently he had seduced their wives. They had invited him to a bar in Meerut, had plied him with country liquor, and had then accompanied him out into the cold air of a December night. It was drizzling a little. Near the bridge over the canal, one of his companions seized him from behind, while the other plunged a knife first into his stomach and then into his chest. When Sunil slumped forward, the other friend stabbed him in the back. A passing cyclist saw the little group, heard a cry and a groan, saw a blade flash in the light from his lamp. He pedalled furiously into town, burst into the kotwali and roused the sergeant on duty. Accompanied by two constables, they ran to the bridge but found the area deserted. It was only as the rising sun drew an open wound across the sky that they found Sunil's body on the canal bank, his head and shoulders on the sand, his legs in running water.

The bar keeper was able to describe Sunil's companions, and they were arrested that same morning in their homes. They had not found time to get rid of their blood-soaked clothes. As they were not known to me, I took very little interest in the proceedings against them; but I understand that they have appealed against their sentences of life imprisonment.

I was in Delhi at the time of the murder, and it was almost a year since I had last seen Sunil. We had both lived in Shahganj and had left the place for jobs; I to work in a newspaper office, he in a paper factory owned by an uncle. It had been hoped that he would in time acquire a sense of responsibility and some stability of character. But I had known Sunil for over two years, and in that time it had been made abundantly clear that he had not been born to fit in with the conventions. And as for character, his had the stability of a grasshopper. He was forever in search of new adventures and sensations, and this appetite of his for every novelty led him into some awkward situations.

He was a product of Partition, of the frontier provinces, of Anglo-Indian public schools, of films Indian and American, of medieval India, knights in armour, hippies, drugs, sex magazines and the subtropical Terai. Had he lived in the time of the Moguls, he might have governed a province with saturnine and spectacular success. Being born into the twentieth century, he was but a juvenile delinquent.

It must be said to his credit that he was a delinquent of charm and originality. I realized this when I first saw him, sitting on the wall of the football stadium, his long legs—looking even longer and thinner because of the tight trousers he wore—dangling over the wall, his chappals trailing in the dust of the road, while his white bush-shirt lay open, unbuttoned, showing his smooth brown chest. He had a smile on his long face, which, with its high cheekbones, gave his cheeks a cavernous look, an impression of unrequited hunger.

We were both watching the wrestling. Two practice bouts were in progress—one between two thin, undernourished boys, and the other between the master of the *akhara* and a bearded Sikh who drove trucks for a living. They struggled in the soft mud of the wrestling pit, their well-oiled bodies glistening in the sunlight that filtered through a massive banyan tree. I had been standing near the akhara for a few minutes when I became conscious of the young man's gaze. When I turned round to look at him, he smiled satanically.

'Are you a wrestler, too?' he asked.

'Do I look like one?' I countered.

'No, you look more like an athlete,' he said. 'I mean a long-distance runner. Very thin.'

'I'm a writer. Like long-distance runners, most writers are very thin.'

'You're an Anglo-Indian, aren't you?'

'My family history is very complicated, otherwise I'd be delighted to give you all the details.'

'You could pass for a European, you know. You're quite fair. But you have an Indian accent.'

'An Indian accent is very similar to a Welsh accent,' I observed. 'I might pass for Welsh, but not many people in India have met Welshmen!'

He chuckled at my answer, then stared at me speculatively. 'I say,' he said at length, as though an idea of great weight and importance had occurred to him. 'Do you have any magazines with pictures of dames?'

'Well, I may have some old *Playboy*s. You can have them if you like.'

'Thanks,' he said, getting down from the wall. 'I'll come and fetch them. This wresting is boring, anyway.'

He slipped his hand into mine (a custom of no special significance), and began whistling snatches of Hindi film tunes and the latest American hits.

I was living at the time in a small flat above the town's main shopping centre. Below me there were shops, restaurants and a cinema. Behind the building lay a junkyard littered with the framework of vintage cars and broken-down tongas. I was paying thirty rupees a month for my two rooms, and sixty to the Punjabi restaurant where I took my meals. My earnings as a freelance writer were something like a hundred and fifty rupees a month, sufficient to enable me to make both ends meet, provided I remained in the backwater that was Shahganj.

Sunil (I had learnt his name during our walk from the stadium) made himself at home in my flat as soon as he entered it. He went through all my magazines, books and photographs with the thoroughness of an executor of a will. In India, it is customary for people to try and find out all there is to know about you, and Sunil went through the formalities with considerable thoroughness. While he spoke, his roving eyes made a mental inventory of all my belongings. These were few—a typewriter, a small radio and a cupboard full of books and clothes, besides the furniture that went with the flat. I had no valuables. Was he disappointed? I could not be sure. He wore good clothes and spoke fluent English, but good clothes and good English are no criteria for honesty. He was a little too glib to inspire confidence. Apparently, he was still at college. His father owned a cloth shop—a strict man who did not give his son much spending money.

But Sunil was not seriously interested in money, as I was shortly to discover. He was interested in experience, and searched for it in various directions.

'You have a nice view,' he said, leaning over my balcony

and looking up and down the street. 'You can see everyone on parade. Girls! They're becoming quite modern now. Short hair and small blouses. Tight salwars. Maxis, minis. Falsies. Do you like girls?'

'Well...' I began, but he did not really expect an answer to his question.

'What are little girls made of? That's an English poem, isn't it? "Sugar and spice and everything nice..." And I don't remember the rest.' He lowered his voice to a confidential undertone. 'Have you had any girls?'

'Well...'

'I had fun with a girl, you know, my cousin. She came to stay with us last summer. Then there's a girl in college who's stuck on me. But this is such a backward country. We can't be seen together in public and I can't invite her to my house. Can I bring her here some day?'

'Well, I don't know...' I hadn't lived in a small town like Shahganj for some time, and wasn't sure if morals had changed along with the fashions.

'Oh, not now,' he said. 'There's no hurry. I'll give you plenty of warning, don't worry.' He put an arm around my shoulders and looked at me with undisguised affection. 'We are going to be great friends, you and I.'

After that I began to receive almost daily visits from Sunil. His college classes got over at three in the afternoon, and though it was seldom that he attended them, he would stop at my place after putting in a brief appearance at the study hall. I could hardly blame him for neglecting his books: Shakespeare and Chaucer were prescribed for students who had but a rudimentary knowledge of modern English usage. Vast numbers of graduates were produced every year, and most of them became clerks or bus conductors or, perhaps, schoolteachers. But Sunil's father wanted the best for his son. And in Shahganj that meant as many degrees as possible.

Sunil would come stamping into my rooms, waking me from the siesta which had become a habit during summer afternoons. When he found that I did not relish being woken up, he would leave me to sleep while he took a bath under the tap. After making liberal use of my hair cream and aftershave lotion (he had just begun shaving, but used the lotion on his body), he would want to go to a picture or restaurant, and would sprinkle me with cold water so that I leapt off the bed.

One afternoon he felt more than usually ebullient, and poured a whole bucket of water over me, soaking the sheets and mattress. I retaliated by flinging the water jug at his head. It missed him and shattered itself against the wall. Sunil then went berserk and started splashing water all over the room, while I threatened and shouted. When I tried restraining him by force, we rolled over on the ground, and I banged my head against the bedstead and almost lost consciousness. He was then full of contrition and massaged the lump on my head with hair cream and refused to borrow any money from me that day.

Sunil's 'borrowing' consisted of extracting a few rupees from my wallet, saying he needed the money for books or a tailor's bill or a shopkeeper who was threatening him with violence, and then spending it on something quite different. Before long I gave up asking him to return anything, just as I had given up asking him to stop seeing me.

Sunil was one of those people best loved from a distance. He was born with a special talent for trouble. I think it pleased his vanity when he was pursued by irate creditors, shopkeepers, brothers whose sisters he had insulted and husbands whose wives he had molested. My association with him did nothing to improve my own reputation in Shahganj.

My landlady, a protective motherly Punjabi widow said: 'Son, you are in bad company. Do you know that Sunil has already been expelled from one school for stealing, and from another for sexual offences?'

'He's only a boy,' I said. 'And he's taking longer than most boys to grow up. He doesn't realize the seriousness of what he does. He will learn as he grows older.'

'If he grows older,' said my landlady darkly. 'Do you know that he nearly killed a man last year? When a fruit seller who had been cheated threatened to report Sunil to the police, he threw a brick at the man's head. The poor man was in hospital for three weeks. If Sunil's father did not have political influence, the boy would be in jail now, instead of climbing your stairs every afternoon.'

Once again I suggested to Sunil that he come to see me less often.

He looked hurt and offended. 'Don't you like me any more?'

'I like you immensely. But I have work to do...'

'I know. You think I am a crook. Well, I am a crook.' He spoke with all the confidence of a young man who has never been hurt or disillusioned; he had romantic notions about swindlers and gangsters. 'I'll be a big crook one day, and people will be scared of me. But don't worry, old boy, you're my friend. I wouldn't harm you in any way. In fact, I'll protect you.'

'Thank you, but I don't require protection, I want to be left alone. I have work, and you are a worry and a distraction.'

'Well, I'm not going to leave you alone,' he said, assuming the posture of a spoilt child. 'Why should you be left alone? Who do you think you are? If we're friends now, it's your fault. I'm not going to buzz off just to suit your convenience.'

'Come less often, that's all.'

'I'll come more often, you old snob! I know, you're thinking of your reputation—as if you had any. Well, you don't have to worry, *mon ami*—as they say in Hollywood. I'll be very discreet, Daddyji!'

Whenever I complained or became querulous, Sunil would call me daddy or uncle or sometimes mum, and make me feel more ridiculous. If he was in a good mood, he would use the Hindi word chacha (uncle). All it did was to make me feel much older than my twenty-five years.

Sunil turned up one afternoon with blood streaming from his nose and from a gash across his forehead. He sat down at the foot of the bed and began dabbing his face with the bedsheet.

'What have you done to yourself?' I asked in some alarm.

'Some fellows beat me up. There were three of them. They followed me on their cycles.'

'Who were they?' I asked, looking for iodine on the dressing table.

'Just some fellows...'

'They must have had a reason.'

'Well, a sister of one of them had been talking to me.'

'Well, that isn't a reason, even in Shahganj. You must have said or done something to offend her.'

'No, she likes me,' he said, wincing as I dabbed iodine on his forehead. 'We went to the guava orchard near my uncle's farm.'

'She went out there alone with you?'

'Sure. I took her on my bike. They must have followed us. Anyway, we weren't doing much except kissing and fooling around. But some people seem to think that's worse than...'

Both he and the other boys of Shahganj had grown up to look upon girls as strange, exotic animals, who must be seized at the first opportunity. Experimenting in sex was like playing a surreptitious game of marbles.

Sunil produced a clasp knife from his pocket, opened it

and held the blade against the flat of his hand.

'Don't worry, Uncle, I can look after myself. The next fellow who tries to interfere with me will get this in his guts.'

'Don't be silly,' I said. 'You will go to prison for ten years. Listen, I'm going up to Shimla for a couple of weeks, just for a change. Why don't you come with me? It will be a pleasant change from Shahganj, and in the meantime all this fuss will die down.'

It was one of those invitations which I make so readily and instantly regret. As soon as I had made the suggestion, I realized that Sunil in Shimla might be even more of a problem than Sunil in Shahganj. But it was too late for me to back out.

'Shimla! Why not? The college is closing for the summer holidays, and my father won't mind my going with you. He believes you're the only respectable friend I've got. Boy! We'll have a good time in Shimla.'

'You'll have to behave yourself there, if you want to come with me. No girls, Sunil.'

'No girls, Sir. I'll be very good, Chachaji. Please take me to Shimla.'

'I think two hundred rupees should be enough for a fortnight for both of us,' I said.

'Oh, too much,' said Sunil modestly.

And a week later we were actually in Shimla, putting up at a moderately priced, middle-class hotel.

Our first few days in the hill station were pleasant enough. We went for long walks, tired ourselves out and acquired enormous appetites. Sunil, in the hills for the first time in his life, declared that they were wonderful, and thanked me a score of times for bringing him along. He took a genuine interest in exploring remote valleys, forests and waterfalls, and seemed to be losing some of his self-centredness. I believe that mountains do affect one's personality, if one can remain among them long enough; and if Sunil had grown up in the hills instead of in a refugee township, I have no doubt he would have been a completely different person.

There was one small waterfall I rather liked. It was down a ravine, in a rather inaccessible spot, where very few people ever went. The water fell about thirty feet into a small pool. We bathed here on two occasions, and Sunil quite forgot the attractions of the town. And we would have visited the spot again had I not slipped and sprained my ankle. This accident confined me to the hotel balcony for several days, and I was afraid that Sunil, for want of companionship, would go in search of more mundane distractions. But though he went out often enough, he came back dusty and sunburnt; and the fact that he asked me for very little money was evidence enough of his fondness for the outdoors. Striding through forests of oak and pine, with all the world stretched out far below, was no doubt a new and exhilarating experience for him. But how long would it be before the spell was broken?

'Don't you need any money?' I asked him uneasily, on the third day of his Thoreau-like activities.

'What for, Uncle? Fresh air costs nothing. And besides, I don't owe money to anyone in Shimla. We haven't been here long enough.'

'Then perhaps we should be going,' I said.

'Shahganj is a miserable little dump.'

'I know, but it's your home. And for the time being, it's mine.'

'Listen, Uncle,' he said, after a moment of reflection, 'yesterday, on one of my walks, I met a schoolteacher. She's over thirty, so don't get nervous. She doesn't have any brothers or relatives who will come chasing after me. And she's much fairer than you, Uncle. Is it all right if I'm friendly with her?'

'I suppose so,' I said uncertainly. Schoolteachers can usually take care of themselves (if they want to), and, besides, an older woman might have a sobering influence on Sunil.

He brought her over to see me that same evening, and seemed quite proud of his new acquisition. She was indeed fair, perhaps insipidly so, with blonde hair and light blue eyes. She had a young face and a healthy body, but her voice was peculiarly toneless and flat, giving an impression of boredom, of lassitude. I wondered what she found attractive in Sunil apart from his obvious animal charm. They had hardly anything in common, but perhaps the absence of similar interests was an attraction in itself. In six or seven years of teaching, Maureen must have been tired of the usual scholastic types. Sunil was refreshingly free from all classroom associations.

Maureen let her hair down at the first opportunity. She switched on the bedroom radio and found Ceylon. Soon she was teaching Sunil to dance. This was amusing, because Sunil, with his long legs, had great difficulty in taking small steps; nor could Maureen cope with his great strides. But he was very earnest about it all, and inserting an unlighted cigarette between his lips, did his best to move rhythmically around the bedroom. I think he was convinced that by learning to dance he would reach the high watermark of Western culture. Maureen stood for all that was remote and romantic, and for all the films that he had seen, to conquer her would, for Sunil, be a voyage of discovery, not a mere gratification of his senses. And for Maureen, this new unconventional friendship must have been a refreshing diversion from the dreariness of her school routine. She was old enough to realize that it was only a diversion. The intensity of emotional attachments had faded with her early youth and love could wound her heart no more. But for Sunil, it was only the beginning of something that stirred him deeply, moved him inexorably towards manhood.

It was unfortunate that I did not then notice this subtle change in my friend. I had known him only as a shallow creature, and was certain that this new infatuation would disappear as soon as the novelty of it wore off. As Maureen had no encumbrances, no relations that she would speak of, I saw no harm in encouraging the friendship and seeing how it would develop.

'I think we'd better have something to drink,' I said, and ringing the bell for the room bearer, ordered several bottles of beer.

Sunil gave me an odd, whimsical look. I had never before encouraged him to drink. But he did not hesitate to open the bottles, and, before long, Maureen and he were drinking from the same glass.

'Let's make love,' said Sunil, putting his arm around Maureen's shoulders and gazing adoringly into her dreamy blue eyes.

They seemed unconcerned by my presence; but I was embarrassed, and, getting up, said I would be going for a walk.

'Enjoy yourself,' said Sunil, winking at me over Maureen's shoulder.

'You ought to get yourself a girlfriend,' said the young woman in a conciliatory tone.

'True,' I said, and moved guiltily out of the room I was paying for.

Our stay in Shimla lasted several days longer than we had planned. I saw little of Sunil and Maureen during this time. As Sunil had no desire to return to Shahganj any earlier than was absolutely necessary, he avoided me during the day but I managed to stay awake late enough one night to confront him when he crept quietly into the room.

'Dear friend and familiar,' I said. 'I hate to spoil your beautiful romance, but I have absolutely no money left, and unless you have resources of your own—or if Maureen can support you—I suggest that you accompany me back to Shahganj the day after tomorrow.'

'How mean you are, Chachaji. This is something serious. I mean Maureen and me. Do you think we should get married?'

'No.'

'But why not?'

'Because she cannot support you on a teacher's salary. And she probably isn't interested in a permanent relationship—like ours.'

'Very funny. And you think I'd let my wife slave for me?'

'I do. And besides...'

'And besides,' he interrupted, grinning, 'she's old enough to be my mother.'

'Are you really in love with her?' I asked him. 'I've never known you to be serious about anything.'

'Honestly, Uncle.'

'And what about her?'

'Oh, she loves me terribly, really she does. She's ready to come down with us if it's possible. Only I've told her that I'll first have to break the news to my father, otherwise he might kick me out of the house.'

'Well, then,' I said shrewdly, 'the sooner we return to Shahganj and get your father's blessings, the sooner you and Maureen can get married, if that's what both of you really want.'

Early next morning Sunil disappeared, and I knew he would be gone all day. My foot was better, and I decided to take a walk on my own to the waterfall I had liked so much. It was almost noon when I reached the spot and began descending the steep path to the ravine. The stream was hidden by dense foliage, giant ferns and dahlias, but the water made a tremendous noise as it tumbled over the rocks. When I reached a sharp promontory, I was able to look down on the pool. Two people were lying on the grass.

I did not recognize them at first. They looked very beautiful together, and I had not expected Sunil and Maureen to look so beautiful. Sunil, on whom no surplus flesh had as yet gathered, possessed all the sinuous grace and power of a young god; and the woman, her white flesh pressed against young grass, reminded me of a painting by Titian that I had seen in a gallery in Florence. Her full, mature body was touched with a tranquil intoxication, her breasts rose and fell slowly, and waves of muscle merged into the shadows of her broad thighs. It was as though I had stumbled into another age, and had found two lovers in a forest glade. Only a fool would have wished to disturb them. Sunil had for once in his life risen above mediocrity, and I hurried away before the magic was lost.

The human voice often shatters the beauty of the most tender passions; and when we left Shimla the next day, and Maureen and Sunil used all the stock cliches to express their love, I was a little disappointed. But the poetry of life was in their bodies, not in their tongues.

Back in Shahganj, Sunil actually plucked up the courage to speak to his father. This, to me, was a sign that he took the affair very seriously, for he seldom approached his father for anything. But all the sympathy that he received was a box on the ears. I received a curt note suggesting that I was having a corrupting influence on the boy and that I should stop seeing him. There was little I could do in the matter, because it had always been Sunil who had insisted on seeing me.

He continued to visit me, bring me Maureen's letters (strange, how lovers cannot bear that the world should not know their love), and his own to her, so that I could correct his English!

It was at about this time that Sunil began speaking to me about his uncle's paper factory and the possibility of working in it. Once he was getting a salary, he pointed out, Maureen would be able to leave her job and join him.

Unfortunately, Sunil's decision to join the paper factory took months to crystallize into a definite course of action, and in the meantime he was finding a panacea for lovesickness in rum and sometimes cheap country spirit. The money that he now borrowed was used not to pay his debts, or to incur new ones, but to drink himself silly. I regretted having been the first person to have offered him a drink. I should have known that Sunil was a person who could do nothing in moderation.

He pestered me less often now, but the purpose of his occasional visits became all too obvious. I was having a little success, and thoughtlessly gave Sunil the few rupees he usually demanded. At the same time I was beginning to find other friends, and I no longer found myself worrying about Sunil, as I had so often done in the past. Perhaps this was treachery on my part…

When finally I decided to leave Shahganj for Delhi, I went in search of Sunil to say goodbye. I found him in a small bar, alone at a table with a bottle of rum. Though barely twenty, he no longer looked a boy. He was a completely different person from the handsome, cocksure youth I had met at the wrestling pit a year previously. His cheeks were hollow and he had not shaved for days. I knew that when I first met him he had been without scruples, a shallow youth, the product of many circumstances. He was no longer so shallow and he had stumbled upon love, but his character was too weak to sustain the weight of disillusionment. Perhaps I should have left him severely alone from the beginning. Before me sat a ruin, and I had helped to undermine the foundations. None of us can really avoid seeing the outcome of our smallest actions…

'I'm off to Delhi, Sunil.'

He did not look up from the table.

'Have a good time,' he said.

'Have you heard from Maureen?' I asked, certain that he had not.

He nodded, but for once did not offer to show me the letter.

'What's wrong?' I asked.

'Oh, nothing,' he said, looking up and forcing a smile. 'These dames are all the same, Uncle. We shouldn't take them too seriously, you know.'

'Why, what has she done, got married to someone else?'

'Yes,' he said scornfully. 'To a bloody teacher.'

'Well, she wasn't young,' I said. 'She couldn't wait for you forever, I suppose.'

'She could if she had really loved me. But there's no such thing as love, is there, Uncle?'

I made no reply. Had he really broken his heart over a woman? Were there, within him, unsuspected depths of feeling and passion? You find love when you least expect to and lose it when you are sure that it is in your grasp.

'You're a lucky beggar,' he said. 'You're a philosopher. You find a reason for every stupid thing and so you are able to ignore all stupidity.'

I laughed. 'You're becoming a philosopher yourself. But don't think too hard, Sunil, you might find it painful.'

'Not I, Chachaji,' he said, emptying his glass. 'I'm not going to think. I'm going to work in a paper factory. I shall become respectable. What an adventure that will be!'

And that was the last time I saw Sunil.

He did not become respectable. He was still searching like a great discoverer for something new, someone different, when he met his pitiful end in the cold rain of a December night.

Though murder cases usually get reported in the papers, Sunil was a person of such little importance that his violent end was not considered newsworthy. It went unnoticed, and Maureen could not have known about it. The case has already been forgotten, for in the great human mass that is India, hundreds of people disappear every day and are never heard of again. Sunil will be quickly forgotten by all except those to whom he owed money.

Panther's Moon

I

In the entire village, he was the first to get up. Even the dog, a big hill mastiff called Sheroo, was asleep in a corner of the dark room, curled up near the cold embers of the previous night's fire. Bisnu's tousled head emerged from his blanket. He rubbed the sleep from his eyes and sat up on his haunches. Then, gathering his wits, he crawled in the direction of the loud ticking that came from the battered little clock which occupied the second most honoured place in a niche in the wall. The most honoured place belonged to a picture of Ganesha, the god of learning, who had an elephant's head and a fat boy's body. Bringing his face close to the clock, Bisnu could just make out the hands. It was five o'clock. He had half an hour in which to get ready and leave.

He got up, in vest and underpants, and moved quietly towards the door. The soft tread of his bare feet woke Sheroo and the big black dog rose silently and padded behind the boy. The door opened and closed and then the boy and the dog were outside in the early dawn. The month was June and the nights were warm, even in the Himalayan valleys, but there was fresh dew on the grass. Bisnu felt the dew beneath his feet. He took a deep breath and began walking down to the stream.

The sound of the stream filled the small valley. At that early hour of the morning, it was the only sound; but Bisnu was hardly conscious of it. It was a sound he lived with and took for granted. It was only when he had crossed the hill, on his way to the town—and the sound of the stream grew distant—that he really began to notice it. And it was only when the stream was too far away to be heard that he really missed its sound.

He slipped out of his underclothes, gazed for a few moments at the goose pimples rising on his flesh, and then dashed into the shallow stream. As he went further in, the cold mountain water reached his loins and navel and he gasped with shock and pleasure. He drifted slowly with the current, swam across to a small inlet which formed a fairly deep pool and plunged into the water. Sheroo hated cold water at this early hour. Had the sun been up, he would not have hesitated to join Bisnu. Now he contented himself with sitting on a smooth rock and gazing placidly at the slim brown boy splashing about in the clear water, in the widening light of dawn.

Bisnu did not stay long in the water. There wasn't time. When he returned to the house, he found his mother up, making tea and chapattis. His sister, Puja, was still asleep. She was a little older than Bisnu, a pretty girl with large black eyes, good teeth, and strong arms and legs. During the day, she helped her mother in the house and in the fields. She did not go to the school with Bisnu. But when he came home in the evenings, he would try teaching her some of the things he had learnt. Their father was dead. Bisnu, at twelve, considered himself the head of the family.

He ate two chapattis, after spreading butter-oil on them. He drank a glass of hot, sweet tea. His mother gave two thick chapattis to Sheroo and the dog wolfed them down in a few minutes. Then she wrapped two chapattis and a gourd curry in some big green leaves and handed these to Bisnu. This was his lunch packet. His mother and Puja would take their meal afterwards.

When Bisnu was dressed, he stood with folded hands before the picture of Ganesha. Ganesha is the god who blesses all beginnings. The author who begins to write a new book, the banker who opens a new ledger, the traveller who starts on a journey, all invoke the kindly help of Ganesha. And as Bisnu made a journey every day, he never left without the goodwill of the elephant-headed god.

How, one might ask, did Ganesha get his elephant's head? When born, he was a beautiful child. Parvati, his mother, was so proud of him that she went about showing him to everyone.

Unfortunately, she made the mistake of showing the child to that envious planet, Saturn, who promptly burnt off poor Ganesha's head. Parvati in despair went to Brahma, the Creator, for a new head for her son. He had no head to give her but advised her to search for some man or animal caught in a sinful or wrong act. Parvati wandered about until she came upon an elephant sleeping with its head the wrong way, that is, to the south. She promptly removed the elephant's head and planted it on Ganesha's shoulders, where it took root.

Bisnu knew this story. He had heard it from his mother. Wearing a white shirt and black shorts and a pair of worn white keds, he was ready for his long walk to school, five miles up the mountain.

His sister woke up just as he was about to leave. She pushed the hair away from her face and gave Bisnu one of her rare smiles.

'I hope you have not forgotten,' she said.

'Forgotten?' said Bisnu, pretending innocence. 'Is there anything I am supposed to remember?'

'Don't tease me. You promised to buy me a pair of bangles,

remember? I hope you won't spend the money on sweets, as you did last time.'

'Oh, yes, your bangles,' said Bisnu. 'Girls have nothing better to do than waste money on trinkets. Now, don't lose your temper! I'll get them for you. Red and gold are the colours you want?'

'Yes, Brother,' said Puja gently, pleased that Bisnu had remembered the colours.

'And for your dinner tonight we'll make you something special. Won't we, Mother?'

'Yes. But hurry up and dress. There is some ploughing to be done today. The rains will soon be here, if the gods are kind.'

'The monsoon will be late this year,' said Bisnu. 'Mr Nautiyal, our teacher, told us so. He said it had nothing to do with the gods.'

'Be off, you are getting late,' said Puja, before Bisnu could begin an argument with his mother. She was diligently winding the old clock. It was quite light in the room. The sun would be up any minute.

Bisnu shouldered his school bag, kissed his mother, pinched his sister's cheeks, and left the house. He started climbing the steep path up the mountainside. Sheroo bounded ahead; for he, too, always went with Bisnu to school.

Five miles to school. Every day, except Sunday, Bisnu walked five miles to school; and in the evening, he walked home again. There was no school in his own small village of Manjari, for the village consisted of only five families. The nearest school was at Kempty, a small township on the bus route through the district of Garhwal. A number of boys walked to school, from distances of two or three miles; their villages were not quite as remote as Manjari. But Bisnu's village lay right at the bottom of the mountain, a drop of over two thousand feet from Kempty. There was no proper road between the village and the town.

In Kempty, there was a school, a small mission hospital, a post office, and several shops. In Manjari village there were none of these amenities. If you were sick, you stayed at home until you got well; if you were very sick, you walked or were carried to the hospital, up the five-mile path. If you wanted to buy something, you went without it; but if you wanted it very badly, you could walk the five miles to Kempty.

Manjari was known as the Five-Mile Village.

Twice a week, if there were any letters, a postman came to the village. Bisnu usually passed the postman on his way to and from school.

There were other boys in Manjari village, but Bisnu was the only one who went to school. His mother would not have fussed if he had stayed at home and worked in the fields. That was what the other boys did; all except lazy Chittru, who preferred fishing in the stream or helping himself to the fruit off other people's trees. But Bisnu went to school. He went because he wanted to. No one could force him to go; and no one could stop him from going. He had set his heart on receiving a good schooling. He wanted to read and write as well as anyone in the big world, the world that seemed to begin only where the mountains ended. He felt cut off from the world in his small valley. He would rather live at the top of a mountain than at the bottom of one. That was why he liked climbing to Kempty, it took him to the top of the mountain; and from its ridge he could look down on his own valley to the north and to the wide, endless plains stretching towards the south.

The plainsman looks to the hills for the needs of his spirit but the hillman looks to the plains for a living. Leaving the village and the fields below him, Bisnu climbed steadily up the bare hillside, now dry and brown. By the time the sun was up, he had entered the welcome shade of an oak and rhododendron forest. Sheroo went bounding ahead, chasing squirrels and barking at langurs.

A colony of langurs lived in the oak forest. They fed on oak leaves, acorns, and other green things, and usually remained in the trees, coming down to the ground only to play or bask in the sun. They were beautiful, supple-limbed animals, with black faces and silver-grey coats and long, sensitive tails. They leapt from tree to tree with great agility. The young ones wrestled on the grass like boys.

A dignified community, the langurs did not have the cheekiness or dishonest habits of the red monkeys of the plains; they did not approach dogs or humans. But they had grown used to Bisnu's comings and goings and did not fear him. Some of the older ones would watch him quietly, a little puzzled. They did not go near the town, because the Kempty boys threw stones at them. And anyway, the oak forest gave them all the food they required. Emerging from the trees, Bisnu crossed a small brook. Here he stopped to drink the fresh clean water of a spring. The brook tumbled down the mountain and joined the river a little below Bisnu's village. Coming from another direction was a second path and at the junction of the two paths Sarru was waiting for him. Sarru came from a small village about three miles from Bisnu's and closer to the town. He had two large milk cans slung over his shoulders. Every morning he carried this milk to town, selling one can to the school and the other to Mrs Taylor, the lady doctor at the small mission hospital. He was a little older than Bisnu but not as well built.

They hailed each other and Sarru fell into step beside Bisnu. They often met at this spot, keeping each other company for the remaining two miles to Kempty.

'There was a panther in our village last night,' said Sarru.

This information interested but did not excite Bisnu. Panthers were common enough in the hills and did not usually present a problem except during the winter months, when their natural prey was scarce. Then, occasionally, a panther would take to haunting the outskirts of a village, seizing a careless dog or a stray goat.

'Did you lose any animals?' asked Bisnu.

'No. It tried to get into the cowshed but the dogs set up an alarm. We drove it off.'

'It must be the same one which came around last winter. We lost a calf and two dogs in our village.'

'Wasn't that the one the shikaris wounded? I hope it hasn't become a cattle lifter.'

'It could be the same. It has a bullet in its leg. These hunters are the people who cause all the trouble. They think it's easy to shoot a panther. It would be better if they missed altogether but they usually wound it.'

'And then the panther's too slow to catch the barking deer and starts on our own animals.'

'We're lucky it didn't become a man-eater. Do you remember the man-eater six years ago? I was very small then. My father told me all about it. Ten people were killed in our valley alone. What happened to it?'

'I don't know. Some say it poisoned itself when it ate the headman of another village.'

Bisnu laughed. 'No one liked that old villain. He must have been a man-eater himself in some previous existence!' They linked arms and scrambled up the stony path. Sheroo began barking and ran ahead. Someone was coming down the path. It was Mela Ram, the postman.

II

'Any letters for us?' asked Bisnu and Sarru together. They never received any letters but that did not stop them from asking. It was one way of finding out who had received letters.

'You're welcome to all of them,' said Mela Ram, 'if you'll carry my bag for me.'

'Not today,' said Sarru. 'We're busy today. Is there a letter from Corporal Ghanshyam for his family?'

'Yes, there is a postcard for his people. He is posted on the Ladakh border now and finds it very cold there.'

Postcards, unlike sealed letters, were considered public property and were read by everyone. The senders knew that too, and so Corporal Ghanshyam Singh was careful to mention that he expected a promotion very soon. He wanted everyone in his village to know it.

Mela Ram, complaining of sore feet, continued on his way and the boys carried on up the path. It was eight o'clock when they reached Kempty. Dr Taylor's outpatients were just beginning to trickle in at the hospital gate. The doctor was trying to prop up a rose creeper which had blown down during the night. She liked attending to her plants in the mornings, before starting on her patients. She found this helped her in her work. There was a lot in common between ailing plants and ailing people.

Dr Taylor was fifty, white-haired but fresh in the face and full of vitality. She had been in India for twenty years and ten of these had been spent working in the hill regions.

She saw Bisnu coming down the road. She knew about the boy and his long walk to school and admired him for his keenness and sense of purpose. She wished there were more like him.

Bisnu greeted her shyly. Sheroo barked and put his paws up on the gate.

'Yes, there's a bone for you,' said Dr Taylor. She often put aside bones for the big black dog, for she knew that Bisnu's people could not afford to give the dog a regular diet of meat—though he did well enough on milk and chapattis.

She threw the bone over the gate and Sheroo caught it before it fell. The school bell began ringing and Bisnu broke into a run.

Sheroo loped along behind the boy.

When Bisnu entered the school gate, Sheroo sat down on the grass of the compound. He would remain there until the lunch break. He knew of various ways of amusing himself during school hours and had friends among the bazaar dogs. But just then he didn't want company. He had his bone to get on with.

Mr Nautiyal, Bisnu's teacher, was in a bad mood. He was a keen rose grower and only that morning, on getting up and looking out of his bedroom window, he had been horrified to see a herd of goats in his garden. He had chased them down the road with a stick but the damage had already been done. His prize roses had all been consumed.

Mr Nautiyal had been so upset that he had gone without his breakfast. He had also cut himself whilst shaving. Thus, his mood had gone from bad to worse. Several times during the day, he brought down his ruler on the knuckles of any boy who irritated him. Bisnu was one of his best pupils. But even Bisnu irritated him by asking too many questions about a new sum which Mr Nautiyal didn't feel like explaining.

That was the kind of day it was for Mr Nautiyal. Most schoolteachers know similar days.

'Poor Mr Nautiyal,' thought Bisnu. 'I wonder why he's so upset. It must be because of his pay. He doesn't get much money. But he's a good teacher. I hope he doesn't take another job.'

But after Mr Nautiyal had eaten his lunch, his mood

improved (as it always did after a meal) and the rest of the day passed serenely. Armed with a bundle of homework, Bisnu came out from the school compound at four o'clock and was immediately joined by Sheroo. He proceeded down the road in the company of several of his class-fellows. But he did not linger long in the bazaar. There were five miles to walk and he did not like to get home too late. Usually, he reached his house just as it was beginning to get dark.

Sarru had gone home long ago and Bisnu had to make the return journey on his own. It was a good opportunity to memorize the words of an English poem he had been asked to learn. Bisnu had reached the little brook when he remembered the bangles he had promised to buy for his sister.

'Oh, I've forgotten them again,' he said aloud. 'Now I'll catch it—and she's probably made something special for my dinner!'

Sheroo, to whom these words were addressed, paid no attention but bounded off into the oak forest. Bisnu looked around for the monkeys but they were nowhere to be seen.

'Strange,' he thought, 'I wonder why they have disappeared.'

He was startled by a sudden sharp cry, followed by a fierce yelp. He knew at once that Sheroo was in trouble. The noise came from the bushes down the khud, into which the dog had rushed but a few seconds previously.

Bisnu jumped off the path and ran down the slope towards the bushes. There was no dog and not a sound. He whistled and called but there was no response. Then he saw something lying on the dry grass. He picked it up. It was a portion of a dog's collar, stained with blood. It was Sheroo's collar and Sheroo's blood.

Bisnu did not search further. He knew, without a doubt, that Sheroo had been seized by a panther. No other animal could have attacked so silently and swiftly and carried off a big dog without a struggle. Sheroo was dead—must have been dead within seconds of being caught and flung into the air. Bisnu knew the danger that lay in wait for him if he followed the blood trail through the trees. The panther would attack anyone who interfered with its meal.

With tears starting in his eyes, Bisnu carried on down the path to the village. His fingers still clutched the little bit of bloodstained collar that was all that was left to him of his dog.

III

Bisnu was not a very sentimental boy but he sorrowed for his dog who had been his companion on many a hike into the hills and forests. He did not sleep that night but turned restlessly from side to side, moaning softly. After some time he felt Puja's hand on his head. She began stroking his brow. He took her hand in his own and the clasp of her rough, warm, familiar hand gave him a feeling of comfort and security.

Next morning, when he went down to the stream to bathe, he missed the presence of his dog. He did not stay long in the water. It wasn't as much fun when there was no Sheroo to watch him.

When Bisnu's mother gave him his food, she told him to be careful and hurry home that evening. A panther, even if it is only a cowardly lifter of sheep or dogs, is not to be trifled with. And this particular panther had shown some daring by seizing the dog even before it was dark.

Still, there was no question of staying away from school. If Bisnu remained at home every time a panther put in an appearance, he might just as well stop going to school altogether.

He set off even earlier than usual and reached the meeting of the paths long before Sarru. He did not wait for his friend because he did not feel like talking about the loss of his dog. It was not the day for the postman and so Bisnu reached Kempty without meeting anyone on the way. He tried creeping past the hospital gate unnoticed, but Dr Taylor saw him and the first thing she said was: 'Where's Sheroo? I've got something for him.'

When Dr Taylor saw the boy's face, she knew at once that something was wrong.

'What is it, Bisnu?' she asked. She looked quickly up and down the road. 'Is it Sheroo?'

He nodded gravely.

'A panther took him,' he said.

'In the village?'

'No, while we were walking home through the forest. I did not see anything—but I heard.'

Dr Taylor knew that there was nothing she could say that would console him and she tried to conceal the bone which she had brought out for the dog, but Bisnu noticed her hiding it behind her back and the tears welled up in his eyes. He turned away and began running down the road.

His school-fellows noticed Sheroo's absence and questioned Bisnu. He had to tell them everything. They were full of sympathy but they were also quite thrilled at what had happened and kept pestering Bisnu for all the details. There was a lot of noise in the classroom, and Mr Nautiyal had to call for order. When he learnt what had happened, he patted Bisnu on the head and told him that he need not attend school for the rest of the day. But Bisnu did not want to go home. After school, he got into a fight with one of the boys, and that helped him forget.

IV

The panther that plunged the village into an atmosphere of gloom and terror may not have been the same panther that took Sheroo. There was no way of knowing and it would have made no difference, because the panther that came by night and struck at the people of Manjari was that most feared of wild creatures, a man-eater.

Nine-year-old Sanjay, son of Kalam Singh, was the first child to be attacked by the panther.

Kalam Singh's house was the last in the village and nearest the stream. Like the other houses, it was quite small, just a room above and a stable below, with steps leading up from outside the house. He lived there with his wife, two sons (Sanjay was the youngest), and little daughter Basanti, who had just turned three.

Sanjay had brought his father's cows home after grazing them on the hillside in the company of other children. He had also brought home an edible wild plant, which his mother cooked into a tasty dish for their evening meal. They had their food at dusk, sitting on the floor of their single room, and soon after settled down for the night. Sanjay curled up in his favourite spot, with his head near the door, where he got a little fresh air. As the nights were warm, the door was usually left a little ajar. Sanjay's mother piled ash on the embers of the fire and the family was soon asleep.

No one heard the stealthy padding of a panther approaching the door, pushing it wider open. But suddenly there were sounds of a frantic struggle, and Sanjay's stifled cries were mixed with the grunts of the panther. Kalam Singh leapt to his feet with a shout. The panther had dragged Sanjay out of the door and was pulling him down the steps, when Kalam Singh started battering at the animal with a large stone. The rest of the family screamed in terror, rousing the entire village. A number of men came to Kalam Singh's assistance and the panther was driven off. But Sanjay lay unconscious.

Someone brought a lantern and the boy's mother screamed when she saw her small son with his head lying in a pool of blood. It looked as if the side of his head had been eaten off by the panther. But he was still alive, and as Kalam Singh plastered ash on the boy's head to stop the bleeding, he found that though the scalp had been torn off one side of the head, the bare bone was smooth and unbroken.

'He won't live through the night,' said a neighbour. 'We'll have to carry him down to the river in the morning.'

The dead were always cremated on the banks of a small river which flowed past Manjari village.

Suddenly, the panther, still prowling about the village, called out in rage and frustration, and the villagers rushed to their homes in panic and barricaded themselves in for the night.

Sanjay's mother sat by the boy for the rest of the night, weeping and watching. Towards dawn he started to moan and show signs of coming round. At this sign of returning consciousness, Kalam Singh rose determinedly and looked around for his stick.

He told his elder son to remain behind with the mother and daughter, as he was going to take Sanjay to Dr Taylor at the hospital.

'See, he is moaning and in pain,' said Kalam Singh. 'That means he has a chance to live if he can be treated at once.'

With a stout stick in his hand, and Sanjay on his back, Kalam Singh set off on the two miles of hard mountain track to the hospital at Kempty. His son, a bloodstained cloth around his head, was moaning but still unconscious. When at last Kalam Singh climbed up through the last fields below the hospital, he asked for the doctor and stammered out an account of what had happened.

It was a terrible injury, as Dr Taylor discovered. The bone over almost one-third of the head was bare and the scalp was torn all around. As the father told his story, the doctor cleaned and dressed the wound, and then gave Sanjay a shot of penicillin to prevent sepsis. Later, Kalam Singh carried the boy home again.

V

After this, the panther went away for some time. But the people of Manjari could not be sure of its whereabouts. They kept to their houses after dark and shut their doors. Bisnu had to stop going to school, because there was no one to accompany him and it was dangerous to go alone. This worried him because his final exam was only a few weeks away and he would be missing important classwork. When he wasn't in the fields, helping with the sowing of rice and maize, he would be sitting in the shade of a chestnut tree, going through his well-thumbed second-hand schoolbooks. He had no other reading, except for a copy of the Ramayana and a Hindi translation of *Alice in Wonderland*. These were well-preserved, read only in fits and starts and usually kept locked in his mother's old tin trunk.

Sanjay had nightmares for several nights and woke up screaming. But with the resilience of youth, he quickly recovered. At the end of the week he was able to walk to the hospital, though his father always accompanied him. Even a desperate panther will hesitate to attack a party of two. Sanjay, with his thin, little face and huge bandaged head, looked a pathetic figure, but he was getting better and the wound looked like it was healing.

Bisnu often went to see him, and the two boys spent long

hours together near the stream. Sometimes Chittru would join them, and they would try catching fish with a home-made net. They were often successful in taking home one or two mountain trout. Sometimes, Bisnu and Chittru wrestled in the shallow water or on the grassy banks of the stream. Chittru was a chubby boy with a broad chest, strong legs and thighs, and when he used his weight he got Bisnu under him. But Bisnu was hard and wiry and had very strong wrists and fingers. When he had Chittru in a vice, the bigger boy would cry out and give up the struggle. Sanjay could not join in these games.

He had never been a very strong boy and he needed plenty of rest if his wounds were to heal well.

The panther had not been seen for over a week and the people of Manjari were beginning to hope that it might have moved on over the mountain or further down the valley.

'I think I can start going to school again,' said Bisnu. 'The panther has gone away.'

'Don't be too sure,' said Puja. 'The moon is full these days and perhaps it is only being cautious.'

'Wait a few days,' said their mother. 'It is better to wait. Perhaps you could go the day after tomorrow when Sanjay goes to the hospital with his father. Then you will not be alone.'

And so, two days later, Bisnu went up to Kempty with Sanjay and Kalam Singh. Sanjay's wound had almost healed over. Little islets of flesh had grown over the bone. Dr Taylor told him that he need come to see her only once a fortnight, instead of every third day.

Bisnu went to his school and was given a warm welcome by his friends and by Mr Nautiyal.

'You'll have to work hard,' said his teacher. 'You have to catch up with the others. If you like, I can give you some extra time after classes.'

'Thank you, sir, but it will make me late,' said Bisnu. 'I must get home before it is dark, otherwise my mother will worry. I think the panther has gone but nothing is certain.'

'Well, you mustn't take risks. Do your best, Bisnu. Work hard and you'll soon catch up with your lessons.'

Sanjay and Kalam Singh were waiting for him outside the school. Together they took the path down to Manjari, passing the postman on the way. Mela Ram said he had heard that the panther was in another district and that there was nothing to fear. He was on his rounds again.

Nothing happened on the way. The langurs were back in their favourite part of the forest. Bisnu got home just as the kerosene lamp was being lit. Puja met him at the door with a winsome smile.

'Did you get the bangles?' she asked.

But Bisnu had forgotten again.

VI

There had been a thunderstorm and some rain—a short, sharp shower which gave the villagers hope that the monsoon would arrive on time. It brought out the thunder lilies—pink, crocus-like flowers which sprang up on the hillsides immediately after a summer shower.

Bisnu, on his way home from school, was caught in the rain. He knew the shower would not last, so he took shelter in a small cave and, to pass the time, began doing sums, scratching figures in the damp earth with the end of a stick.

When the rain stopped, he came out from the cave and continued down the path. He wasn't in a hurry. The rain had made everything smell fresh and good. The scent from fallen pine needles rose from the wet earth. The leaves of the oak trees had been washed clean and a light breeze turned them about, showing their silver undersides. The birds, refreshed and high-spirited, set up a terrific noise. The worst offenders were the yellow-bottomed bulbuls who squabbled and fought in the blackberry bushes. A barbet, high up in the branches of a deodar, set up its querulous, plaintive call. And a flock of bright green parrots came swooping down the hill to settle on a wild plum tree and feast on the unripe fruit. The langurs, too, had been revived by the rain. They leapt friskily from tree to tree, greeting Bisnu with little grunts.

He was almost out of the oak forest when he heard a faint bleating. Presently, a little goat came stumbling up the path towards him. The kid was far from home and must have strayed from the rest of the herd. But it was not yet conscious of being lost. It came to Bisnu with a hop, skip, and jump and started nuzzling against his legs like a cat.

'I wonder who you belong to,' mused Bisnu, stroking the little creature. 'You'd better come home with me until someone claims you.'

He didn't have to take the kid in his arms. It was used to humans and followed close at his heels. Now that darkness was coming on, Bisnu walked a little faster.

He had not gone very far when he heard the sawing grunt of a panther.

The sound came from the hill to the right and Bisnu judged the distance to be anything from a hundred to two hundred yards. He hesitated on the path, wondering what to do. Then he picked the kid up in his arms and hurried on in the direction of home and safety.

The panther called again, much closer now. If it was an ordinary panther, it would go away on finding that the kid was with Bisnu. If it was the man-eater, it would not hesitate to attack the boy, for no man-eater fears a human. There was no time to lose and there did not seem much point in running. Bisnu looked up and down the hillside. The forest was far behind him and there were only a few trees in his vicinity. He chose a spruce.

The branches of the Himalayan spruce are very brittle and snap easily beneath a heavy weight. They were strong enough to support Bisnu's light frame. It was unlikely they would take the weight of a full-grown panther. At least that was what Bisnu hoped.

Holding the kid with one arm, Bisnu gripped a low branch and swung himself up into the tree. He was a good climber. Slowly but confidently he climbed halfway up the tree, until he was about twelve feet above the ground. He couldn't go any higher without risking a fall.

He had barely settled himself in the crook of a branch when the panther came into the open, running into the clearing at a brisk trot. This was no stealthy approach, no wary stalking of its prey. It was the man-eater, all right. Bisnu felt a cold shiver run down his spine. He felt a little sick.

The panther stood in the clearing with a slight thrusting forward of the head. This gave it the appearance of gazing intently and rather short-sightedly at some invisible object in the clearing. But there is nothing short-sighted about a panther's vision. Its sight and hearing are acute.

Bisnu remained motionless in the tree and sent up a prayer to all the gods he could think of. But the kid began bleating. The panther looked up and gave its deep-throated, rasping grunt—a fearsome sound, calculated to strike terror in any tree-borne animal. Many a monkey, petrified by a panther's roar, has fallen from its perch to make a meal for Mr Spots. The man-eater was trying the same technique on Bisnu. But though the boy was trembling with fright, he clung firmly to the trunk of the spruce tree.

The panther did not make any attempt to leap into the tree. Perhaps, it knew instinctively that this was not the type of tree that it could climb. Instead, it described a semicircle around the tree, keeping its face turned towards Bisnu. Then it disappeared into the bushes.

The man-eater was cunning. It hoped to put the boy off his guard, perhaps entice him down from the tree. For, a few seconds later, with a half-pitched growl, it rushed back into the clearing and then stopped, staring up at the boy in some surprise. The panther was getting frustrated. It snarled, and putting its forefeet up against the tree trunk, began scratching at the bark in the manner of an ordinary domestic cat. The tree shook at each thud of the beast's paw.

Bisnu began shouting for help.

The moon had not yet come up. Down in Manjari village, Bisnu's mother and sister stood in their lighted doorway, gazing anxiously up the pathway. Every now and then, Puja would turn to take a look at the small clock.

Sanjay's father appeared in a field below. He had a kerosene lantern in his hand.

'Sister, isn't your boy home as yet?' he asked.

'No, he hasn't arrived. We are very worried. He should have been home an hour ago. Do you think the panther will be about tonight? There's going to be a moon.'

'True, but it won't be dark for another hour. I will fetch the other menfolk and we will go up the mountain for your boy. There may have been a landslide during the rain. Perhaps the path has been washed away.'

'Thank you, brother. But arm yourselves, just in case the panther is about.'

'I will take my spear,' said Kalam Singh. 'I have sworn to spear that devil when I find him. There is some evil spirit dwelling in the beast and it must be destroyed!'

'I am coming with you,' said Puja.

'No, you cannot go,' said her mother. 'It's bad enough that Bisnu is in danger. You stay at home with me. This work is for men.'

'I shall be safe with them,' insisted Puja. 'I am going, Mother!'

And she jumped down the embankment into the field and followed Sanjay's father through the village.

Ten minutes later, two men armed with axes had joined Kalam Singh in the courtyard of his house and the small party moved silently and swiftly up the mountain path. Puja walked in the middle of the group, holding the lantern. As soon as the village lights were hidden by a shoulder of the hill, the men began to shout—both to frighten the panther, if it was about, and to give themselves courage.

Bisnu's mother closed the front door and turned to the image of Ganesha for comfort and help.

Bisnu's calls were carried on the wind and Puja and the men heard him while they were still half a mile away. Their own shouts increased in volume and, hearing their voices, Bisnu felt strength return to his shaking limbs. Emboldened by the approach of his own people, he began shouting insults at the snarling panther, then throwing twigs and small branches at the enraged animal. The kid added its bleats to the boy's shouts, the birds took up the chorus. The langurs squealed and grunted, the searchers shouted themselves hoarse and the panther howled with rage. The forest had never before been so noisy.

As the search party drew near, they could hear the panther's savage snarls, and hurried, fearing that perhaps Bisnu had been seized. Puja began to run.

'Don't rush ahead, girl,' said Kalam Singh. 'Stay between us.'

The panther, now aware of the approaching humans, stood still in the middle of the clearing, head thrust forward in a familiar stance. There seemed too many men for one panther. When the animal saw the light of the lantern dancing between the trees, it turned, snarled defiance and hate, and without another look at the boy in the tree, disappeared into the bushes. It was not yet ready for a showdown.

VII

Nobody turned up to claim the little goat, so Bisnu kept it. A goat was a poor substitute for a dog, but, like Mary's lamb, it followed Bisnu wherever he went, and the boy couldn't help being touched by its devotion. He took it down to the stream, where it would skip about in the shallows and nibble the sweet grass that grew on the banks.

As for the panther, frustrated in its attempt on Bisnu's life, it did not wait long before attacking another human.

It was Chittru who came running down the path one afternoon, bubbling excitedly about the panther and the postman.

Chittru, deeming it safe to gather ripe bilberries in the daytime, had walked about half a mile up the path from the village, when he had stumbled across Mela Ram's mailbag lying on the ground. Of the postman himself there was no sign. But a trail of blood led through the bushes.

Once again, a party of men headed by Kalam Singh and accompanied by Bisnu and Chittru, went out to look for the postman. But though they found Mela Ram's bloodstained clothes, they could not find his body. The panther had made no mistake this time.

It was to be several weeks before Manjari had a new postman.

A few days after Mela Ram's disappearance, an old woman was sleeping with her head near the open door of her house. She had been advised to sleep inside with the door closed but the nights were hot and anyway the old woman was a little deaf, and in the middle of the night, an hour before moonrise, the panther seized her by the throat. Her strangled cry woke her grown-up son, and all the men in the village woke up at his shouts and came running.

The panther dragged the old woman out of the house and down the steps, but left her when the men approached with their axes and spears, and made off into the bushes. The old woman was still alive and the men made a rough stretcher of bamboo and vines and started carrying her up the path. But they had not gone far when she began to cough, and because of her terrible throat wounds, her lungs collapsed and she died.

It was the 'dark of the month'—the week of the new moon when nights are darkest.

Bisnu, closing the front door and lighting the kerosene lantern, said, 'I wonder where that panther is tonight!'

The panther was busy in another village: Sarru's village.

A woman and her daughter had been out in the evening bedding the cattle down in the stable. The girl had gone into the house and the woman was following. As she bent down to go in at the low door, the panther sprang from the bushes. Fortunately, one of its paws hit the doorpost and broke the force of the attack, or the woman would have been killed. When she cried out, the men came around shouting and the panther slunk off. The woman had deep scratches on her back and was badly shocked.

The next day, a small party of villagers presented themselves in front of the magistrate's office at Kempty and demanded that something be done about the panther. But the magistrate was away on tour and there was no one else in Kempty who had a gun. Mr Nautiyal met the villagers and promised to write to a well-known shikari but said that it would be at least a fortnight before the shikari would be able to come.

Bisnu was fretting because he could not go to school. Most boys would be only too happy to miss school, but when you are living in a remote village in the mountains, and having an education is the only way of seeing the world, you look forward to going to school, even if it is five miles from home. Bisnu's exams were only two weeks off and he didn't want to remain in the same class while the others were promoted. Besides, he knew he could pass even though he had missed a number of lessons. But he had to sit for the exams. He couldn't miss them.

'Cheer up, Brother,' said Puja, as they sat drinking glasses of hot tea after their evening meal. 'The panther may go away once the rains break.'

'Even the rains are late this year,' said Bisnu. 'It's so hot and dry. Can't we open the door?'

'And be dragged down the steps by the panther?' said his mother. 'It isn't safe to have the window open, let alone the door.'

And she went to the small window—through which a cat would have found difficulty in passing—and bolted it firmly.

With a sigh of resignation, Bisnu threw off all his clothes except his underwear and stretched himself out on the earthen floor.

'We will be rid of the beast soon,' said his mother. 'I know it in my heart. Our prayers will be heard, and you shall go to school and pass your exams.'

To cheer up her children, she told them a humorous story which had been handed down to her by her grandmother. It was all about a tiger, a panther, and a bear, the three of whom were made to feel very foolish by a thief hiding in the hollow trunk of a banyan tree. Bisnu was sleepy and did not listen very attentively. He dropped off to sleep before the story was finished.

When he woke, it was dark and his mother and sister were asleep on the cot. He wondered what it was that had woken him. He could hear his sister's easy breathing and the steady ticking of the clock. Far away, an owl hooted—an unlucky sign, his mother would have said; but she was asleep and Bisnu was not superstitious.

And then he heard something scratching at the door, and the hair on his head felt tight and prickly. It was like a cat scratching, only louder. The door creaked a little whenever it felt the impact of the paw—a heavy paw, as Bisnu could tell from the dull sound it made.

'It's the panther,' he muttered under his breath, sitting up on the hard floor.

The door, he felt, was strong enough to resist the panther's weight. And if he set up an alarm, he could rouse the village. But the middle of the night was no time for the bravest of men to tackle a panther.

In a corner of the room stood a long bamboo stick with a sharp knife tied to one end, which Bisnu sometimes used for spearing fish. Crawling on all fours across the room, he grasped the homemade spear, and then scrambling on to a cupboard, he drew level with the skylight window. He could get his head and shoulders through the window.

'What are you doing up there?' said Puja, who had woken up at the sound of Bisnu shuffling about the room.

'Be quiet,' said Bisnu. 'You'll wake Mother.'

Their mother was awake by now. 'Come down from there, Bisnu. I can hear a noise outside.'

'Don't worry,' said Bisnu, who found himself looking down on the wriggling animal which was trying to get its paw in under the door. With his mother and Puja awake, there was no time to lose.

He had got the spear through the window, and though he could not manoeuvre it so as to strike the panther's head, he brought the sharp end down with considerable force on the animal's rump.

With a roar of pain and rage the man-eater leapt down from the steps and disappeared into the darkness. It did not pause to see what had struck it. Certain that no human could have come upon it in that fashion, it ran fearfully to its lair, howling until the pain subsided.

VIII

A panther is an enigma. There are occasions when it proves itself to be the most cunning animal under the sun and yet the very next day it will walk into an obvious trap that no self-respecting jackal would ever go near. One day a panther will prove itself to be a complete coward and run like a hare from a couple of dogs, and the very next, it will dash in among half a dozen men sitting around a campfire and inflict terrible injuries on them.

It is not often that a panther is taken by surprise, as its power of sight and hearing are very acute. It is a master at the art of camouflage and its spotted coat is admirably suited for the purpose. It does not need heavy jungle to hide in. A couple of bushes and the light and shade from surrounding trees are enough to make it almost invisible.

Because the Manjari panther had been fooled by Bisnu, it did not mean that it was a stupid panther. It simply meant that it had been a little careless. And Bisnu and Puja, growing in confidence since their midnight encounter with the animal, became a little careless themselves.

Panther's Moon

Puja was hoeing the last field above the house and Bisnu, at the other end of the same field, was chopping up several branches of green oak, prior to leaving the wood to dry in the loft. It was late afternoon and the descending sun glinted in patches on the small river. It was a time of day when only the most desperate and daring of man-eaters would be likely to show itself.

Pausing for a moment to wipe the sweat from his brow, Bisnu glanced up at the hillside and his eye caught sight of a rock on the brow of the hill which seemed unfamiliar to him. Just as he was about to look elsewhere, the round rock began to grow and then alter its shape, and Bisnu watching in fascination was at last able to make out the head and forequarters of the panther. It looked enormous from the angle at which he saw it and for a moment he thought it was a tiger. But Bisnu knew instinctively that it was the man-eater.

Slowly, the wary beast pulled itself to its feet and began to walk around the side of the great rock. For a second it disappeared and Bisnu wondered if it had gone away. Then it reappeared and the boy was all excitement again. Very slowly and silently the panther walked across the face of the rock until it was in direct line with the corner of the field where Puja was working.

With a thrill of horror Bisnu realized that the panther was stalking his sister. He shook himself free from the spell which had woven itself around him and shouting hoarsely ran forward.

'Run, Puja, run!' he called. 'It's on the hill above you!'

Puja turned to see what Bisnu was shouting about. She saw him gesticulate to the hill behind her, looked up just in time to see the panther crouching for his spring.

With great presence of mind, she leapt down the banking of the field and tumbled into an irrigation ditch.

The springing panther missed its prey, lost its foothold on the slippery shale banking and somersaulted into the ditch a few feet away from Puja. Before the animal could recover from its surprise, Bisnu was dashing down the slope, swinging his axe and shouting, 'Maro, maro!'

Two men came running across the field. They, too, were armed with axes. Together with Bisnu they made a semi-circle around the snarling animal, which turned at bay and plunged at them in order to get away. Puja wriggled along the ditch on her stomach. The men aimed their axes at the panther's head and Bisnu had the satisfaction of getting in a well-aimed blow between the eyes. The animal then charged straight at one of the men, knocked him over and tried to get at his throat. Just then Sanjay's father arrived with his long spear. He plunged the end of the spear into the panther's neck.

The panther left its victim and ran into the bushes, dragging the spear through the grass and leaving a trail of blood on the ground.

The men followed cautiously—all except the man who had been wounded, and who lay on the ground, while Puja and the other womenfolk rushed up to help him.

The panther had made for the bed of the stream and Bisnu, Sanjay's father, and their companion were able to follow it quite easily. The water was red where the panther had crossed the stream and the rocks were stained with blood. After they had gone downstream for about a furlong, they found the panther lying still on its side at the edge of the water. It was mortally wounded but it continued to wave its tail like an angry cat. Then, even the tail lay still.

'It is dead,' said Bisnu. 'It will not trouble us again in this body.'

'Let us be certain,' said Sanjay's father and he bent down and pulled the panther's tail.

There was no response.

'It is dead,' said Kalam Singh. 'No panther would suffer such an insult were it alive!'

They cut down a long piece of thick bamboo and tied the panther to it by its feet. Then, with their enemy hanging upside down from the bamboo pole, they started back for the village.

'There will be a feast at my house tonight,' said Kalam Singh. 'Everyone in the village must come. And tomorrow we will visit all the villages in the valley and show them the dead panther, so that they may move about again without fear.'

'We can sell the skin in Kempty,' said their companion. 'It will fetch a good price.'

'But the claws we will give to Bisnu,' said Kalam Singh, putting his arm around the boy's shoulders. 'He has done a man's work today. He deserves the claws.'

A panther's or tiger's claws are considered to be lucky charms.

'I will take only three claws,' said Bisnu. 'One each for my mother and sister, and one for myself. You may give the others to Sanjay and Chittru and the smaller children.'

As the sun set, a big fire was lit in the middle of the village of Manjari and the people gathered around it, singing and laughing. Kalam Singh killed his fattest goat and there was meat for everyone.

IX

Bisnu was on his way home. He had just handed in his first paper, arithmetic, which he had found quite easy. Tomorrow it would be algebra, and when he got home he would have to practise square roots and cube roots and fractional coefficients.

Mr Nautiyal and the entire class had been happy that he had been able to sit for the exams. He was also a hero to them for his part in killing the panther. The story had spread through the villages with the rapidity of a forest fire, a fire which was now raging in Kempty town.

When he walked past the hospital, he was whistling cheerfully.

Dr Taylor waved to him from the verandah steps.

'How is Sanjay now?' she asked.

'He is well,' said Bisnu.

'And your mother and sister?'

'They are well,' said Bisnu.

'Are you going to get yourself a new dog?'

'I am thinking about it,' said Bisnu. 'At present I have a baby goat—I am teaching it to swim!'

He started down the path to the valley. Dark clouds had gathered and there was a rumble of thunder. A storm was imminent.

'Wait for me!' shouted Sarru, running down the path behind Bisnu, his milk pails clanging against each other. He fell into step beside Bisnu.

'Well, I hope we don't have any more man-eaters for some time,' he said. 'I've lost a lot of money by not being able to take milk up to Kempty.'

'We should be safe as long as a shikari doesn't wound another panther. There was an old bullet wound in the man-eater's thigh. That's why it couldn't hunt in the forest. The deer were too fast for it.'

'Is there a new postman yet?'

'He starts tomorrow. A cousin of Mela Ram's.'

When they reached the parting of their ways, it had begun to rain a little.

'I must hurry,' said Sarru. 'It's going to get heavier any minute.'

'I feel like getting wet,' said Bisnu. 'This time it's the monsoon, I'm sure.'

Bisnu entered the forest on his own and at the same time

the rain came down in heavy, opaque sheets. The trees shook in the wind and the langurs chattered with excitement.

It was still pouring when Bisnu emerged from the forest, drenched to the skin. But the rain stopped suddenly, just as the village of Manjari came into view. The sun appeared through a rift in the clouds. The leaves and the grass gave out a sweet, fresh smell.

Bisnu could see his mother and sister in the field transplanting the rice seedlings. The menfolk were driving the yoked oxen through the thin mud of the fields while the children hung on to the oxen's tails, standing on the plain wooden harrows, and with weird cries and shouts sending the animals almost at a gallop along the narrow terraces.

Bisnu felt the urge to be with them, working in the fields. He ran down the path, his feet falling softly on the wet earth. Puja saw him coming and waved at him. She met him at the edge of the field.

'How did you find your paper today?' she asked.

'Oh, it was easy.' Bisnu slipped his hand into hers and together they walked across the field. Puja felt something smooth and hard against her fingers and, before she could see what Bisnu was doing, he had slipped a pair of bangles on her wrist.

'I remembered,' he said with a sense of achievement.

Puja looked at the bangles and blurted out: 'But they are blue, Bhai, and I wanted red and gold bangles!' And then, when she saw him looking crestfallen, she hurried on: 'But they are very pretty and you did remember... Actually, they are just as nice as red and gold bangles! Come into the house when you are ready. I have made something special for you.'

'I am coming,' said Bisnu, turning towards the house. 'You don't know how hungry a man gets, walking five miles to reach home!'

The Night Train at Deoli

When I was at college I used to spend my summer vacations in Dehra, at my grandmother's place. I would leave the plains early in May and return late in July. Deoli was a small station about thirty miles from Dehra. It marked the beginning of the heavy jungles of the Indian Terai.

The train would reach Deoli at about five in the morning when the station would be dimly lit with electric bulbs and oil lamps and the jungle across the railway tracks would just be visible in the faint light of dawn. Deoli had only one platform, an office for the stationmaster and a waiting room. The platform boasted a tea stall, a fruit vendor, and a few stray dogs; not much else because the train stopped there for only ten minutes before rushing on into the forests.

Why it stopped at Deoli, I don't know. Nothing ever happened there. Nobody got off the train and nobody got in. There were never any coolies on the platform. But the train would halt there a full ten minutes and then a bell would sound, the guard would blow his whistle, and presently Deoli would be left behind and forgotten.

I used to wonder what happened in Deoli behind the station walls. I always felt sorry for that lonely little platform and for the place that nobody wanted to visit. I decided that one day I would get off the train at Deoli and spend the day there just to please the town.

I was eighteen, visiting my grandmother, and the night train stopped at Deoli. A girl came down the platform selling baskets.

It was a cold morning and the girl had a shawl thrown across her shoulders. Her feet were bare and her clothes were old but she was a young girl, walking gracefully and with dignity.

When she came to my window, she stopped. She saw that I was looking at her intently but at first she pretended not to notice. She had a pale skin, set off by shiny black hair and dark, troubled eyes. And then those eyes, searching and eloquent, met mine.

She stood by my window for some time and neither of us said anything. But when she moved on, I found myself leaving my seat and going to the carriage door. I stood waiting on the platform looking the other way. I walked across to the tea stall. A kettle was boiling over on a small fire but the owner of the stall was busy serving tea somewhere on the train. The girl followed me behind the stall.

'Do you want to buy a basket?' she asked. 'They are very strong, made of the finest cane...'

'No,' I said, 'I don't want a basket.'

We stood looking at each other for what seemed a very long time and she said, 'Are you sure you don't want a basket?'

'All right, give me one,' I said and took the one on top and gave her a rupee, hardly daring to touch her fingers.

As she was about to speak, the guard blew his whistle. She said something but it was lost in the clanging of the bell and the hissing of the engine. I had to run back to my compartment. The carriage shuddered and jolted forward.

I watched her as the platform slipped away. She was alone on the platform and she did not move, but she was looking at me and smiling. I watched her until the signal-box came in the way and then the jungle hid the station. But I could still see her standing there alone...

I stayed awake for the rest of the journey. I could not rid my mind of the picture of the girl's face and her dark, smouldering eyes.

But when I reached Dehra the incident became blurred and distant, for there were other things to occupy my mind. It was only when I was making the return journey, two months later, that I remembered the girl.

I was looking out for her as the train drew into the station and I felt an unexpected thrill when I saw her walking up the platform. I sprang off the footboard and waved to her.

When she saw me, she smiled. She was pleased that I remembered her. I was pleased that she remembered me. We were both pleased and it was almost like a meeting of old friends.

She did not go down the length of the train selling baskets but came straight to the tea stall. Her dark eyes were suddenly filled with light. We said nothing for some time but we couldn't have been more eloquent.

I felt the impulse to put her on the train there and then and take her away with me. I could not bear the thought of having to watch her recede into the distance of Deoli station. I took the baskets from her hand and put them down on the ground. She put out her hand for one of them but I caught her hand and held it.

'I have to go to Delhi,' I said.

She nodded. 'I do not have to go anywhere.'

The guard blew his whistle for the train to leave and how I hated the guard for doing that.

'I will come again,' I said. 'Will you be here?'

She nodded again and, as she nodded, the bell clanged and the train slid forward. I had to wrench my hand away from the girl and run for the moving train.

This time I did not forget her. She was with me for the remainder of the journey and for long after. All that year she was a bright, living thing. And when the college term finished I packed in haste and left for Dehra earlier than usual. My grandmother would be pleased at my eagerness to see her.

I was nervous and anxious as the train drew into Deoli because I was wondering what I should say to the girl and what I should do. I was determined that I wouldn't stand helplessly before her, hardly able to speak or do anything about my feelings.

The train came to Deoli and I looked up and down the platform but I could not see the girl anywhere.

I opened the door and stepped off the footboard. I was deeply disappointed and overcome by a sense of foreboding. I felt I had to do something and so I ran up to the stationmaster and said, 'Do you know the girl who used to sell baskets here?'

'No, I don't,' said the stationmaster. 'And you'd better get on the train if you don't want to be left behind.'

But I paced up and down the platform and stared over the railings at the station yard. All I saw was a mango tree and a dusty road leading into the jungle. Where did the road go? The train was moving out of the station and I had to run up the platform and jump for the door of my compartment. Then, as the train gathered speed and rushed through the forests, I sat brooding in front of the window.

What could I do about finding a girl I had seen only twice, who had hardly spoken to me, and about whom I knew nothing—absolutely nothing—but for whom I felt a tenderness and responsibility that I had never felt before?

My grandmother was not pleased with my visit after all because I didn't stay at her place more than a couple of weeks. I felt restless and ill at ease. So I took the train back to the plains, meaning to ask further questions of the stationmaster at Deoli.

But at Deoli there was a new stationmaster. The previous man had been transferred to another post within the past week. The new man didn't know anything about the girl who sold baskets. I found the owner of the tea stall, a small, shrivelled-up man, wearing greasy clothes, and asked him if he knew anything about the girl with the baskets.

'Yes, there was such a girl here. I remember quite well,' he said. 'But she has stopped coming now.'

'Why?' I asked. 'What happened to her?'

'How should I know?' said the man. 'She was nothing to me.'

And once again I had to run for the train.

As Deoli platform receded, I decided that one day I would have to break journey there, spend a day in the town, make enquiries, and find the girl who had stolen my heart with nothing but a look from her dark, impatient eyes.

With this thought I consoled myself throughout my last term in college. I went to Dehra again in the summer and when, in the early hours of the morning, the night train drew into Deoli station, I looked up and down the platform for signs of the girl, knowing I wouldn't find her but hoping just the same.

Somehow, I couldn't bring myself to break journey at Deoli and spend a day there. (If it was all fiction or a film, I reflected, I would have got down and cleaned up the mystery and reached a suitable ending for the whole thing.) I think I was afraid to do this. I was afraid of discovering what really happened to the girl. Perhaps she was no longer in Deoli, perhaps she was married, perhaps she had fallen ill...

In the last few years I have passed through Deoli many times and I always look out of the carriage window half expecting to see the same unchanged face smiling up at me. I wonder what happens in Deoli, behind the station walls. But I will never break my journey there. It may spoil my game.

I prefer to keep hoping and dreaming and looking out of the window up and down that lonely platform, waiting for the girl with the baskets.

I never break my journey at Deoli but I pass through as often as I can.

Killer with a Knife

Blood-red, the fallen blossoms lay on the snow, even more striking when laid bare. On the trees they blended with the foliage. On the ground, on those patches of recent snow, they seemed to be bleeding.

It had been a harsh winter in the hills, and it was still snowing at the end of March. But this was flowering time for the rhododendron trees, and they blossomed in sun, snow, or pelting rain. By mid-afternoon the hill station was shrouded in a heavy mist, and the trees stood out like ghostly sentinels.

The hill station wasn't Shimla, where I had gone to school, or Mussoorie, where I was to settle later on. It was Dalhousie, a neglected and almost forgotten hill station in the western Himalaya. But Dalhousie had the best rhododendron trees, and they grew all over the mountain, showing off before the colourless oaks and drooping pines.

But I wasn't in Dalhousie for the rhododendrons. It was 1959, and the Dalai Lama had just fled from Tibet, seeking sanctuary in India. Thousands of his followers and fellow-Tibetans had fled with him, and these refugees had to be settled somewhere. Dalhousie, with its many empty houses, was ideal for this purpose, and a carpet-weaving centre had been set up on one of the estates. The Tibetans made beautiful rugs and carpets. I know nothing about carpet-weaving, but I was working for CARE, an American relief organization, and I had been sent to Dalhousie (with the approval of the Government of India) to assess the needs of the refugees.

This is not the story of my tryst with the Tibetans, although I did suffer greatly from drinking large quantities of butter tea, which travels very slowly down the gullet and feels like lead by the time it reaches your stomach. The carpet-weaving centre became a great success, and I went on to work for CARE for several years; but that's another story. Out of one experience came another experience, as often happens during our peregrinations on planet earth, and it was during my stay in Dalhousie that I had a strange and rather unsettling experience.

I was staying at a small hotel which was quite empty as no one visited Dalhousie in those days and certainly not at the end of March. The hill station had been convenient for visitors from Lahore, but Partition had put an end to that.

◆

The hotel had a small garden, bare at this time of the year. But on the second day of my stay, returning from the carpet-weaving centre, I noticed that there was a gardener working on the flower beds, digging around and transplanting some seedlings. He looked up as I passed, and for a moment I thought I knew him. There was something familiar about his features—the slit eyes, the broad, flattened nose, the harelip—yes, the cleft lip was very noticeable—but he wasn't anyone I knew or had known, at least I didn't think so.... He was just a likeness to someone I had seen somehow, somewhere else. It was a bit of a tease.

And it would have remained just that if he hadn't looked up and met my gaze.

A flood of recognition crossed his face. But then he looked away, almost as though he did not want to recognize me; or be recognized.

I passed him. It was curious, but it didn't bother me. We keep bumping into people who look slightly familiar. It is said that everyone has a double somewhere on this planet. I had yet to meet mine—God forbid!—but perhaps I was seeing someone else's double.

I was relaxing in the verandah later that evening, browsing through an old magazine, when the gardener passed me on his way to the garden shed to put away his tools. There was something about his walk that brought back an image from the past. He had a slight limp. And when he looked at me again, his harelip registered itself on my memory. And now I recognized him. And of course he knew me.

I was the man who'd caught him riffling through my landlady's cupboards and drawers in Dehradun, some three years previously. I had exposed him, reported him, suggested she dismiss him; but the old lady, a widow, had grown quite fond of the youth, and had kept him in her service. He was good at running about and making himself useful, and, in spite of his cleft lip, he was not unattractive.

When I left Dehradun to take up my job in Delhi, I had forgotten the matter, almost forgotten the young man and my landlady; it was another tenant who informed me that the youth—his name was Sohan—had stabbed the old lady and made off with the contents of her jewel case and other valuables. She had died in hospital a few days later.

Sohan hadn't been caught. He had obviously left the town and taken to the hills or a large city. The police had made sporadic attempts to locate him, but as time passed the case lost its urgency. The victim was not a person of importance. The criminal was a stranger, a shadowy figure of no known background.

But here he was three years later, staring me in the face. What was I to do about him? Or what was he to do about me?

Killer with a Knife

◆

After Sohan had gone to his quarters, somewhere behind the hotel, I went in search of the manager. I would tell him what I knew and together we could decide on a course of action. But he had gone to a marriage and would be back late. The hotel was in charge of the cook who, a little drunk, served dinner in a hurry and retired to his quarters. 'Don't you have a night-watchman?' I asked him before he took off. 'Yes, of course,' he replied, 'Sohan, the gardener. He's the chowkidar too!'

An early retirement seemed the best thing all round, especially as I had to leave the next day. So I went to my room and made sure all the doors and windows were locked. I pushed the inside bolts all the way. I made sure the antiquated window frames were locked. As I peered out of the window, I noticed that a heavy mist had descended on the hillside. The trees stood out like ghostly apparitions, here and there a rhododendron glowing like the embers of a small fire. Then darkness enveloped the hillside. I felt cold, and wondered how much of it was fear.

I went to the bathroom and bolted the back door. Now no one could get in. Even so, I felt uneasy. Sohan was still a fugitive from the law, I had recognized him, and I was a threat to his freedom. He had killed once—perhaps more than once—and he could kill again.

I read for some time, then put out the light and tried to sleep. From a distance came the strains of music from a wedding band. Someone knocked on the door. I switched on the light and looked at my watch. It was only 10 p.m. Perhaps the manager had returned.

There was another knock, and I went to the door and was about to open it when some childhood words of warning from my grandmother came to mind: 'Never open the door unless you know who's there!'

'Who's there?' I called.

No answer. Just another knock.

'Who's there?' I called again.

There was a cough, a double-rap on the door.

'I'm sleeping,' I said. 'Come in the morning.' And I returned to my bed. The knocking continued but I ignored it, and after some time the person went away.

I slept a little. A couple of hours must have passed when I was woken by further knocking. But it did not come from the door. It was above me, high up on the wall. I'd forgotten there was a skylight.

I switched on the light and looked up. A face was outlined against the glass of the skylight. I could make out the flat rounded face and the harelip. It appeared to be grinning at me—rather like the disembodied head of the Cheshire Cat in *Alice in Wonderland*.

The skylight was very small and I knew he couldn't crawl through the opening. But he could show me a knife—and that was what he did. It was a small clasp knife and he held it between his teeth as he peered down at me. I felt very vulnerable on the bed. So I switched off the light and moved to an old sofa at the far end of the room, where I couldn't be seen. There didn't seem to be any point in shouting for help. So I just sat there, waiting.... And presumably, without a sound, he slipped away, and I remained on the sofa until the first glimmer of dawn penetrated the drawn window curtains.

◆

The manager was apologetic. 'You should have rung the bell,' he said, 'someone would have come.'

'The bell doesn't work. And someone did come…'

'I'm sorry, I'm sorry. The fellow's a villain, no doubt about it. And he's missing this morning. Your presence here must have frightened him off. So he's wanted for theft and murder. Well, we shall inform the police. Perhaps they can pick him up before he leaves the town.'

And we did inform the police. But Sohan had already taken off. The milkman had seen him boarding the early morning bus to Pathankot.

Pathankot was a busy little town on the plain below Dehradun. From there one road goes to Jammu, another to Dharamshala, a narrow-gauge railway to Kangra, and the main railway to Amritsar or Delhi. Sohan could have taken any of those routes. And no one was going to go looking for him. A police alert would be put out—a mere formality. He wasn't on their list of current criminals.

That afternoon I took a taxi to Pathankot and whiled away the evening at the railway station. My train, an overnight express to Delhi, left at 8 p.m. There was no rush at that time of the year. I had a first-class compartment to myself.

In those days our trains were somewhat different from what they are today. A first, second or third class compartment was usually a single carriage or bogey. We did not have corridor trains. Bogeys were connected by steel couplings, otherwise you were not connected in any way to the other compartments. But there was an emergency cord above the upper berths, and if you pulled it, the train might stop. There were always troublemakers on the trains, just as there are today, and sometimes the chain was pulled out of mischief. As a result it was often ignored.

As the train began moving out of the station I went to all the windows and made sure that they were fastened. Then I bolted the carriage door. I was becoming adept at bolting doors and windows. Sohan was probably hiding out in some distant town or village, but I wasn't taking any chances.

The train gathered speed. The lights of Pathankot receded as we plunged into a dark and moonless night. I had a pillow and a blanket with me, and I stretched out on one of the bunks and tried to think about pleasant things such as scarlet geraniums, fragrant sweet peas, and the beautiful Nimmi, star of the silver screen; but instead I kept seeing the grinning face of a young man with a harelip. All the same, I drifted into sleep. The rocking movement of the carriage, the rhythm of the wheels on the rails, have always had a soothing effect on my nerves. I sleep well in trains and rocking chairs.

But not that night.

I woke to the sound of that familiar tapping; not at the door, but on the window glass not far from my head. The insistent tapping of someone who wanted to get in.

It was common enough for ticketless travellers to hang on to the carriage of a moving train, in the hope that someone would let them in. But they usually chose the crowded second or third-class compartments; a first-class traveller, often alone, was unlikely to let in a stranger who might well turn out to be a train robber.

I raised my head from my pillow, and there he was, clinging to the fast-moving train, his face pressed to the glass, his harelip revealing part of a broken tooth…. I pulled down the shutters, blotting out his face. But, agile as a cat, he moved to the next window, the sneer still on his face. I pulled down that shutter too.

I pulled down all the shutters on his side of the carriage. He couldn't get in, bodily. But mentally, he was all over me.

Mind over matter. Well, I could apply my mind too. I shut my eyes and willed my tormentor to fall off the train!

No one fell off the train (at least no one was reported to

have done so), but presently we slowed to a gradual stop and, when I pulled up the shutters of the window, I saw that we were at a station. Jalandhar, I think. The platform was brightly lit and there was no sign of Sohan. He must have jumped off the train as it slowed down. It was about one in the morning. A vendor brought me a welcome glass of hot tea, and life returned to normal.

♦

I did not see Sohan in the years that followed. Or rather, I saw many Sohans. For two or three years I was pursued by my 'familiar'. Wherever I went—and my work took me to different parts of the country—I found myself encountering young men with harelips and a menacing look. Pure imagination, of course. He had every reason to stay as far from me as possible.

Gradually, the 'sightings' died down. Young men with harelips became extremely rare. Perhaps they were all going in for corrective surgery.

The years passed, and I had forgotten my familiar. I had given up my job in Delhi and moved to the hills. I was a moderately successful writer, and a familiar figure on Mussoorie's Mall Road. Sometimes other writers came to see me in my cottage under the deodars. One of them invited me to have dinner with him at the old Regal hotel, where he was staying. Before dinner, he took me to the bar for a drink.

'What will you have, whisky or vodka?'

No one seemed to drink anything else. I asked for some dark rum, and the barman went off in search of a bottle. When he returned and began pouring my drink, I noticed something slightly familiar about his features, his stance. He was almost bald, and he had a grey, drooping moustache which concealed most of his upper lip. He glanced at me and our eyes met. There was no sign of recognition. He smiled politely as he poured my drink. No, it definitely wasn't Sohan. He was too refined, for one thing. And he went about his duties without another glance in my direction.

Dinner over, I thanked my writer friend for his hospitality, and took the long walk home to my cottage. It was a dark, moonless night. No one followed me, no one came tapping on my bedroom window.

◆

Mussoorie had its charms. In my mind, every hill station is symbolized by a particular tree, even if it's not the dominant one. Dalhousie has its rhododendrons, Shimla its deodars, Kasauli its pines and Mussoorie its horse chestnuts. The monkeys would do their best to destroy the chestnuts, but I would collect those that were whole and plant them in people's gardens, whether they wanted them or not. The horse chestnut is a lovely tree to look at, even if you can't do anything with it!

My walks took me to the Regal from time to time, and occasionally I would relax in the bar, chatting to an old resident or a casual visitor, while the barman poured me a rum and soda. He never looked twice at me. And I never saw him outside that bar room. He appeared to be as much of a fixture as the moth-eaten antler-head on the wall, only he wasn't quite as moth-eaten.

'Efficient chap,' said Colonel Bhushan indicating the barman. 'And a great favourite with his mistress.'

'You mean the owner of this place?' I had only a vague idea of who owned what in the town. And in some cases the ownership was rather vague. But in the case of the Regal—Mrs Kapoor, a wealthy widow in her fifties, was very much in charge, all too visible an owner; well fleshed-out, ample-bosomed, with arms like rolling pins. Her staff trembled at her approach; but not, it seemed, the bartender, who led a charmed life, incapable of doing any wrong.

The lights went out, as they frequently do in this technological age, and the barman brought over our next round of drinks by candlelight.

By the light of a candle I caught a glimpse of the barman's features as he hovered over me. There was only the hint of a harelip, and the candle lit up his slanting eyes and prominent cheekbones. This was the only time I had a really close look at him.

♦

A week later I met Colonel Bhushan on the Mall. This was where all the gossip took place.

'Have you heard what happened last night at the Regal?' He wasted no time in getting to the news of the day.

A twinge of fear, of anticipation, ran through me. 'Nothing too terrible, I hope?'

'That barman chap—always thought he was a bit too smooth—stabbed the old lady, stabbed her two or three times, then plundered her room and made off with jewellery worth lakhs—as well as all the cash he could find!'

'How's the lady?'

'She'll survive. Tough old buffalo. But the rascal got away. By now he must be in Sirmur, or even across the Nepal border. Probably belongs to some criminal tribe.'

Yes, I thought, possibly a descendant of one of those robber gangs who harassed pilgrims on their way to the sacred shrines, or plundered traders from Tibet, or caravans to Samarkand.... To rob and plunder still runs in the blood of the most harmless looking people.

So the barman at the Regal was the same man I'd known in

Dehradun and then encountered in Dalhousie. The passing of time had altered his features but not his way of life. By now he would probably be far from Mussoorie. But I had a feeling I'd see him again—if not here, then somewhere else. Each one of us had a 'familiar'—a presence we would rather do without—an unwelcome and menacing guest—and for me it is Sohan.

Where does he come from, where does he go? I doubt if I shall ever know.

But I have a feeling he'll turn up again one of these days. And then?

Born Evil

'Can someone be born evil?' asked Mr Lobo, handing Miss Ripley-Bean a glass of nimbu paani as they sat on the sunny verandah lounge of the Royal. 'Be totally evil, that is—from birth through manhood and into old age. Someone without a conscience, someone who inflicts cruelty without a qualm, who cares a damn for what the world would think of him. Someone like Hitler, perhaps?'

'Hitler was vegetarian,' said Miss Ripley-Bean, helping herself to a cracker and giving it to her Tibetan terrier, Fluff, who gobbled it up. A notice in the hotel lobby said "No dogs allowed', but this was blissfully ignored by Miss Ripley-Bean. After all, Fluff was no ordinary dog.

'What has that to do with it?' asked Mr Lobo, curious. 'Being a vegetarian?'

'Well, presumably he was kind to animals. Didn't approve of killing and eating them. But of course he hated Jews—and Russians—and gypsies—and Black people.'

'And killed them without compunction, or had his lackeys do the job for him. He thought that was his duty. Or rather, his policy.'

'And he was driven by hatred. Don't forget that.'

'So would you say he was born evil?'

'I think the evil grew in him,' said Miss Ripley-Bean, giving Fluff another cracker. The plate of crackers would soon be empty.

Neither Miss Ripley-Bean nor Mr Lobo were hotel guests. Miss Ripley-Bean's father had sold the hotel to Nandu's father at the time of Independence, on condition that she, May Ripley-Bean, could continue to live there for the rest of her days. He had died shortly afterwards. And Mr Lobo was the hotel pianist. He had been there for a couple of years. Every evening he would sit at the piano in the lounge, strumming out old favourites or popular film tunes for the benefit of a dwindling clientele. In the late 1960s hill stations were going through a slump, and classier hotels like the Royal were feeling the pinch.

Miss Ripley-Bean and Mr Lobo had struck up a quaint friendship. She was almost seventy and he was just forty. Neither had ever been married. Mr Lobo enjoyed listening to Miss Ripley-Bean's tales of old Mussoorie and the Doon valley, and she enjoyed listening to him play Viennese waltzes and romantic ballads from old movies. Miss Ripley-Bean had been quite a movie buff once—a fan of Eddie Cantor, Al Jolson, Fred Astaire, Nelson Eddy and of course Greta Garbo, but that had been back in the thirties and forties, when the cinemas had been flooded with Hollywood's best. But over the years her eyesight had deteriorated, and now, unless she sat in the front row with the rickshaw boys and shop assistants she couldn't see very much. Also, she couldn't take Fluff into a cinema hall; he might want to pee on people's legs.

'I have never known anyone who was completely evil,' said Mr Lobo reflectively. 'Even Hitler had his softer side. He could love Eva Braun—and die beside her. Have you known anyone who was completely evil? Born evil—evil to the end of his days?'

'Evil is an aberration of personality, often ingrained in the mind at birth,' said Miss Ripley-Bean.

'You mean it's in the genes—it can't be helped?'

'I am not sure. I knew a couple who were both very good

people. And yet they had a son who took to crime like a duck to water.'

'It could go far back, to earlier forebears—that propensity for crime.

'Quite possibly. You see, this young man—or rather boy, as he was when I knew him—had the most charming and innocent-looking face that you could imagine. It was almost angelic. Everyone fell for him—old ladies, young women, strict headmasters, peppery old colonels, older boys, younger boys, schoolgirls. And he smiled at everyone and was oh-so-polite and well mannered. But he hated all of them—he hated everyone!'

'But why—was there any reason for it?'

'None at all. He was just made that way. The rest of humanity meant absolutely nothing to him. They were just his playthings, his toys. He played with them and then threw them away. But not before damaging them a little—sometimes more than a little.'

'And who was this paragon of evil? You seem to have known him well.'

Miss Ripley-Bean gave Fluff another cracker. 'Young Alexander. Yes, I knew him. But I did not really know him. No one did. In a way he lived in a world of his own making—he made things happen. Like dropping a lighted match in the petrol tank of a motorcycle and watching it go up in flames. Or firing Diwali rockets through the open window of the headmaster's bedroom and destroying all the bed linen.'

'He must have been crackers,' said Mr Lobo.

'Yes, but not this sort of cracker'—and Miss Ripley-Bean slipped another Royal cracker to Fluff, who accepted graciously. 'He was cracked in the head all right, but in an evil way—like Emperor Nero, who loved to watch his slaves being torn apart by lions. It was fire that excited Alexander. Conflagrations! If he heard that there was a building on fire, in Mussoorie or

Dehradun or wherever his family happened to be staying, he'd rush to watch. Sometimes he'd pretend to help the firefighters, get involved in what was happening, but it was the spreading fire that he really enjoyed—and the screams of people who were trapped inside or running about on the roof or jumping from windows.

'There was this big fire at Green's Hotel back in the late forties. The ballroom went up in flames. Alexander was just a boy then, home from school; his family lived in one wing of the hotel. Out front was a ballroom that had come up during the war. American and British soldiers would come over in the evenings—Dehra was a recreation centre for Allied soldiers—and dance with the Anglo-Indian girls. They were great dancers, those girls, and so pretty. Fights broke out over them. Of course the Americans had more money to spend and that was part of the trouble.

'Alexander was fourteen at the time, too young to be familiar with that lot, but he liked listening to the band—Jimmy Cotton and his Band, they came from the Imperial in Delhi, just to play at Green's.

'No one knows how the fire started. And no one believed Alexander had anything to do with it—he looked so charming, so cute, just sitting there behind the band, his eyes sparkling with excitement as he tapped his feet to a tango or swayed to the rhythms of a rumba. The air was full of cigarette smoke, so at first no one noticed the smoke rising from an alcove near the bar. Had someone thrown a lighted cigarette on to a rug? Very careless but common enough at these dance parties. Rugs were always being ruined, Only this time the rug was already soaked in kerosene—a spill from an oil lamp, probably—and in no time at all the rug caught fire and the ballroom was full of smoke.

'"Fire! Fire!" It was Alexander shouting.

'And sure enough, the curtains were on fire, and the dancing stopped and the band stopped playing. Yes, the dancing had stopped, but now Alexander was dancing, doing a tap dance of his own, as he grew more and more excited.

'There was panic in the ballroom. Girls, soldiers, musicians, waiters, everyone rushed for the exit. There was only one exit, and in the melee two of the girls fell to the ground and were crushed to death. By the time a fire engine arrived, the flames were out of control. Young Alexander made a big show of helping the firefighters—giving instructions, directing the water hoses, dashing about with a fire extinguisher—oh, he was quite the hero. Later, everyone commended him for his efforts. It was all an act of course. No one had any idea that he was the real culprit.'

'Diabolical,' said Mr Lobo.

'Exactly. The face of an angel and the mind of the devil. You know, the world is full of criminals and many end up behind bars so that society is protected from them. But they are, for the most part, ordinary people—people like you and me—who have transgressed, crossed the line of decency, given in to their animal instincts or succumbed to human greed and paid the price for it. But Alexander was consistently evil. He went from one brazen act of evil to another—and got away with it, time after time.'

'What happened next?'

'There were minor incidents—a fire in a cinema, at a railway station—but these were detected in time and brought under control, Alexander's school gymnasium burnt down quite mysteriously. He was sixteen when he set fire to his parents' house. This was down in Rajpur, where they lived at the time. It was a lovely old mansion, so big that Alexander's parents were able to use part of it as a guest house. But the guests did not stay very long—not with Alexander around. He would introduce snakes into their rooms, or monitor lizards, or stink bombs that he made himself. The paying guests were happy to pay their bills and go elsewhere. He would even torment his little sister. One day, while she was asleep, he cut most of her hair off, leaving just shreds and patches. He was well thrashed for this by his father.

'Vengeful by nature, he waited until they had all gone out to a Sunday church service. Then he sent the cook and the gardener out on errands and set about making a pile of all the best furniture in the front room before setting it alight.

'"I am Guy Fawkes today," he declared, addressing an invisible audience. Guy Fawkes, who had once tried to burn down the English Parliament, was his history-book hero.

'The furniture made a great bonfire. It spread from the sofas and tables to the costly rugs that his mother had collected and then to the curtains, and then from room to room, upstairs and downstairs, rapidly spreading through the entire house.

'The cook returned from his errand to find his kitchen ablaze, and flames leaping from the bedroom windows. Was the Baba safe? He was a good man and feared for the safety of the errant youth. He could not believe that it was Alexander who had started it all. He dashed about, calling out to the Baba, the name by which Alexander was known to the servants. Presently Alexander emerged from a wing of the house, covered in soot.

'"House on fire," he said calmly. "Better call the fire brigade."

'But there was no fire brigade in Rajpur. And there was not much that the cook and the gardener and the helpful neighbours could do with buckets of water. When Alexander's parents and sister returned from church, they were confronted by the smoking ruin of their old home. And their pet Alsatian had disappeared in the flames.'

Mr Lobo poured out another glass of nimbu paani for Miss Ripley-Bean, and she in turn gave Fluff another cracker.

'So what happened to Alexander? Did they send him to a reform home?'

'Oh no, they doted on him and wouldn't accept that he was responsible for it, although in the back of their minds they must have known that he was the devil incarnate. We can never believe the worst of our own progeny, can we?'

'I wouldn't know, said Mr Lobo, a confirmed bachelor.

'Nor would I, really,' said Miss Ripley-Bean. 'But over the years I've seen it in so many people who rush to the defence of their beloved Tom, Dev or Danny, in spite of their having committed the most heinous of crimes. So Alexander's parents covered up for their diabolic boy even though it was their own house he'd burnt down!

'Well, he couldn't go to college. He'd already been expelled from two schools. So they sent him to a Bible school in Landour, run by a couple of homely American missionaries. Poor boy, they said, he has had a bad time of it—misunderstood by his parents and teachers; we'll put him in the Lord's way and, who knows, one day he might make a good preacher! And they put him in charge of the community library.'

'That should have cured him.'

'Hardly. Books! All those books. Such a temptation to the little firebug. What could make a better fire? Books burn so well—and who needs them anyway, or so reasons Alexander, who values everything on the basis of inflammability. Some of the world's greatest libraries have been lost to fires, or so he's heard, so why not add this little one to the list? Most of them are religious books anyway, and no one bothers to read them. The ragman buys up the old ones and turns them into paper bags.

'So there is quite a conflagration, and although the students of the nearby Pinewood School turn out in force, with buckets and jerrycans of water, they can do nothing to put out the fire. And meanwhile, Alexander is sitting on the hillside singing an old sea-shanty that he'd learnt in his nursery days:

> Fire in the galley, fire down below,
> Fetch a bucket of water, boys,
> there's fire down below.
> Fire up aloft, and fire down below,
> Fetch a bucket of water, boys,
> there's fire down below.

'He'd also heard the good missionary lady speak of this wicked old world being consumed by "fire and brimstone", and he felt that this was a good beginning.

'Once again, no blame attached to Alexander. It was a short circuit, obviously. Or a careless smoker. And Alexander did not smoke.

'But with the library gone, some other occupation had to be found for him. And since he was the outdoor type, why not appoint him as assistant to the estate manager of Pinewood School, Mr Rajan, who was due for retirement in a few months? The missionaries were directors of the school and could easily arrange things. The estate was extensive, taking in the entire hillside and a large tract of pine forest. Mr Rajan had a hard time keeping away the villagers who would slip in at night to cut branches for firewood. He needed help.

'And Alexander turned out to be a handy helper. He kept the villagers away by strutting about with a loaded rifle, occasionally firing it at random. In the autumn, pine needles covered the ground, and by December the pine cones were falling.

'The school people used the pine cones in their fireplaces, and Alexander kept them well supplied. He had also discovered that pine cones burn beautifully. School was about to close for winter when a fire broke, out in the forest. It hadn't rained for weeks, the grass had turned yellow, the pine needles dry and brittle, and Alexander had made a little bonfire of cones just for his private amusement, and he couldn't resist watching it spread.

'A boy stuck his head out of a dormitory window and exclaimed, "Look! There are flames in the forest!" And soon, everyone was running around, eager to see the forest fire and speculating on whether or not it would reach the school building.

'The village was actually more in danger than the school, for the trees were close to the fields. But a strong wind carried the flames towards the school, burning leaves and floating embers leaping from one tree to another, while the grass beneath was a carpet of fire. A flock of sheep, returning to the village, perished in the smoke and flames. Their attendants, two youngsters, were lucky to escape. The school servants and some of the bigger boys ran about with buckets of sand or water. Several pine martens and a barking deer fled the forest in panic, as did a party of flying squirrels and several large brown owls.

'Alexander was very prominent in all this activity, at times directing the firefighters and at times running about wildly and without any clear sense of purpose. Standing on a cliff edge and waving his arms to a crowd of spectators, he slipped on the pine needles and went tumbling down the steep slope into the burning undergrowth. His clothes on fire, he ran here and there screaming for help, but he was overcome by the smoke and flames and vanished from sight.

'Eventually the wind shifted and the fire burnt itself out. Mr Rajan and his helpers went in search of Alexander and found his charred body at the edge of the forest.

'So all things wicked must come to an end, commented Mr Lobo. 'It's all a matter of time. And time must pass…'

'Time has nothing else to do, except pass,' said Miss Ripley-Bean wryly. 'And as for Alexander, he was accounted a hero and, being dead, he could not change his status to that of villain. They gave him a grand funeral and a headstone with an inscription that mentioned his bravery in helping to prevent a forest fire from enveloping the school. His grave is up there in the Landour cemetery.'

Miss Ripley-Bean gave Fluff the last of the crackers and rose to go. 'Time for my afternoon nap,' she said. 'It's always nice to talk to you, Mr Lobo.'

That evening Mr Lobo went for a long walk, which took him to the Landour cemetery. After wandering around for some time, he found Alexander's tombstone. As he returned to the hotel, the sun fell away to the west, which now reddened to receive it. He looked very thoughtful as he tapped on Miss Ripley-Bean's front door.

He found the old lady sipping a crème de menthe. She made her own liqueur and treated herself to a couple of glasses every evening.

'Have some crème de menthe, Mr Lobo. There is nothing else, I'm afraid, she said by way of greeting.

'No, thanks,' said Mr Lobo, who hated crème de menthe. 'I won't stay. Just wanted to tell you that I visited the Landour cemetery.

'And did you find the grave?'

'Yes, I did. It was quite clearly inscribed. But it gave his full name. John Alexander Bean. Is that correct?'

'Yes, that was his name,' said Miss Ripley-Bean. 'He was my brother.'

The Late Night Show

According to the crime novels I used to read, there there are four principal reasons for committing murder:

1. Money
2. Property
3. Revenge
4. Insanity, temporary or otherwise

In that order of priority.

But according to the crime movies I used to see, the priorities were a little different:

1. Passion (hate/jealousy)
2. Insanity (serial killing)
3. Money (bank hold-ups)
4. Espionage

Having grown up on crime fiction (both in literature and on film) I think my assessments are not far off the mark. When I put it to my friend Inspector Keemat Lal a few years ago, he said 50 per cent of murders were the result of greed—for money, property or another person's possessions. He was right, of course, but something as mundane as that doesn't make for great films or novels.

♦

In the year I finished school, I was still staying with my mother in the old Green's Hotel in Dehradun. Just across the road was the Odeon, a small cinema showing English and American films. Every winter, during the school holidays, I had been a regular picture-goer. Now that I had finished school, I was still a patron of the cinema, but preferred going to the night shows, from nine thirty to twelve. At night, the hall was usually half-empty, and the usher-cum-ticket-collector, who had become a friend of mine, would let me in without a ticket—provided I occupied one of the cheaper seats. As pocket money was in short supply (my mother's salary was both poor and irregular), I readily accepted my friend's assistance. In this way I saw almost every Hollywood or British film made around that period.

Just as much of my reading was centred around Agatha Christie, Ellery Queen, and Edgar Wallace, so did my taste in films veer towards the slick thrillers in which stars such as James Cagney, Humphrey Bogart and Edward G. Robinson portrayed various colourful characters from the underworld. Back then, I remember how strange it felt watching these actors transition from their roles as gangsters or outlaws to portraying detective-heroes (as Bogart did in *The Maltese Falcon*) or even appearing in musicals (like Cagney in *Yankee Doodle Dandy*).

If today I have an almost encyclopaedic knowledge of films made in the 1940s and 1950s, it is due largely to my usher friend who allowed me into the Odeon night after night, putting his job at some risk in doing so. I reciprocated by bringing him the occasional bottle of beer from the Green's bar. The barman, too, was a friend of mine.

There were other regulars who came to the night shows—salesmen, shopkeepers, waiters, those who did not get much time off during the day. And some old characters too—like the retired postmaster who never missed a film but always fell asleep after a couple of reels and whose snoring drowned out the sound from the projection room; or the hunchback who always sat in the front row because he couldn't see anything from the back; or the man who drank endless cups of tea throughout the show. Mostly menfolk. Women seldom came to the night show, unless escorted by husbands or family.

One regular always intrigued me. He was a man in his thirties who sat through the show without ever removing his hat. Presumably he was bald and felt the cold draught that ran through the hall whenever one of the doors were opened. In January the hall could be cold. He wore an overcoat too, which also served as a receptacle for packets of channa which he munched assiduously during the film. Those were the days before fast foods of various descriptions took over. You had a choice between peanuts and channa. And apart from tea, there was a crimson- coloured cold drink called Vimto, which had a raspberry flavour. The gentleman with the hat always drank Vimto.

There was no social intercourse during the film. Either you saw the picture or you left the hall. The hatted gentleman almost always took the same seat, not far from one of the exit doors. Occasionally he would have a companion, but not for long. Mr Hat watched the film in its entirety, but the companions came and went. Sometimes he would offer them something from the folds of his overcoat. They would pocket the offering and leave after a few minutes.

One night there was a little more activity than usual in the row where Mr Hat was sitting. He came with a companion, who left after a few minutes. A little later he was joined by another person. I did not pay much attention to them was engrossed in

The Third Man, Anton Karas's haunting zither music building up to the chase in the sewers of Vienna, with Joseph Cotten hunting down his black-marketeer friend Orson Welles. Cotten, not Welles, was my favourite actor.

The activity around Mr Hat was something of a distraction, and one or two in the hall shouted to them to shut up or go home. One of his companions, a tall individual, got up suddenly and walked towards the exit. He passed in front of me. And when he pushed open the door, the light from the foyer fell on his face and I caught a glimpse of narrow eyes, a large hooked nose, and a jutting chin. Then the door closed and I was back in the world of post-war Vienna. Ten minutes later the film was over and the lights came on, We began moving slowly out of the theatre—reluctantly, as it was freezing outside.

Mr Hat hadn't moved. He was hunched forward, his hat tilted over his head. I thought he'd fallen asleep. Curious as ever, I took a few steps down the central aisle and looked down at him. At first I thought he'd spilled a bottle of Vimto over his unbuttoned coat and shirt front. Then I realized that it was blood, not Vimto, that had gushed out of his torn and still bleeding throat. I cried out, and my usher friend came running. Then the manager. Then the tea-stall owner. Then those who were still in the hall.

'His throat's been cut,' said someone. 'He's dead or dying'

And by the time a policeman and a doctor arrived, Mr Hat's life-blood had seeped away.

♦

It was two or three weeks before I visited the Odeon again, and then too only for a matinée.

'No more night shows,' said my mother. 'You must be in the hotel by nine, and preferably in your bed.'

'But it had nothing to do with me,' protested. 'He was just another film-goer.'

'No ordinary film-goer gets stabbed to death in the middle of a picture. Wasn't someone with him?'

'Sometimes. I didn't really notice.'

But I had noticed the tall, hawk-nosed man who had left before the show ended. I would recognize him again. But I did not tell my mother this.

With nothing much to do late in the evening began hanging around the Green's Hotel bar, where the bartender, Melaram, often chatted to me if he wasn't too busy. I sat by myself in a corner of the large, dimly lit room, watching the customers and sipping a shandy. I would have preferred a beer, but my mother had given Melaram instructions to serve me with nothing stronger than shandy.

'A pity you can't go to the Odeon any more,' he said sympathetically. 'Not at night, anyway. Why don't you go to the afternoon shows?'

'The free pass was only for the night shows,' I told him. 'The hall is practically empty at night.'

'Not surprising, with people getting murdered in their seats.'

'It only happened once.'

'True ... So how would you like to see a Hindi movie? You can come with me. We'll go to the Filmistan. Your mother won't mind.'

So Melaram took me to see an extravaganza called *Ali Baba aur Chalees Chor*, which was the sort of film Melaram enjoyed. All I remember is that it had a nifty little heroine called Shakeela, who was easy on the eye.

The following week we saw another film, and this time we were accompanied by my friend Sitaram, one of the room boys. We sat in the cheaper seats and clapped with the tongawallas and labourers whenever the dashing hero (Dilip Kumar) rescued the coy heroine (Nalini Jaywant) from the menacing villain (Pran, as usual).

As we left the cinema and were about to cross the road, I thought I saw the man who had passed me in the Odeon the night Mr Hat had been killed. He looked at me, hesitated for a moment, and then passed on. Had he recognized me?

'Someone you know?' asked Melaram at my side.

'That fellow who just passed,' I said. 'I think he was with the man who got killed that night.'

'Well, better keep quiet about it,' said Melaram. 'I think he's from one of the drug gangs. If you see him again, don't let him think you recognize him.'

◆

To my suprise, the next time I saw him was in the Green's bar. He strode in as though looking for someone, then shrugged, sat down on a bar stool and ordered a beer. I was in my dark corner and probably he would not have noticed me just then, had I not got up and left the room by the service door. I felt his eyes on me. I thought it best not to hang around, so went to my room (my mother had allowed me to use one of the smaller hotel rooms), locked the door, switched on the bedlight, and immersed myself in *Wuthering Heights*.

It was the right sort of book for such a night. Outside, a storm had broken, thunder rolled across the heavens, and the rain came rattling down on the corrugated tin roof. I read for an hour or two, then looked at my watch—given to me recently for having passed out of school. It was only eleven o'clock. I switched off the light and tried to sleep. Presently the thunder grew more distant, the rain lessened. A breeze sprang up, and a bunch of bougainvillea kept tapping against the window panes.

And then someone was tapping on my door.

A light tap to begin with, and then louder, more insistent. 'Who's there?' I called, but no one answered.

Had it been the night-watchman, or Sitaram at a loose end, they would have said something. Perhaps Sitaram up to tricks?

'Go to bed,' I called out. 'I'm sleepy.'

No answer. But after a little while, more knocking. Then silence. Then footsteps receding.

I switched on my bedside radio and lay awake, listening to popular songs that held no special meaning for me. But at least the radio was company. Finally I fell asleep, the music still playing.

It must have been towards dawn that I woke again. The radio was still on, but the station had gone off the air and there was a lot of static coming over the airwaves. I switched it off.

That tapping again. But now it came from the window, not the door.

I got up on my knees and drew aside the window curtain. There was a face pressed against the glass. An outside light fell upon it and made it look more hideous than it really was. The slit eyes, hooked nose and wide sensual mouth seemed more sinister than ever. Boris Karloff as Frankenstein couldn't have been more frightening.

The apparition smiled at me, and I let the curtain fall.

And then I did a foolish thing. I leapt out of bed, opened my door, and ran barefoot down the corridor, calling for Sitaram, Melaram, the chowkidar, anyone!

But no one came. It was the hour before dawn, and no one stirred.

I ran out on to the back verandah, and he was waiting there—Hook Nose was waiting. In his right hand he held a *kukri*, its blade shining in the lamplight.

I turned and ran into the wilderness behind the hotel. A path ran down the slope and into a tangle of jungle. I knew it well.

He was running after me, crashing clumsily through the lantana, but I was faster than him, and I kept running until I came to an abandoned cowshed that stood at the edge of the jungle.

I did not enter it. He would have caught me there. Instead I crouched behind some bushes—and waited.

He was not long in coming. He stopped in front of the open door—the shed's only door—then stepped inside. I could hear him stumbling around in the dark.

I crept up to the door, pulled it shut, and slid the bolt in. It was an old door, but strong, made of deodar wood. There were no windows in the shed, just a small slit high up on the wall. Mr Hook Nose would have to break the door down in order to get out. He'd need an axe to do that. Already he was hammering away with his fists and cursing.

I left him to it, and returned to the hotel.

Dawn was breaking. A cock crowed near the kitchen outhouse, while an early riser emerged from his room, yelling for his morning tea.

◆

I went to Bareilly to spend a month with one of my aunts. There were no bookshops in Bareilly, and no English cinema, and I was soon restless and eager to return to Dehradun.

When I got down at the station, Sitaram was there to meet me.

He told me that Melaram had gone to a new and bigger hotel, and that Green's had a new but inexperienced bartender. He also brought me up to date on all the films that were running in town.

Was it fear, curiosity, a morbid fascination that took me down to the old cowshed that very afternoon? Somehow I had to know if Hook Nose had escaped, or if he was still there, now a bag of bones!

I had lunch with my mother, then said I was going for a walk—it was a bracing February afternoon in the Doon—and took the jungle path down to the shed.

It was still locked. Dared I open that door? Would the revenant of Hook Nose come rushing out at me? Worse still, would I find his remains putrefying in the dust?

Well, I had to find out.

I opened the door and stepped inside.

It was so dark I could hardly see anything. In the stale air there was the smell of muskrats and rotting vegetation. But nothing that I would describe as a human smell.

I looked around. Toadstools grew on the floor. There was a pile of wood in one corner. A large grey rat ran out from under the woodpile and out through the open door. No sign of Hook Nose anywhere. Either he'd escaped on his own or someone had set him free. I felt relieved, but also apprehensive. What if he came looking for me again?

That evening, as I emerged from my room, Sitaram took me by the hand and said, 'Come on, the bar's open. I'll get you a beer. No customers as yet.'

I was still a year under the legal limit for drinking in a bar, but that didn't stop me from perching on a bar stool while Sitaram went in search of something for me to eat.

The bartender had his back to me. When he turned, a bottle of Golden Eagle in his hands, received the shock of my life. It was Hook Nose!

I almost fell off my stool. My first impulse was to get up and run. But his face was expressionless. All he did was open the bottle and top up a glass with beer, and place it before me. Was it possible that he did not recognize me?

Sitaram was beckoning me to a table in a dark alcove.

I hurried towards him.

'Who's the new bartender?' I asked urgently.

'Don't know his name,' said Sitaram, speaking rapidly in Hindustani. 'I don't think he knows it himself. Your mother felt sorry for him and gave him the job. Somehow he'd got locked into that old shed behind the hotel. Must have been there for several days before he was found, just by chance, when we went there for some firewood—he'd had nothing to eat and drink, and he'd hurt his head trying to get out. Lost his memory. Couldn't remember a thing. Had nowhere to go. So your mother gave him a job. He goes about in a bit of a daze, but he's all right for serving drinks. Perhaps he'll start remembering things one of these days ... Why are you looking worried? It's no concern of yours. Come on, finish your beer and we'll go to the pictures. I've got the night off. There's a new film with Nimmi in it. You like her, don't you?'

The Last Truck Ride

[Twice a day Pritam Singh takes his battered old truck on the narrow, mountainous roads to the limestone quarry. He is in the habit of driving fast. The brakes of his truck are in good condition. What happens when a stray mule suddenly appears on the road?]

A horn blared, shattering the silence of the mountains, and a truck came round the bend in the road. A herd of goats scattered left and right.

The goatherds cursed as a cloud of dust enveloped them, and then the truck had left them behind and was rattling along the stony, unpaved hill road.

At the wheel of the truck, stroking his grey moustache, sat Pritam Singh, a turbaned Sikh. It was his own truck. He did not allow anyone else to drive it. Every day he made two trips to the limestone quarries, carrying truckloads of limestone back to the depot at the bottom of the hill. He was paid by the trip and he was always anxious to get in two trips every day.

Sitting beside him was Nathu, his cleaner-boy. Nathu was a sturdy boy, with a round cheerful face. It was difficult to guess his age. He might have been twelve or he might have been fifteen—he did not know himself, since no one in his village had troubled to record his birthday—but the hard life he led probably made him look older than his years. He belonged to the hills, but his village was far away, on the next range.

Last year the potato crop had failed. As a result there was no money for salt, sugar, soap and flour, and Nathu's parents and small brothers and sisters couldn't live entirely on the onions and artichokes which were about the only crops that had survived the drought. There had been no rain that summer. So Nathu waved goodbye to his people and came down to the town in the valley to look for work. Someone directed him to the limestone depot. He was too young to work at the quarries, breaking stones and loading them on the trucks; but Pritam Singh, one of the older drivers, was looking for someone to clean and look after his truck. Nathu looked like a bright, strong boy, and he was brought on board at ten rupees a day.

That had been six months ago, and now Nathu was an experienced hand at looking after trucks, riding in them and even sleeping in them. He got on well with Pritam Singh, the grizzled, fifty-year-old Sikh, who had well-to-do sons in Punjab, but whose sturdy independence kept him on the road in his battered old truck.

Pritam Singh pressed hard on his horn. Now there was no one on the road—no animals, no humans—but Pritam was fond of his horn and liked blowing it. It was music to his ears.

'One more year on this road,' said Pritam. 'Then I'll sell my truck and retire.'

'Who will buy this truck? said Nathu. 'It will retire before you do.'

'Don't be cheeky, boy. She's only twenty years old. There are still a few years left in her!' And as though to prove it, he blew his horn again. Its strident sound echoed and re-echoed down the mountain gorge. A pair of wild fowl, disturbed by the noise, flew out from the bushes and glided across the road in front of the truck.

Pritam Singh's thoughts went to his dinner. 'Haven't had a good meal for days,' he grumbled.

'Haven't had a good meal for weeks,' said Nathu, although he looked quite well fed.

'Tomorrow I'll give you dinner,' said Pritam. 'Tandoori chicken and pulao.'

'I'll believe it when I see it,' said Nathu.

Pritam Singh sounded his horn again before slowing down. The road had become narrow and precipitous, and trotting ahead of them was a train of mules. As the horn blared, one mule ran forward, one ran backwards. One went uphill, one went downhill. Soon there were mules all over the place.

'You can never tell with mules,' said Pritam, after he had left them behind.

The hills were bare and dry. Much of the forest had long since disappeared. Just a few scraggy old oaks still grew on the steep hillside. This particular range was rich in limestone, and the hills were scarred by quarrying.

'Are your hills as bare as these?' asked Pritam.

'No, they have not started blasting there as yet,' said Nathu. 'We still have a few trees. And there is a walnut tree in front of our house, which gives us two baskets of walnuts every year'.

'And do you have water?'

'There is a stream at the bottom of the hill. But for the fields, we have to depend on the rainfall. And there was no rain last year.'

'It will rain soon,' said Pritam. 'I can smell rain. It is coming from the north.'

'It will settle the dust.'

The dust was everywhere. The truck was full of it. The leaves of the shrubs and the few trees were thick with it. Nathu could feel the dust near his eyelids and on his lips. As they approached the quarries, the dust increased—but it was a different kind of dust now—whiter, stinging the eyes, irritating the nostrils—limestone dust, hanging in the air.

The blasting was in progress.

Pritam Singh brought the truck to a halt. 'Let's wait a bit,' he said.

They sat in silence, staring through the windscreen at the scarred cliffs about a hundred yards down the road. There was no sign of life around them.

Suddenly, the hillside blossomed outwards, followed by a sharp crack of explosives. Earth and rock hurtled down the hillside.

Nathu watched in awe as shrubs and small trees were flung into the air. It always frightened him—not so much the sight of the rocks bursting asunder, but the trees being flung aside and destroyed. He thought of his own trees at home—the walnut, the pines—and wondered if one day they would suffer the same fate and whether the mountains would all become a desert like this particular range. No trees, no grass, no water—only the choking dust of the limestone quarries.

Pritam Singh pressed hard on his horn again to let the people at the site know he was coming. Soon they were parked outside a small shed, where the contractor and the overseer were sipping cups of tea. A short distance away some labourers were hammering at chunks of rock, breaking them up into manageable blocks. A pile of stones stood ready for loading, while the rock that had just been blasted lay scattered about the hillside.

'Come and have a cup of tea,' called out the contractor.

'Get on with the loading,' said Pritam. 'I can't hang about all afternoon. There's another trip to make and it gets dark early these days.'

But he sat down on a bench and ordered two cups of tea from the stall owner. The overseer strolled over to the group of labourers and told them to start loading. Nathu let down the grid at the back of the truck.

Nathu stood back while the men loaded the truck with limestone rocks. He was glad that he was chubby: thin people seemed to feel the cold much more—like the contractor, a skinny fellow who was shivering in his expensive overcoat.

To keep himself warm, Nathu began helping the labourers with the loading.

'Don't expect to be paid for that,' said the contractor, for whom every extra paise spent was a paisa off his profits.

'Don't worry,' said Nathu, 'I don't work for contractors. I work for Pritam Singh.'

'That's right,' called out Pritam. 'And mind what you say to Nathu—he's nobody's servant!'

It took them almost an hour to fill the truck with stones. The contractor wasn't happy until there was no space left for a single stone. Then four of the six labourers climbed on the pile of stones. They would ride back to the depot on the truck. The contractor, his overseer and the others would follow by jeep. 'Let's go!' said Pritam, getting behind the steering wheel. 'I want to be back here and then home by eight o'clock. I'm going to a marriage party tonight!'

Nathu jumped in beside him, banging his door shut. It never opened at a touch. Pritam always joked that his truck was held together with Sellotape.

He was in good spirits. He started his engine, blew his horn and burst into a song as the truck started out on the return journey.

The labourers were singing too, as the truck swung round the sharp bends of the winding mountain road. Nathu was feeling quite dizzy. The door beside him rattled on its hinges.

'Not so fast,' he said.

'Oh,' said Pritam, 'And since when did you become nervous about fast driving?'

'Since today,' said Nathu.

'And what's wrong with today?'

'I don't know. It's just that kind of day, I suppose.'

'You are getting old,' said Pritam. 'That's your trouble.'

'Just wait till you get to be my age,' said Nathu.

'No more cheek,' said Pritam, and stepped on the accelerator and drove faster. As they swung round a bend, Nathu looked out of his window. All he saw was the sky above and the valley below. They were very near the edge. But it was always like that on this narrow road. After a few more hairpin bends, the road started descending steeply to the valley.

'I'll just test the brakes,' said Pritam and jammed down on there so suddenly that one of the labourers almost fell off at the back.

They called out in protest.

'Hang on!' shouted Pritam.

'You're nearly home!'

'Don't try any shortcuts,' said Nathu.

Just then a stray mule appeared in the middle of the road. Pritam swung the steering wheel over to his right; but the road turned left, and the truck went straight over the edge.

As it tipped over, hanging for a few seconds on the edge of the cliff, the labourers leapt from the back of the truck.

The truck pitched forward, bouncing over the rocks, turning over on its side and rolling over twice before coming to rest against the trunk of a scraggy old oak tree. Had it missed the tree, the truck would have plunged a few hundred feet down to the bottom of the gorge.

Two labourers sat on the hillside, stunned and badly shaken. The other two had picked themselves up and were running back to the quarry for help.

Nathu had landed in a bed of nettles. He was smarting all over, but he wasn't really hurt.

His first impulse was to get up and run back with the labourers. Then he realized that Pritam was still in the truck. If he wasn't dead, he would certainly be badly injured.

Nathu skidded down the steep slope, calling out, 'Pritam, Pritam, are you all right?'

There was no answer.

Then he saw Pritam's arm and half his body jutting out of the open door of the truck. It was a strange position to be in, half in and half out. When Nathu came nearer, he saw Pritam was jammed in the driver's seat, held there by the steering wheel which was pressed hard against his chest. Nathu thought he was dead. But as he was about to turn away and clamber back up the hill, he saw Pritam open one blackened swollen eye. It looked straight up at Nathu.

'Are you alive?' whispered Nathu, terrified.

'What do you think?' muttered Pritam. He closed his eye again.

When the contractor and his men arrived, it took them almost an hour to get him to a hospital in the town. He had a broken collarbone, a dislocated shoulder and several fractured ribs. But the doctors said he was repairable—which was more than what could be said for his truck.

'The truck's finished,' said Pritam, when Nathu came to see him a few days later. 'Now 'I'll have to go home and live with my sons. But you can get work on another truck.'

'No,' said Nathu. 'I'm going home too.'

'And what will you do there?'

'I'll work on the land. It's better to grow things on the land than to blast things out of it.'

They were silent for some time.

'Do you know something?' said Pritam finally. 'But for that tree, the truck would have ended up at the bottom of the hill and I wouldn't be here, all bandaged up and talking to you. It was the tree that saved me. Remember that, boy.'

'I'll remember,' said Nathu.